Louder than Words

Also by Laura Jarratt

Skin Deep
By Any Other Name

Louder than Words

LAURA JARRATT

First published in paperback in Great Britain 2014
by Electric Monkey, an imprint of Egmont UK Limited
The Yellow Building, 1 Nicholas Road, London W11 4AN

ISBN 978 1 4052 6912 4

1 3 5 7 9 10 8 6 4 2

www.egmont.co.uk

A CIP catalogue record for this title is available from the British Library

Typeset by Avon DataSet Ltd, Bidford on Avon, Warwickshire
Printed and bound by CPI Group (UK) Ltd, Croydon, CR0 4YY

56735/1

EGMONT

Our story began over a century ago, when seventeen-year-old
Egmont Harald Petersen found a coin in the street. He was on
his way to buy a flyswatter, a small hand-operated printing
machine that he then set up in his tiny apartment.

The coin brought him such good luck that today Egmont has
offices in over 30 countries around the world. And that lucky
coin is still kept at the company's head offices in Denmark.

For Orlaith.
I wrote this while you were sleeping.

RAFAELA

When I grow up I'd like to be a writer. I guess a lot of people my age say that and I also guess they're told that fourteen isn't old enough to know what you want to do with your life. That might be correct for most people, but not for me – I do know and it's a really important deal for me.

I love words. I love the patterns they form on a page, the rhythms, the way they dance into formation: a ballet in one book, hip hop in another, or tap, jazz, all different. I love finding new words. To find a word I didn't know before, a word that perfectly describes something that I never even knew there was a word for, that gives me such a buzz.

Words on a page . . . they're beautiful, powerful. They blow me away.

Words in my mouth . . . they don't work. They're the barrel of a gun, the point of a dagger held to my throat. They choke up inside me and won't come out.

My pen has a freedom my mouth has never had.

Sometimes Silas sneaks into my room when I'm reading and I don't hear him. I'm locked away in my own space in time. And he stands there watching me with what I call his big brother grin. When I finally feel his eyes on me and look up, I know he's caught me mouthing words soundlessly to myself again.

'One day, Rafi,' he'll say as he bounces on to the bed next to me and musses my hair. He never says more than that, but I know what he means all the same: one day he'll walk in and hear me *say* the words, maybe only in a whisper, but he'll really hear me say them.

I don't know if that will ever happen. I don't know if I'll ever talk again, even in private. The worst part is I'm not sure any more that I want to.

Some days I do and I want to be just like everyone else at school – I can't wait to get back after the weekend to trade gossip, chattering away, forgetting how loud I'm being. Maybe even squealing a bit like the other girls in my class do when they get overexcited, making the quiet boys who sit near the door wince when they hear them.

But when I think about all the nasty, aggressive stuff that people use their words for it makes me not want to speak at all. Ever.

It didn't start that way. When it began I wanted to speak. I wanted it desperately. I just couldn't. The very thought of forcing words out made the strangled feeling in my throat stronger so my vocal cords tightened over the sounds and nothing, *nothing* would come out.

The last person I spoke to was my brother Silas, and I was six. Even then I think it was only a whispered, 'No.' Since then, not a word.

Silas says he'd give anything to hear me speak again.

Strange now how I sit here and think the same thing about him.

I've gone on and on about me when really this story isn't about me at all. It's about Silas. I'm just the pen on the page telling his story now that he can't speak either.

When I wiped Silas's computer clean as he asked me to, I found some emails he'd saved in draft. He wrote them to Dad when I guess there were things he needed to say that he couldn't say to me. Of course he couldn't send them because he hasn't got Dad's contact details either. But those emails are important. I cried when I read them for they're the only words he has.

This is my brother's story and it might be the most important story I ever write.

RAFI'S TRUTH BOOK

It is the little rift within the lute,

That by and by will make the music mute,

And ever widening slowly silence all.

(Alfred, Lord Tennyson)

CHAPTER 1

It all started that Wednesday on the school bus, if you can ever pinpoint a moment when something like this begins.

We were on our way home. I was tucked next to the window beside Silas on the long back seat with a bunch of his sixth-form friends. Occasionally I listened to whatever they were talking about, but mostly I stared out of the window unless one of them spoke to me directly. Not that I wasn't interested in what they were saying, but it wasn't fair to my brother otherwise. His friends didn't want to be stuck with a fourteen-year-old, but Silas wouldn't leave me sitting on my own so this was my compromise – I sat with them, but didn't bug them by listening in to conversations like I was part of their group. Silas said they wouldn't mind if I did, but nobody else's little sister sat back there with them and I didn't want things to be different for him because of me.

For instance, today his friend Toby was spreading a rumour about a girl from another school and it was obvious I wasn't supposed to hear any of it. It's funny how being mute has that effect on some people – they behave as if you're deaf, even when they know perfectly well that you're not. I get that a lot. It isn't really Toby's fault – I can do such a good impersonation of being

5

totally oblivious to everything around me that Silas's friends sometimes forget that I can hear them.

'So what Josie did, right, was to . . .' Toby glanced over at me and then got his phone out to show them. '. . . totally strip off and beg Lloyd to take pictures of her. Look at her, she's loving it. What a slut!'

'OMG! She is such a tramp.' The girl next to Silas sat back in disgust. My brother, I noticed, didn't even look at the phone.

Another girl, Rachel, began arguing with Toby.

'That's so harsh,' she said. 'If those pictures had been of a guy then you'd be different about it, but because it's a girl you're being a sexist pig and calling her names.'

The other girls laughed. 'Are you having one of your Feminazi moments again?' her friend said to her.

Rachel wouldn't back down though. 'No, I am right about this. If a guy did that, waving his dick about and grinning, then they'd all be laughing with him and saying what a great lad he was. You know they would. But because she's female, she's a slut. It's not fair.'

The other girls stopped giggling.

'It's such double standards. It doesn't matter whether she should have posed for those pictures or not. What matters is that if it was a boy nobody would be bothered. They can do whatever they want, sleep around as much as they want, cheat, and nobody ever calls them out on it. I can't believe we're in the twenty-first century and we've got no further than when our grandparents were our age!'

There was a pause, followed by the girls collectively rounding on Toby.

'Rachel's right, Toby. You're being so sexist and you know it.'

'It's not even like that girl did it herself. It was her ex who posted those pictures, wasn't it?'

'So what she's actually guilty of is having bad taste in boys! What names are you going to call him now?'

'Rach is totally right and you don't want to admit it. You're all so twentieth century in your attitudes towards women. Except Silas.'

'Oh yeah, except Silas.'

The boys pulled faces. And whined, 'Yeah, except Silas,' in chorus.

My brother just grinned. If the other boys had a dig at him because of what the girls said, he never cared. I couldn't imagine what it must feel like to be so self-assured and together that you weren't bothered what others thought of you.

'People make mistakes,' he said easily. 'And we don't know both sides of the story.'

Even Toby shrugged, with a grin, and nodded. 'Yeah, well, her boyfriend *is* a complete loser.'

'How do you know this Josie?' Silas asked.

'I don't *know* her. I've met her once for about five minutes.

Her dad's a mate of mine's – both in the force.'

Silas raised his eyebrows. 'So her loser ex decides to mess with a policeman's kid? Is he dumb or what?'

Toby laughed. 'Her dad's an inspector, so yeah, he must be dumb. But then he probably knows she'd never tell her dad cos he'd go insane at her for letting Lloyd take those pictures in the first place.'

One of the girls shuddered. 'Yeah, your topless photo on the internet is not something you'd ever want your dad to know about.'

'Oh, our stop!' Silas got up and I shuffled out behind him. 'See you!'

As they said goodbye to us, I gave them a quick smile without directing it at any face in particular and we hopped off the bus at the corner of Edgecombe Road.

Edgecombe is a long, broad residential road on the outskirts of our town that leads down to a footpath out into open countryside. It's tree-lined on both sides and the houses are mostly large Victorian or Edwardian villas, often behind heavy laurel hedges and tall gates. There's the odd new-build where someone has sold off part of their garden, but even Mum acknowledges they've been designed to tie in with the surrounding houses – she tends to get on her artistic high horse over things like that.

We set off down the street – our house is right at the bottom backing on to the fields – but we'd only gone a couple of houses when Silas nudged me and nodded towards a figure standing ahead of us on the pavement, dressed in the green uniform of the church high school on the other side of town.

I looked up at him questioningly.

'I don't know – didn't a new family move into the Claxtons' old house?'

I frowned and nodded – I thought so.

'Maybe she's one of them. Doesn't look very happy, does she?'

This was a definite understatement. As we got closer it was clear the girl was in tears, and not just a few, but great big heaving sobs. She'd dropped her school bag by her feet and covered her face with her hands, and now she stood there, shaking and sobbing.

I shrugged at my brother. What did we do? We couldn't just walk past and leave her there.

Silas looked like most seventeen-year-old boys would if faced with a crying stranger. Or he did for about five seconds, then he squared his shoulders. 'Come on, we'd better see what's up.'

This is one of the reasons why I love my brother. He won't walk past on the other side of the road. Even when that leads him places he doesn't want to go. Sometimes I wonder in retrospect whether I wish he had ignored her that day, despite what it would have cost me if he had, but then if he had he wouldn't be Silas.

I trailed after him, determined to be supportive.

'Excuse me, are you OK?' He stood a careful distance from the girl. She started at the sound of his voice and looked up, her face streaming with tears that she just couldn't stem.

'Are you OK?' he repeated while I smiled what I hoped was a comforting smile. I was quite amazed at myself for being so brave.

'What are you laughing at?' she snapped through the sobbing. 'Get lost. Leave me alone!'

'She's not laughing at you,' Silas said gently. 'She's trying to be nice. She can't speak.'

'Oh!' The girl stopped as she was halfway through turning away from us. She looked at me and I dredged up the remains of my shattered courage to smile again. 'S-s-sorry.' She took a big sniff and scrubbed her hand over her face to dash away as many of the free-flowing tears as she could.

'Look,' said Silas, 'you're obviously not all right and I don't want to interfere, but . . .'

'I'll be fine,' the girl said quickly, rubbing her hands over her face again. I ferreted inside my bag for a tissue because her nose was streaming too. I felt for her, confronted by a strange boy with snot and tears all over her face. 'Thank you.' She took the tissue from me. 'I'm sorry I was nasty. I've . . . I've just had a bit too much today of people laughing at me.' Her eyes began to water again.

I nudged Silas. 'Oh, don't worry. She hasn't taken offence,' he said on my behalf. 'She's more concerned about whether you're going to be OK.'

The girl blew her nose hard. 'I'll be fine. I had a bad day.'

Silas smiled at her as she bit down on her bottom lip to stop it shaking. 'Must have really sucked.'

She managed a weak laugh. 'Yeah, it really did.'

'I'm Silas and this is my little sister, Rafaela, but we all call her Rafi. We live down there in the house round the bend. Are you from The Poplars?'

'Yes, we moved in a couple of weeks ago. Um, is your sister deaf?'

'No, she can hear perfectly well. She's mute – she used to talk, but she stopped when she was little. Why is quite complicated, but basically she doesn't speak at all now.'

You could see the girl didn't know what to say. People never do. In the end she probably got it as right as anyone can, by just saying, 'Oh, OK then . . . hi, Rafi, I'm Josie.'

I saw my brother stiffen slightly out of the corner of my eye at the exact same time I froze my face so the girl – Josie – couldn't read it. Because right then we both knew why she was crying. It couldn't be a coincidence. Josie wasn't that common a name. And she was about the right age – sixteen – and from that school . . .

'Some days do stink more than you think possible,' Silas said lightly, nodding in the direction we'd been walking.

She fell in beside us. 'Yup.'

'Rafi says – oh, not in words,' he added when he saw Josie's look of confusion. 'Rafi tells you what she means in other ways . . . that on a day that stinks the answer is always chocolate. Don't you, Raf?'

Josie smiled at me. 'Lucky there's some in my fridge, then.'

She was prettier than I'd first thought, though it's hard to say when someone's cried as much as she had. Her brown eyes were still raw-rimmed and her face was blotchy, marring what looked like very clear and soft skin, the colour of milky coffee under normal circumstances. Her crinkly black hair was twisted up into a knot on the top of her head – the severity would have looked terrible on me, but she had a softness around her cheekbones that could take it. Yes, a pretty girl. Not stunning, not breath-taking, but a girl a lot of boys would look twice at.

We stopped when we reached her house.

'I hope you are all right,' Silas said, looking completely unconvinced.

'I will be,' Josie said with a sad twist to her mouth that I doubt she knew was there.

'You should come round and talk to Rafi if you're not. She's a good listener,' he said. I practically dropped dead there on the spot, but the girl was looking at me so I faked it and nodded as enthusiastically as I could given I'd nearly expired with shock and the need to freak out. Had my brother gone mad? Come round and talk to *me*!

Josie looked genuinely pleased. 'Oh, thank you,' she said directly to me. 'That's so nice of you.'

I rummaged in my bag again for a Twix I'd had there since break and not got round to eating yet. I put it in her hand with trepidation.

She managed a little laugh. 'You're great, you know that?'

'If you do come round, the name of the house is Elands. So you know you've got the right one.' Silas gave her a last smile and she slipped inside the heavy gate with a final thanks and a little wave.

'That was so weird,' he said, once we were out of hearing. 'Toby tells us about this girl and then . . .' He looked down at me. 'I feel so sorry for her. She's in bits.'

And that's my brother again. He doesn't care if he's supposed to feel sorry for her, whether that's a 'boy' thing to do. He just does, so that's it. All the same I glared at him for that trick of inviting her round.

'Don't look at me like that. I hope she does come round to see you. From what Toby said nobody in her school is speaking to her any more, especially the other girls. You know how mean girls can be about things like that and she looks like she could use a friend.'

He didn't add that I could too.

Back at home, my mother was nowhere in sight and there was a note on the fridge. 'Back at seven. Make food. Seeing a gallery about a sculpture.'

Silas sighed and opened the fridge. 'What do you fancy for

dinner? I could do pasta and meatballs. Needs to be something quick – I've got an essay to write for tomorrow.'

That was fine with me so he whipped up some food while I sat at the dining table and got my homework out of my bag. It was typical of Mum to disappear off to London without telling us this morning. She was quite capable of simply forgetting to communicate things like that.

Silas threw a quick bowl of salad together as well as the pasta and sat down with me to eat while he read through the text he had to write the essay on. He had a frown crease between his eyes so I left him to get on with it and flicked through a magazine while I ate. The food tasted good – he wasn't a bad cook when it came to simple stuff. Much better than me anyway. And better than Mum.

Sitting round this table, that was my first real memory of my family. I must have been about three because Silas looks around six in my mind. We were all sitting down for Sunday lunch. The others were still at home then: my oldest sister Carys, who played the flute so well that she'd be off to a specialist music academy soon and then on to a glittering international career as a soloist; Gideon, who inherited Mum's artistic talent and had already had his first exhibition, aged twelve; Kerensa, who did her maths A level before she was ten; and Silas, who was flicking peas at me when Mum wasn't looking.

Silas at six was beautiful. So much so that people stopped

Mum in the street to tell her. He had dark hair that waved a little, but was cropped short enough so that no one mistook him for a girl, eyes the blue of the Mediterranean Sea when it's painted by the light of a summer sky – a colour I would kill to have – with curling black eyelashes so long they looked as if they'd rest on his cheeks when he was asleep. I don't of course remember these details from when I was three. I've seen the photos and at seventeen he's sickeningly unchanged. I do look a little like him, people say, but what they mean is, if he's a painting, I look like a practice version that's had water spilled on it and is left washed out and smudged.

But I didn't know any of this in the memory. What I knew then was that Silas had just hit me in the face with a pea and it was funny. About two seconds later, when Mum noticed the gravy stain on my clean T-shirt, she found it less funny and exploded into one of her legendary rants. The family stopped eating and winced, and Silas burst into tears.

I didn't like the shouting and the big, fat, salty drops rolling down my brother's cheeks so I started to cry too. Dad stormed from the table, shouting, 'Is there never any peace in this wretched house?' and another Ramsey family lunch was ruined.

Mum didn't have any more babies after me because not long after that Sunday lunch, Dad left us. He ran away with an ordinary woman who didn't stress about gravy stains on a child's T-shirt and he didn't see us any more. Silas told me he'd wanted to, but Mum wouldn't let him so that was that. Dad didn't fight for us, but then Mum says he never fought for anything except to get away from her.

I wonder if I'd have become mute if he'd still been around. Probably. I don't think him abandoning us had too much to do with it. Except he was more ordinary than the rest, like me, so maybe it would have been easier for me if he'd stayed – that would have made two of us the boring ones among the exceptional Ramseys.

JOSIE'S PINTEREST BOARD

Making a hundred friends is not a miracle. The miracle is to make a single friend who will stand by your side even when hundreds are against you.

CHAPTER 2

It could all have ended there, with a girl we met on the street, crying because of a stupid Facebook prank, and I suppose it would have done if Josie hadn't come round to our house. But Silas had invited her and that set in motion the whole chain of events leading to now.

She didn't come over that evening or the next day or even the one after that. But on Saturday morning the bell on our front gates rang shortly after breakfast and Mum answered.

'Hello?'

'Hi, um, this is Josie. I live down the street. I've come to see Rafi.'

There was a stunned pause. My mother raised an eyebrow at the intercom receiver in her hand and then she buzzed Josie in. She turned to find me standing in the kitchen doorway. 'Apparently it's for you.'

I nodded, faking nonchalance. Suddenly I was a whirl of nerves inside. Josie had come to see me, but how would I communicate with her? This was why I didn't have friends. Without Silas as my interpreter, how could I make myself heard? Nobody but Silas understood me.

'Well, this should be interesting,' my mother remarked tartly as she sat down at the kitchen table and began flipping through the culture supplement in the newspaper.

I could feel my hands begin to tremble and my throat tightened.

'You should let her in,' my mother added and I heard the exasperation in her voice.

Of course I should. Josie must be at the door by now and wondering whether to ring the bell there too. How stupid of me. I hurried to the front door and wrenched it open just as Josie's hand hovered over the brass bell button.

'Ah, hi!' she said, and to my surprise she looked as nervous as I felt. 'Hope you don't mind me coming over. I wasn't sure if you really meant it when you invited me, but then I thought if you did it would be so rude if I didn't after you guys were nice to me when I was upset and —' She paused to gulp in a breath. 'I should shut up. I talk too much.'

And me not enough, I thought. I smiled uselessly and shook my head to say I didn't think so. She looked confused for a moment and then I think she figured out what that meant because she nodded and said, 'That's kind of you, but I know I do really. Sometimes I should just, you know, stop babbling on.'

I stood aside and beckoned her in. There wasn't a day that went by when my lack of words didn't make me feel stupid at some time or other, but I rarely felt the loss as acutely as I did at this precise moment. And my throat felt more closed than ever.

'Thanks.' She looked around our hall with interest. 'Wow, I've never seen so many paintings.'

Like every room in the house, the walls were lined with pictures. None of them were my mother's — she wasn't that vain — but all of them were chosen by her. Some were free, from artist friends, others she'd bought over the years and several were Gideon's. Probably even Gideon's finger paintings when he was two were special. Unlike other mothers, she'd never put any of her other children's attempts up — Silas's and my portraits of cats and houses and Christmas trees had never defaced the kitchen cupboards. Gideon's efforts had earned their place through merit alone.

'Our mother's an artist.'

We turned round to see a sleep-ruffled Silas coming down the stairs wearing a pair of boxers and, thankfully, a T-shirt. On Saturdays, my brother didn't rise from his pit until the sun was well up in the sky, usually because he was messing around online most of Friday night, doing some geeky computer stuff with his geeky internet friends. For that was Silas's special thing: he wasn't an artist or a musician or a maths boffin; he did things with computers. What exactly he did was beyond my understanding, but whatever it was I knew he was good at it from the reverential way his friends spoke to him about that kind of thing.

Josie looked flustered. 'Oh, right.'

'Want coffee or juice or something?'

Of course. That's what normal people did — offered their guests a drink. Doh! I sucked in a breath and tried to work out how to operate in some kind of normal girl mode. I could give up and just leave it all to Silas or let Josie go away and not have the stress of working out how I was going to communicate with her. But here she was, standing in my hall, and I had this crazy feeling that I was this close, *this* close, to making a connection. It was terrifying, but at the same time so exciting I thought I might burst.

I jerked my head at her, smiling again, and my face was starting to freeze up from the effort of grinning to replace the useless words that never escaped my throat. I walked through to the kitchen and she followed me, with Silas trailing behind, rubbing sleep from his eyes. I wondered what she thought of my brother in that state. I noticed she avoided looking at him directly, seeming to find her feet more interesting.

My mother gave her a polite but distant nod as she folded up the newspaper. I thought for a moment I detected a flash of curiosity from her, but then she got up to leave. 'I must get on. I need to get those three pieces finished for the Bartlett commission.' She drifted out of the room in a suitably 'arty' fashion. Josie looked impressed, if a little intimidated. Silas and I rolled our eyes at each other. It was less impressive when you lived with it.

'Exit stage left,' muttered Silas and flicked the kettle on.

He was about to ask Josie what she wanted to drink, but

that was wrong. She was my guest and I should be doing it. I yanked the fridge door open and held up the juice carton, and simultaneously pointed to the coffee jar on the worktop.

'Oh, juice would be great, thanks.'

I beamed. It felt as if the grin exploded across my face. Such a stupid little thing that would seem to anyone else, but to me at that moment it was a breakthrough of the highest order. I had done it. Normal communication established. Me! I connected!

I was so happy that I almost forgot to pour the juice for her, but then I pulled myself together. It was a good job she couldn't see how thrilled I was or she'd think I was a complete loser.

Why did her opinion matter to me? I didn't know her at all, only met her once and then very briefly. Was it a premonition of friendship or just that a chance seemed – incredibly – to be presenting itself and I so badly didn't want to blow it? I don't think I ever worked out the answer. But it didn't matter: what was to be would be.

I set her juice down on the table and got myself a glass too, as Silas mooched around making coffee and toast and tactfully ignoring us. I could have hugged him for that.

'So I figured I should come and say thank you for . . . oh, that you stopped to see if I was OK the other day, that you *cared*,' Josie said, sipping juice. 'I mean, most people wouldn't. Even my so-called friends don't. They all think it's one great big joke. Easy for them when it's not them on the receiving end!'

I pulled a puzzled face, which was a bit duplicitous of me, but what was I supposed to do — let her know I knew what she was talking about and the gossip was all over my school too?

'Oh yeah, sorry, this won't make any sense to you.' She sighed heavily. 'I don't really want to explain because it hurts to even talk about it, but . . .' She took a deep breath. 'Well, we can't be friends if I'm pretending about why I was upset that day, can we?'

I shook my head, dazed. So she really did want to be friends. It wasn't some silly daydream I was having. She honestly, truly wanted to be friends with me.

Nobody had ever wanted to be friends with me before.

Unless she had other motives.

I looked up at Silas leaning against the kitchen counter and munching toast with peanut butter. Maybe it was Silas that Josie really wanted to be around. Was I just a convenient way to get closer to him?

I frowned. Hmm, maybe my nasty, suspicious mind was just that — nasty and suspicious. But why would a Year 11 girl — who was pretty and, according to Toby, had been popular before her ex trashed her reputation — want to be friends with me?

Josie looked at me with a puzzled expression so I tried to wipe the frown away.

It worked. As my frown disappeared, so did her puzzlement and she took a deep breath in. 'Look, I don't normally talk like this to complete strangers I meet in the street, but I think gut reactions are really important and, this is going to sound mental, but I had a really strong one when I met you, like I just knew we'd be friends. Some kind of instant connection. Did you feel anything like that?'

Did I? Yes, perhaps that was what I was feeling, that unexpected sense of wanting to communicate with a girl I didn't know, a feeling that had come out of nowhere and left me shaken at the strangeness. That kind of need was so foreign to me. Maybe this was how friendships started. I suppose Josie would know that better than me. I nodded slowly.

Josie beamed. She had one of those transformational smiles that turned her into someone you wanted so much to be with. 'Oh good!'

She glanced at Silas, who had picked up our mother's newspaper and was sitting on a stool at the furthest end of the long kitchen counter studiously ignoring us. I wasn't fooled. He 'wasn't listening' with exactly the same face I used when I 'wasn't listening' to his friends. But Josie fell for it.

'I don't normally cry in the street,' she said. 'I said I'd had a really bad day. Well, it was beyond bad. It's been like the most completely sucky week of my whole life.' She paused and added, 'You're a really good listener, do you know that? I mean, you don't nod all the time and obviously you don't answer, but it's in your eyes that you're listening. And there's something else there too . . . that you won't *judge*.' She shook her head slightly as if she'd surprised even herself with that insight and then she went on. 'Even my friends were horrible about what happened. They won't even speak to me now and . . . oh, this will be making no sense at all. I'll have to start at the beginning, but tell me if I'm boring you and I'll stop, OK?'

Yes, that was OK, but I couldn't see myself getting bored. I wanted to know her side of it; after all, Toby's wasn't likely to be totally accurate.

'Have you ever been in love? Dumb question I guess because you probably haven't yet, but I could be wrong. No? You will be one day. I thought I was. It's the strangest feeling. It's like it takes over your whole life. Like you're not even yourself any more. Like you're whoever the person you love wants you to be even if that's not who you know you are deep down. You change.' She checked my face. 'You look doubtful. Maybe you're right. Maybe you don't really change and you just pretend. No? Or do you think that's not really love at all. Yeah, you could be right about that too. I'm not sure either. Like I said, I thought I was in love. Now I'm not so sure I ever was. All I know is I hate him now.'

That wasn't unexpected. If someone had betrayed me like that, I'd hate him too.

'His name's Lloyd and he's in the year above me, but he's not at my school. He goes to college to do engineering. My dad didn't know I was going out with him or he'd have grounded me for life. Dad's in the police and Lloyd got in some trouble last year for under-age driving. That's how I met him – he was driving around the leisure centre car park in his cousin's car one night after I came out from my swim club meet, but this was after he'd got in trouble the first time. So he was doing it again. I know, I know what you're thinking, and yes, obviously he is completely stupid, but so must I be too because all I could think when I met him was how cute he was. I didn't find out about the trouble with the police until later and by then I was so into him that I told myself it didn't matter. I made so many excuses for him.'

At least she could see that now. That was something.

She got her phone out and showed me a picture. 'That's him.' And yes, it was clear what she'd seen in him. He looked as dodgy as anything and I would have run a mile from a boy like him, but he had that bad-boy grin that some girls find irresistible, and he was easy on the eye, I had to admit.

'So I was crazy about him; you have to understand that part or none of this makes any sense and you'll think I'm just some slut who –'

I thought she was going to cry for a moment, but she took a few breaths and managed not to.

'Sorry. We'd been seeing each other a few months when he invited me to his cousin's party. Everyone there was wasted and I know I drank too much too, but I wasn't completely out of it – I can't use that as an excuse. I did know what I was doing, but . . . I trusted him. That's how stupid I am. I trusted that pig and . . .' Her eyes started filling up with tears.

I got up hurriedly and tore off some kitchen roll for her. Silas sat rooted to his stool like a tree, and stared at the paper like he was deaf and invisible. I wondered whether Josie felt more uncomfortable saying this in front of him. Or did she want him to know the truth? If she was interested in him . . .

'Thanks. I didn't mean to cry again. It's so silly. I'm not crying over him. I am so totally over him I can't understand why I ever liked him now. It's because I feel such an *idiot*. Everyone's laughing at me and the more they do, the worse it gets because it encourages him. I begged him to stop, though I hated myself for doing it because I bet it gives him a buzz to make me beg, but he won't. Just keeps putting worse and worse stuff online about me.'

OK, so I knew he'd posted some pictures, but it was still going on? I shook my head at her to show I didn't understand.

'Yeah, I know. I'm being rubbish at explaining.' She wiped her face with the paper towel. 'Basically, after that party I went back to his to get changed before going home. My dad's really strict and I didn't want him smelling smoke and alcohol on me. While I was getting changed, Lloyd sneaked into the bedroom and took some photos of me. I didn't have my bra on in some of them. I sort of yelled at him when I realised he was there, but he made out like it was a big joke and we'd both had too much to drink so, yes, I was dumb and I started laughing too. Then he talked me into posing for a couple of photos. Just messing around, he said, but he kept kissing me and telling me I was beautiful, and he just wanted something to remind him just how beautiful when I wasn't there.'

Her face crumpled and she began to cry properly. Not pretty crying as people do when they're doing it for effect but full-on red-eyed face, streaming and snotty.

As I listened to her, I felt what she did. Felt it through the emotion leaking out of her words. Felt the betrayal, the humiliation and, behind that, the impotent anger that someone she cared about had done – appeared to still be doing – this to her. This is a thing about being silent that I don't think people realise for they spend so much time talking and so little time really listening. You can hear so much, come to know so much from the way words are spoken, as much as from the words themselves. Sometimes more, actually, because people can hide what they really mean inside their choice of words, but they're not as good at hiding it in their faces, their voices, their body language.

Josie's words didn't say nearly as much as her weeping eyes and the way she shook all over.

It was hard for me, faced with her like that, to know what to do. I'd be better at dealing with it now, but then I was so unsure of myself, so clueless about the basics of friendship. I bit my lip as I watched her and half wished Silas would rescue me.

What a coward. How many times had I sat in my room and dreamed of a moment like this? For friendship to be dangled in front of me, waiting to be grabbed at. And now it was here, my mind was whining for Silas to help me. Then again, wasn't cowardice a big part of why I didn't speak?

Josie grabbed the wet paper towel again and rubbed her face. It didn't do much good — you could still see all too well she'd been crying. 'I wish you could tell me what you're thinking,' she said. 'Don't you ever get frustrated that you can't say stuff like that to people?'

Yes. Yes. A thousand times yes.

But never enough to beat the fear. If that's what it was — fear. Even I didn't really know.

'Do you have a phone?' she asked, tears suddenly forgotten as inspiration flashed over her face. 'A mobile I mean, not a house phone.'

A mobile?

Ah, that. I shook my head. Not vehemently, though I wanted to. But that would seem strange to her so I managed to shake it normally. Like it was just any old casual question I was answering. I saw Silas's head come up and he spun round on the stool to face us.

'Why not? I could text you if you did and you could text back and —'

Yes — and . . .

. . . and we could communicate. I started to feel a bit weird.

'She's never had one,' Silas said, coming over quickly.

Josie grinned at us. 'Then it's about time she got one, isn't it?'

Silas opened his mouth to protest. He did try, I knew that, I recognised that and I loved him for it. But he had just come up against the tornado that was Josie and he was unprepared.

She stood up and pushed her chair back, rummaging in her bag until she found her purse. She pulled out a bank card with satisfaction. 'Come on!'

Come on where? my face said.

'We're going to buy you a phone!'

JOSIE'S PINTEREST BOARD

I have loved him too much not to feel any hatred for him.

(Jean Racine)

CHAPTER 3

We had to go into the city to buy the phone, which meant a long bus ride, but our town didn't have much of a high street left any more. It was what they call a dormitory town now, full of people who worked elsewhere but preferred to live somewhere less busy. Silas came along with us.

'So why exactly can't Rafi talk?' Josie asked him as the bus jolted to a halt at another set of traffic lights. 'Is there something wrong with her throat?'

'No, she's what's called a selective mute. Or she was. Now it's progressed further; she's got progressive mutism, which is much rarer.'

'You've lost me.'

Silas cast me an anxious glance. He knew I hated being talked about like this. 'She stopped talking when she was little, not completely, but in certain places and with certain people. It was around when our dad left and when she started school.'

'So she can talk?'

'Yes and no. They used to think that kids did it because they wanted to stop, like it was a choice. Now they think it's maybe that they want to talk, but just can't, like a phobia.'

'Wow, that's . . . horrible. Like she wants to speak to you, but she just can't?'

'Yeah, maybe, but in her case it got worse. Most kids with it will talk to family or one-to-one, but Rafi even stopped doing that. That's progressive mutism. She hasn't spoken at all since she was six.'

He glanced at me again and Josie picked up on it this time. She changed the subject. 'So what kind of phone shall we get you?' she asked me and she got her own mobile out, flicked open the browser and showed me some models. 'Which do you like best?'

The answer: none of them. I didn't want a phone. But how could I, or Silas by proxy, explain that without making me look like an even bigger freak?

Why have a phone when you can't talk? It just sits there laughing at your inadequacy. And text? Who did I have to text? I had no friends, except my brother, and I didn't want to text him badly enough to accept the mockery of that little electronic device sitting in my pocket reminding me every minute how abnormal I was.

Phones are designed for talking. Period.

Not for fruitloops who can't speak.

Silas had tried to talk me round before, showed me games I could play etc. But there was still that big fundamental block. Phones equal talking and Rafi doesn't talk. So just no.

And now Josie had breezed in and turned everything upside

down because she just didn't know – and I was too scared to tell her.

I had butterflies fluttering in the pit of my stomach. COMMUNICATION. Text words were still words after all and this was a big step.

It could be a big step towards a better place, part of me said. And it was only writing, and didn't I want to be a writer?

But the coward part still shied away. Which was funny because the coward part of me was exactly why I was sitting on that bus seat letting Josie railroad me into getting a phone. I didn't have the courage to say no.

The shopping area was busy. Lots of people our age in groups hanging out, window-shopping, having a laugh. If they could read my thoughts on how freaked I felt at something so simple as having a phone, they'd have an even bigger laugh. Maybe Mum was right that day when she lost her temper with me and told me I needed an army of shrinks to sort my brain out and she didn't know what she'd done to deserve such a screwed-up kid. In my head, I screamed back at her: *You wouldn't care how screwed-up I was if I could paint like Gideon, or play music like Carys, or basically if I was more like the others!*

'So you go to the same school?' Josie asked me as we made our way down the main street and Silas waved to a couple of friends from school who were sitting in the window of McDonald's. I started to nod, but Silas beat me to it.

'Yeah, Rafi's in Year 10 and I'm in the sixth form.'

'That must be expensive, both of you there at once.'

'I'm on a scholarship so I get my fees paid.' Like my other brother and sisters had. 'Our dad stumps up for Rafi.'

About the only thing he did do for us, Mum said, and it was because I didn't get high enough marks in the entrance exam or have some redeeming talent, so they wouldn't take me otherwise. In fact, they weren't keen on taking me even with the fees being paid, but as I said, my mother is a force of nature and the thought of the bad publicity that could follow if they turned me down clearly left the Head in a cold sweat. My mother was quite capable of phoning every press office in the country and ranting at length about discrimination and injustice to the . . . *disabled*.

Josie carefully avoided the eyes of a girl we passed who stared at us in shock. My brother nodded slightly to her, as if he knew her, but not very well. I'd never seen her before. I nudged Josie.

'She's from my school,' she whispered, as if the girl could still hear us even though she was some way behind now. 'Didn't they try to make you go to a . . . um, special school?'

'Oh, they tried,' Silas cut in, and for the first time in my life I almost didn't want him to speak for me. 'They recommended some really good schools: one for the deaf, one for school phobics, one for kids with behavioural problems. None for kids who are mute – there just aren't any. But our mother wanted her to go to a normal school.'

'What did Rafi want though?'

And that was the question my mother never asked. She always knew better than me of course.

'To go to the same place as me,' Silas replied as if that should be obvious.

He was right. That's what I had wanted. Had he asked me or had he just known? I couldn't remember now. But the loneliest time of my life was when he went to upper school and I was left alone in the prep and didn't see him all day except for the bus. At least now I didn't have to have lunch alone. I didn't want to think about how it would be when he left after next year.

I never thought about the future at all if I could help it. I suppose then I didn't believe I had one worth thinking about. I mean, I knew I wanted to be a writer, but that was a dream – I never saw myself as any older than I was at that moment. There'd be nobody to speak for me when I grew up so I didn't allow growing up to be real to me.

I hadn't noticed the group of boys coming round the corner, but they certainly noticed us. A burst of male laughter made me turn my head in their direction. There were five of them. I recognised Lloyd immediately from the photo. Josie went rigid beside me as she spotted him.

Lloyd raised an eyebrow at her and gave a mocking wave.

'Just ignore him,' she muttered.

We kept walking.

'Hey, Josieee,' he called, 'the boys were wondering when they get to see it all for real.'

She couldn't help herself. She stopped, her hands shaking with rage, embarrassment or both. 'Go to hell, Lloyd.'

He clapped a hand to his chest, faking a wound, while his mates laughed. 'Damaged goods, babe, that's what you are.' I could have imagined it, but I thought he cast a sly glance at Silas when he said it. 'And the whole world knows it now!'

'You're sick in the head,' she shouted, but her eyes were filling with tears again and I willed her not to cry in front of him.

I looked at Silas, uncertain what to do. I wanted to shout hurtful things at Lloyd myself, but a) I couldn't think of anything and b) well, b was obvious, wasn't it? Silas's face was utterly blank. He was staring straight at Lloyd, but with no discernible expression.

One of Lloyd's mates lifted his T-shirt up. 'I'll show you mine if you show me yours,' he called as they all burst out laughing again.

Silas's face didn't even flicker so I jumped when he actually spoke. 'You want me to get back at him for you?' he said quietly, in a conversational tone.

From Josie's expression, she wondered if he was winding her up. I tugged her sleeve to say, *Let's go*. We weren't going to win anything here.

'I'm serious,' Silas said as she walked off quickly in response, followed by a load of jeering, and veered off into the first of the phone shops.

She stopped in front of one of the displays. 'What do you mean?'

'Just what I said.'

'Why would you do that?'

Silas wore what I called his 'on a high horse' expression and I knew he wasn't going to let go of this. 'I don't like him.'

'I didn't think you knew Lloyd,' Josie said, puzzled.

'I don't, and I don't need to. I don't like him. End of.' He smiled coldly, a far remove from his normal half-lazy grin. 'And I can make him sorry he ever started this.'

JOSIE'S PINTEREST BOARD

We all make mistakes. It's how we come back from the mistakes that matters.

CHAPTER 4

I chose a white phone in the end and Josie dragged me into Starbucks to set it up and show me how to text. It wasn't difficult because it wasn't as if I hadn't seen everyone else in the known universe texting.

Josie sent me my first text message. <How does it feel?>

<Like a miracle. But a bit scary too.>

<Why?>

<Because I'm speaking to someone.>

<Yeah, I get that. xxx>

Silas watched me with anxious eyes, but said nothing. I loved him in that second for letting me try without interference. Unfair, he would tell me later, because before I'd always wanted him to interfere. Unfair, but also kind of great – he'd bolted a grin on the end as he added that last part.

<You're doing great> Josie added. <xoxoxoxo>

I felt a lump in my throat. I stared at the device in my hand with its pretty screensaver that Josie had just loaded for me and now it was here and I was holding it, it didn't seem so awful. It didn't seem to be laughing at me at all. It felt friendly . . . like Josie.

How had I been so scared of this?

40

<So what did Lloyd do with the photos?> I asked.

I just started a conversation.

I. Started. A. Conversation.

Me.

I felt like I was flying through clouds on a magic carpet or some craziness like that. Euphoric. That was the word. I'd never had any use for it before now. I felt like the bravest, cleverest person in the world for a moment.

'I'll go and buy a muffin and then I'll tell you, I promise.' She avoided Silas's eyes as if she'd rather he wasn't there. 'I just need chocolate to get through this. You want one?'

'I'll get them.' Silas got up hastily, still guilting from having to let Josie buy my phone as she wouldn't take no for an answer. He'd argued with her in the shop to let him pay or go halves, but she wasn't having any of it. She hadn't spent her allowance for two months, she said, and she was flush and we were going to be friends with this, so it was for her as much as me. Silas looked over towards the counter and screwed his face up. 'How can there be like ten types of chocolate muffin? Which one do you want?'

'Triple choc,' she said feelingly. 'For this, the more chocolate the better.'

'Rafi?'

I got up and pointed to the white choc and raspberry. I'd never had one before, but it sounded good. I didn't come into the city very often. Silas was no fun to shop with and there really wasn't anyone else for me to go with. I certainly wasn't brave enough to go on my own.

Josie took a big, chocolaty bite of the muffin before she went on with the story. 'It was the little things that broke us up and it started after he took those photos. I'd notice he'd be mean to me in front of his friends or that he wouldn't call or text, like he wanted me to do all the work or his ego wouldn't let him make an effort. And he'd put me down all the time. And you know, I thought I loved him, but I'm not a doormat. I'm not being treated like that by any guy.'

Silas's eyebrows quirked upwards and he hid a slight grin. He hadn't expected that. Actually, me neither. There was more to Josie than met the eye.

She sighed. 'I tried talking to him about it, to let him know how I felt. But every time I did he brushed me off like I was some cheap dumb-ass who was lucky to have got him in the first place.'

I could imagine the Lloyd I'd seen behaving just like that.

But what she said next shocked me and Silas into open-mouthed mirror images of each other.

'And when I thought carefully about it, I understood he didn't love me at all. That was why he treated me badly. Not because he couldn't express his true feelings or it was just the way he and his friends acted around each other, or any of the other stuff he tried to blag me with when I told him we were over.'

She. Told. *Him.*

So it was Josie who broke them up.

Of course. That was why her ex had gone nuclear with the pictures online. She ditched him.

Why had we assumed it was the other way round?

'That's when he got really nasty. He put those pictures I told you about up online and he linked them on Facebook, on all the sites he uses. He made a special website to put them on: www. josieisaho.com. Everyone knows about it.' She fixed us with a look. 'I bet you guys even heard about it, didn't you? I keep getting bitchy messages left on my Facebook page and some of them are from your school.'

I nodded, shamefaced. Silas shrugged. 'People say a lot of stuff. It doesn't mean we believe it.'

'Have *you* ever been in love?' Josie demanded.

Silas looked frankly uncomfortable. 'Er, no.'

'You're lucky,' she said. 'Because it isn't always like it is in books. Sometimes it sucks. In fact, I'm beginning to think it's never like it is in books. I learned something important from Lloyd though – what you want isn't always good for you.'

'Um, yes. I guess so,' Silas replied. It was funny how out of his depth he looked discussing love with her. My brother was seldom uncomfortable and, let's face it, that was my default condition, so I enjoyed the moment. Mean, yes, but hey, I'd spent my life being the poor, damaged one of the family so I don't think Silas would have begrudged me a tiny moment of glee. He's got more empathy in his little finger than the rest of my family put together.

I sucked in my breath and typed <But you asked him to stop?>

Josie waited for the second it took for my message to come through on her phone, smiling despite her watery eyes giving away how hard she was finding this.

'Yes. I asked him. And he laughed in my face and told me I was getting everything I deserved. And then made out that he's such a name online that he'd get the pictures to go viral and then I'd see if any boy would touch me again.'

Silas made a noise of disgust. 'Yeah, well, I've never heard of him so he can't be that big.' He fixed Josie with a stern, big-brother look. 'So do you want me to get him to stop?'

'How could you do that?' She wasn't taking him seriously. I think she knew he was in earnest, but she just didn't see how he could do it. Actually, I didn't have a clue either.

'Because he might think he's a player online, but I'm very sure I can play rougher.' Silas smiled that chilly little smile again that had been unfamiliar to me before today. 'So you want me to do it?'

Josie nodded, still not convinced he could make it happen. I thought differently – I had no idea what Silas was going to do, but if he said he was going to do something and it involved a computer then I was 100 per cent sure he could make it happen. I understood why Josie was sceptical: my brother didn't look like your classic computer geek, but he was as gifted as the rest of my family, me and Dad excepted of course.

Silas grinned. 'Good!' And I swear twin devils danced in his blue eyes. Now that look I *had* seen before and it made me grin.

When we left the coffee shop, Lloyd and his mates were still hanging around the high street. Again I saw Lloyd run an assessing glance over my brother. 'Doesn't he know what a slut you are yet?' he shouted to Josie. 'Or is that what he wants?'

'It's not true,' Josie muttered. 'It's so not true. I never slept with him.' She chewed her lip. 'I've never slept with anyone.'

'She's not that good anyway!' Lloyd yelled to Silas.

My brother held that impassive face with which he'd stared at Lloyd earlier, but those little devils were dancing again as he fixed his eyes on Lloyd's T-shirt. Something about it seemed to please him. I couldn't see what. It was just an average black T-shirt with some kind of graphic on the front and the words CODES OF WAR in yellow letters underneath.

'Pwned,' Silas whispered with a cold smile. 'And you don't even know it yet.'

JOSIE'S PINTEREST BOARD

You and I are more than friends.
We're like a really small gang.

CHAPTER 5

Female bonding, that was what Josie called it. It seemed in this case that meant us hanging out together on Sunday.

'We'll just chill and take in a film,' she said, like it was just nothing to hop on a bus and grab lunch at the pizza place before the 2 p.m. showing, buy popcorn and sit in the reclining seats with a litre cup of Diet Coke.

Well, it was nothing to her. To me, it was a first. Silas was more your 'slob on the sofa at a mate's house and watch a film there' type of guy than the kind who went to the cinema. Consequently, unless there was something I really wanted to see, we never went. I think he'd taken a girl or two on a date there from time to time, but that was it. Silas would probably say he'd have taken me if I'd asked, but that I never did and I suppose that was true. I squirmed on the bus seat as I realised just how much of a hermit I was.

And it was all my own fault.

Josie showed me the app on her phone with the cinema listings. 'Pick one,' she said.

I coloured up and shook my head, pointing to her to tell her to choose.

'No way. You're choosing this time. I'll pick next.'

Wow. There was going to be a next time.

But wait! She was making me make the decision. Because that was another of those many, many things I didn't do.

My throat tightened in panic like it did when I tried to speak, but I didn't want to admit how stupid I was so I pointed randomly at the list.

'Cool,' she said enthusiastically. 'That looks good and the guy in it is *verrrry* hot.'

I breathed out in relief. Partly because I'd made a good decision it seemed, but mostly and more bizarrely, if I had to explain my weirdness to anyone, because the decision-making was over. I was, I realised, more scared of making the choice than the consequences of what I chose.

Now that really was screwed-up.

'How are you doing?' Josie asked. Perhaps more of my feelings showed in my face than I intended.

I made to nod for OK but then . . . <Bit nervous.>

It was important to be honest – I felt that from Josie. She exuded the idea that friendship had to equal honesty or it wasn't friendship at all. It was implicit somehow in her face, the way she stood; everything about her said it.

When I realised that, I stopped wondering if she wanted to use me to get to Silas – it wasn't in her make-up.

'Why?' There was curiosity but no scorn in her voice, which gave me confidence.

<I've been in a bubble.>

I didn't know if she'd understand that. I couldn't have fitted those words to what my life had been until just that point, but it was suddenly and starkly true that I'd hidden myself in my silent world so thoroughly that I was practically a hermit.

'Is that what you want?'

Good question. Was it?

No, I didn't want a bubble life. Never to go shopping or have fun like going to get lunch and see a film. That wasn't what it was about when I stopped speaking all those years ago, but somehow it had morphed into this without me being consciously aware of what I was becoming.

<No.>

She beamed that face-changing smile. 'Good, because I don't want you to be in a bubble either. We'd make a pretty good team, I think, me and you. I've kind of figured that you don't have any other friends, do you?'

I coloured bright red and shook my head.

'Well, that's OK because neither do I any more. I thought I did, but I found out very fast in these last couple of weeks that they weren't real friends at all. Real friends wouldn't have made assumptions like they did. Real friends wouldn't have bitched behind my back. And they wouldn't have dropped me out of their group like I had leprosy or something.'

Nod.

'So we sort of fit together, don't we? OK, you're younger than me but you're pretty smart so –'

Shake of the head.

'You are. It's obvious. You understand stuff, feelings and things. That's just as smart as being like an A-star student at school.'

Bigger shake of the head. I was in no way smart.

'No, we did this in school! This whole thing about how your IQ isn't that important because people with high IQs often end up being employed by a boss who's not as exam-clever as them, but who's really good at understanding people. Honest, it's true! We did it in Careers.'

Um, OK, I hadn't come across that idea before. My face creased up in confusion as I tried to process, get her to understand . . .

'Your phone – use your phone,' she reminded me.

Of course. I swallowed and prepared a text. It wasn't that I didn't want to share this with her. I was just so unused to it that it felt as off balance as driving on the other side of the road.

<Not good with people. Can't talk to them!>

'Hmm, I don't know why that is yet, but I'm not buying that you're not good with people.' She narrowed her eyes. 'There must be a really good reason why you stopped talking, but now isn't the time to, er, talk about it!' She laughed. 'We get off here.'

As the afternoon wore on, I began to think Josie might be right. We did seem to sort of fit. Or at least she seemed like she had fun too, hanging out with me. And there was another thing. Josie talked lots. 'My dad says I have verbal diarrhoea,' she told me. And I didn't, so perhaps that worked better than anyone could have predicted.

I noticed, when we got pizza before the film and on the bus home afterwards, that she talked about her dad a lot.

'He's a policeman. Loads of people have been funny with me about that. Always making little digs that are supposed to be jokes, but it shows that they don't quite trust me because of his job. That might be part of why I was so stupid about Lloyd – trying to prove something, but I'm not sure if it was to them or to myself.'

But she never mentioned her mum.

<Do you get on with your mother?>

'My mum died when I was seven. She had cancer.'

<SORRY!!!>

'No, it's fine. It was a long time ago and of course I still miss her, but it's OK. I don't get upset about it now.'

So that was something else we had in common – only one parent each.

'You and Silas seem . . . hmmm, like you don't get on with your mum so well. Or have I got that totally wrong?'

<She's not around very much and she's really into her work.>

'What about your dad? Silas said he left?'

<Yes, I don't see him now.>

'Now *I'm* sorry,' she said. 'Are you OK with that or do you miss him lots?'

<I don't remember him much.>

There was much more I could have said, like how my mother might have had a whole bunch more of us because she swore that being pregnant enhanced her creativity and she loved the feeling of forming a new life inside her, a whole new kind of artistic creation. But she was a lot less enchanted with us when we came out. Snot-nosed toddlers with sticky fingers obviously didn't inspire her in the same way. Her interest in us when we were small had waned by the time it came to Silas and me even more so than for our brother and sisters. For the others, it returned as they got older and their gifts became apparent, but not with me obviously. I was just the weird but boring one.

'Is your brother serious about stopping Lloyd?' Josie asked me as we walked back home from the bus stop.

Nod.

'But how? I mean, what can he do?'

<I don't know, but if he said he's going to do it then he will.>

'That's pretty nice of him,' she said, half puzzled, half impressed. 'You're lucky to have a brother like that looking out for you. Makes me wish I had one instead of being an only child. I always thought they'd be a nuisance – you know, picking on you and stuff. But yours seems pretty cool.'

Yeah, he was. I was lucky. Him not so much, having to put

up with me tagging along after him. I could see why Josie liked Silas. Most people liked Silas, but obviously if you were Josie, you'd like him even more — standing up for you when all the other boys were just horrible. I couldn't see what she saw in Lloyd at all now after how vile he'd been when we saw him. Even if he was quite good-looking, however did she think he was nice and worth loving?

But I've learned that you're blind most of all to what should be right in front of your face.

I collect truths. I write them down in a book I keep hidden under my bed. And that thought right there is one of them.

FROM JOSIE'S PINTEREST BOARD

A real woman can do it all by herself, but a real man wouldn't let her.

CHAPTER 6

It was at school that I had the first inkling of what Silas had done. It was lunchtime and I was sitting in the corner of the library, reading a book, when Toby and a group of other sixth-form boys rushed in and clustered round the computers.

Toby sat down and typed furiously. I was only a couple of metres away, though of course they paid no attention to me. I knew enough from Silas to see Toby was breaking through the school security via a proxy site.

'So you remember Josie whose ex posted those pictures of her? Well, someone's really mad at her ex because you won't believe what's going on with his website and stuff.'

Rachel and her friends came in at a more leisurely pace and stood behind the boys, and then I saw my brother ambling over too, not a care in the world, totally laid back.

'Look at this!' Toby laughed and they crowded closer. 'Someone really knew how to take him out hard. And fast. I can't believe how this thing has spread.'

Behind them I craned my neck, trying to see through a gap.

'What thing?' Rachel demanded, fed up with his failure to get straight to the point.

'Patience, patience, princess!' Toby said.

She snorted. 'This is why you don't have a girlfriend, Toby! Patronising jerk!'

He grinned. 'Thanks, babe, and I love you too.' He clicked on something and they all gasped.

I was momentarily distracted by the horrible thought of Toby as a boyfriend, but then I scooted round in the chair for a better view. Only Silas noticed, but he didn't seem to mind.

The gasps turned to laughter. On the screen was a gigantic picture of a naked Lloyd . . . having sex with another naked Lloyd. It was laid out like a demotivational poster with the caption underneath: 'Because nobody else will have me.'

Toby clicked again and the page changed to a picture of Lloyd feeling a pair of enormous boobs that he'd suddenly sprouted: 'The only ones I'll ever get near.' And then the page changed again, and again – a long series of pictures of Lloyd or whoever with Lloyd's head superimposed, all with one thing in common. They made him look like the dumbest thing ever.

'Wasn't this the website he set up to trash his girlfriend?' Rachel asked.

'Yup, and now he's had the deed turned on him. Comprehensively.' Toby clicked off a picture captioned 'Micro-penis' as the girls snorted with laughter.

'How?' Rachel asked, trying to stop laughing long enough to speak.

'Hacked,' replied Toby. 'And either he doesn't know it yet

or whoever did it has locked him out of his own stuff because he hasn't tried to fix it. Here, check this out – it links back to his Facebook page. Look how many people have left comments already. It's only been up a few hours and . . .' Toby paused and looked up, shocked. 'Seriously, this is hardcore. It's all over the net already.'

'Good,' Rachel said savagely and there were murmurs of agreement from the other girls.

I cast a sidelong glance at Silas who was wearing the most innocent face imaginable.

'Don't you think whoever did that must have had some serious skills?' Toby asked my brother, as the acclaimed computer guru among the boys.

Silas shrugged. 'More than this Lloyd anyway, and the right software to do the job.'

'Can't wait to see what happens next,' Toby said gleefully as he clicked on one more page, with Lloyd's head on the body of a magnified mosquito and the caption: 'Does a lot of buzzing to get noticed, but when he is . . .' the image rolled over to a splat on a desk '. . . he gets slapped down and squashed dead.'

I sidled up behind Silas and prodded him. He drew me away from the others who were still grouped round the computer and gave me *that* smile. 'Oh, believe me, that's nothing yet. Toby doesn't know the half of it! Watch this space.' He winked and then whizzed off back to the sixth-form block before I could interrogate him further.

When they'd all gone out again, I checked my precious new phone and saw a message from Josie: <OMG what did your brother do? I have had Lloyd SCREAMING at me on the phone. Not that I'm bothered. But he's going mental. Something about his internet accounts!!! LOL!>

I bit back a smile of amusement. I probably shouldn't laugh. Something about all this made me feel nervous, as if it could all turn very nasty. But another part of me was thrilled Lloyd was getting what he deserved.

<Silas is good with computers.> I did smile as I sent the response. I liked how understated it was. So few words and so much said.

<ROFL! Yeah, I figured. You make me laugh – you are so funny.>

A huge grin burst out over my face at her answer, until I looked up and found two of the girls in my year watching with their mouths open at the sight of me texting and grinning. I doused the smile from my face and quickly rammed the phone back in my bag.

RAFI'S TRUTH BOOK

Words have the power to heal or destroy.

When words are both true and kind,

they can change our world.

(Buddha)

CHAPTER 7

Josie came round after school and I whisked her upstairs to my room — that was what normal people did, right? — before my mother, who was rearranging pictures in the sitting room, could pass comment.

'It's all over school,' said Josie, flopping breathlessly on to my bed as if she'd run here the whole way. 'Loads of people were watching Lloyd's stuff because they thought the whole thing with the pictures of me was excellent drama, and so now they've all seen it. They've been tweeting about it all day and this afternoon a Twitter account appeared under Lloyd's name, linked to his website and other stuff, and it keeps tweeting apologies to me and saying what a total dumb-ass he is and please, please forgive him. Lloyd never even *had* a Twitter account. But if that was your brother, how did he do that from school? Don't you have security?'

I smiled and rolled my eyes. The school system was nothing that Silas couldn't get around in a few minutes. The laughable thing about my school was it didn't even teach computing as an A level because it was considered too 'new' a subject for the universities to take it seriously, so all the computing geeks did maths and further maths. We only did a piddly bit of ICT up to GCSE. What this meant was that there wasn't a teacher in the place who had a clue how to stop Silas – or anyone – on a mission.

'So it was him then!' Josie grinned. 'Look at this.' She showed me a series of text messages on her phone, from Lloyd. To say he wasn't happy was an understatement. The amount of abuse he was giving her made me quite angry and I almost growled as I read the messages. 'Oh, don't worry about him. I told you – I don't give a toss about him any more so I don't care what he thinks of me. I just wanted it to stop.'

Yes, but what if Silas actually made it worse by making Lloyd so mad he did something even more awful?

She saw my worried face. 'Don't – I'm sure if your brother can do all this, he can cover his tracks so Lloyd doesn't find out it was him.'

Actually and surprisingly, it wasn't Silas I'd been worrying about but she didn't need to know that. There was no point making her nervous when she obviously hadn't thought of that possibility, and she looked so happy.

'It is very, very awesome of your brother to do this.'

Yes, it probably was, but I didn't like the kind of hero-worshipful face that had appeared on Josie. I wanted to tell her that she really should not fall in love with my brother out of some misguided sense of gratitude. Because you see, Silas does not fall in love back. No girl ever touches his heart. He isn't mean to any of the girls he dates. No, it's not that. But they always end up the ones who get hurt when he realises they like him more than he does them. He tries to break it off gently, but it never works out like that.

It seems to me from what I hear when they cry on the phone at him, when I hear the girls in school sobbing in the toilets before morning registration, that a boy can never break it off gently. It always seems to leave a big, gaping wound. Getting dumped hurts however nicely it's done.

Or maybe it hurts even more if they do it nicely.

'Anyway, enough of me,' Josie said, grabbing my old teddy and settling back on the pillows as if they were cushions on a sofa. 'And more about *you*.'

Er, me. Oh no, no, no. There was absolutely no need to be talking about me at all. Really not. Nothing interesting to see here – move on. Maybe I would prefer her to be mooning over Silas. It would divert her attention away from me at least.

'I'm mostly guessing, but I decided you probably don't like talking about yourself much, given the whole not talking at all thing?'

I nodded, knowing my cheeks were flushing, but unable to stop them.

'So that's OK because most people, including me, talk about themselves far too much and don't listen enough.'

True.

'But friends need to know some stuff about each other so I thought we'd start with some small things. Kind of get to know each other better?'

Tentative nod.

'So I'll ask three questions and then you can do the same. Got it? Good, so number one – what's your favourite colour?'

I let out the breath I'd been holding. OK, this wasn't so bad.

<Yellow.>

'Mine's red. Someone said it suited me once and it cheers me up. Number two – what's your favourite food?'

This was easy. <Pasta with pesto.> The smell of basil always made me feel happy.

Josie grinned ruefully. 'Chips. Or chocolate. I can never decide. Number three – you might have to think about this one – what's your favourite quote? I collect quotes. I try to snag at least one good one a day. I get most of them from Pinterest. My favourite at the moment is, "We forfeit three fourths of ourselves in order to be like other people." That's so cool, especially for just right now in my life because some days I forget that. Some days it seems like it'd be easier to be like everyone else, you know?'

Nod.

Yes, I knew that feeling; except I couldn't be like everyone else so sometimes I thought it'd be easier to fade away so completely I was invisible. Some days I would do that if I could. Perhaps one day I'd have the courage to tell Josie about that. I thought she might understand and that she might not laugh at me for it. After all, it was amazing that she collected quotes because that meant words must be important to her too. I wanted that to be something we had in common.

But my favourite quote? <It's by Robert Frost. 'I write to find out what I didn't know I knew.'>

Her face lit up. 'That's amazing. No, really, I love that. Do you write then?'

Absolutely scarlet-cheeked nod.

'Can I see something you've written?'

Can you see my soul, you mean? That was like asking me to cut myself open and lay everything inside me bare.

I began to shake my head in horror, but then I remembered another quote I loved but would never dare aspire to: 'Speak the truth, even if your voice shakes.' When I came across that one last year, it made my eyes fill up and I had to let the tears roll down my face for a while before I could stand to breathe again.

I couldn't speak the truth. But I could write it maybe.

Plus I could never be a writer if I didn't show anyone my work.

Dare to believe in your future, a voice said in my head. I didn't know where it came from. More than that, I didn't know why I listened to it then, because I never would have done before that moment, but somehow I found myself getting up on wobbly legs and, with shaking hands, taking out my notebooks from the box under the bed.

I flipped open a simple exercise book. I liked to keep my short stories separate, in their own individual books. I shoved the book at Josie with a shrug and retreated to the other side of the room. That story, the one about an adopted girl who was trying to find her birth mother, was one of my better ones. But that didn't mean I wasn't feeling sick and paralysed as I watched Josie read it. Or rather when I didn't watch her because I couldn't stand to look. So I sat by the window and stared determinedly out of it.

I was concentrating so hard on what was outside – our garden looking exactly the same as it did every day – that I all but jumped out of my skin when she said, 'Rafi, this is great. It really, really is!'

I turned round, flustered and shaking my head. Josie was grinning at me.

'No, Rafi, it is. I could never write anything like that. I swear I thought I was going to cry at the end. Can I see another one?'

Was she flattering me or was she serious? She *looked* serious, but I knew my stuff wasn't that good.

Still, I'd shown her one so I might as well dig another out. The one in the red notebook wasn't too awful. I could perhaps let her see that one.

I suppose the feeling you have when someone reads what you've written for the first time is a bit like actors getting stage fright. There's no point writing for it only to sit in a box under your bed, but letting someone else into your world is *terrifying*.

I sat motionless and nauseated again as Josie read the next story. Again she beamed at the end and told me how fantastic it was, but I wasn't at all convinced. Still, it was nice of her.

'I want you to do something,' she said, watching my face. 'Will you try?'

I held my hands up to say I didn't know.

'I want you to write a story about you, about when you stopped talking. I hope one day you'll show it to me, but even if you never do, I want you to write it. Do you think you could try?'

Could I?

I felt a prickle of nervous excitement at the thought. Yes, that was something I should write. I didn't know why, but something inside me told me it was a good thing to do. A *true* thing.

I nodded.

Josie let out a triumphant squeal. 'Awesome! That'll be the most amazing story ever, I know it.' She rushed over and hugged me. 'And I hope you do let me read it when it's ready.'

Now *that* I couldn't do, but I was still buzzing with the notion of writing my story for myself and so I blocked that unwelcome thought out and hugged Josie back.

Hugging a friend felt good. I felt *normal*.

We hung out a while longer and then she went home when it got dark. It was only when she'd gone that I realised I never did ask her the three questions.

If an injury has to be done to a man it should be so severe that his vengeance need not be feared.

(Niccolo Machiavelli)

CHAPTER 8

At lunchtime, the library computers were full. I stared as people crowded around, giggling and nudging each other. The librarian watched from her desk with a frown. She knew they were up to something, but couldn't catch them. And Silas's friends were right in the middle of it all.

I sneaked over and sat down where there was space, near some boys in my year, Ben and Callum.

'So what's this?' Callum asked Ben.

'The *Codes of War* site. Two nights ago, the forum starts buzzing about some guy taking an epic revenge on another so I followed a couple of links until I saw it for myself. Basically some guy made an "I got dumped so I'm acting like a little bitch" website about his ex-girlfriend. Posted some naked pictures of her, to make out she's a mega slut, and tried to get all his mates to spread it around. Then a few days later, someone else, and nobody knows who it is because this guy has completely covered his tracks, comes along and takes him out. Like totally. He hacks all the guy's sites and changes everything – look, see this – to make the guy look like the biggest tool ever, and he gets what he's done everywhere. And I mean everywhere – this thing is all over the net. It started at night, when the US gamers were on the forum. Now it's right round the world.'

'It went viral?'

'Viral like Ebola,' said Ben with a grin. 'What makes this really interesting is this girl goes to the Catholic High and her ex is at the college.'

'What, here?'

'Yeah. So this is global, mate, but right on our doorstep too.'

'So that's why everyone is buzzing about it.'

I got up and left as quietly as I'd come. My text tone had pinged. It was Josie asking me to meet her in town after school. I could, but I'd have to tell Silas and he was still with the others in the library. I took a deep breath and went back in there, pushing my way through the throngs around the computers until I got to him.

Toby pushed back from the screen, nearly running over my foot with his wheeled chair. 'Silas, have you seen this? It is seriously messed up.' He was reading down a messageboard with the *Codes of War* logo at the top. My brother glanced over, but their friend Jake pushed him aside so he could see.

'He's built a botnet,' Jake exclaimed. 'In, what, two days? Whoever he is, he's scary!'

'What's a botnet?' Rachel asked.

Toby scanned through the posts. 'So what he did was clone Lloyd's social media accounts, all of them, and then got all his friends to swap to the cloned accounts before anyone knew what he'd done. And he's created this video which everyone's been watching – no, don't click on it! When this went viral, people opened it and it's got code hidden in there that takes ownership of their machines. That's what the botnet is,' he said, looking up at Rachel who pulled a freaked-out face.

'Looks like they've only found out because he's told everyone on the forum. He's used their machines to relay spam messages supposedly from Lloyd saying how sorry he is and how the pictures were all a fake and will Josie please forgive him,' Jake said with a frown. 'Hey, that means he's got control of my laptop too!'

'And mine,' Toby added, glowering. 'Nobody on here knows how to stop him. He says he'll release the machines as soon as Lloyd apologises publicly to Josie and stops going after her. And that he won't use the botnet for anything other than that.' He yanked his phone out of his pocket and began texting furiously.

'What are you doing?' Rachel asked.

'Texting as many people who know Lloyd as possible to give him some hassle! This is heavy stuff. I tell you, I'm more than a bit scared of what this guy could do. This all hit from nowhere and so fast. I've got no idea how he's done it.'

'Neither has anyone else on here,' Jake said gloomily. 'They're all talking about how they can clean their machines up, but no one's got a solution yet. If I see that Lloyd, he better get out of my way. I don't want this guy messing around inside my PC.'

Toby finished texting. 'Silas, do you know how to fix this? I mean, can you clean us up?'

Silas stretched his legs out. 'Probably. But he may be on the level, you know. He might really release them once he's got what he wants.'

'Yeah, and he might sell all my payment details halfway round the world too,' Jake snapped.

Silas rolled his sea-blue eyes. 'I'll come round to yours later and see what I can do,' he said. 'Hey, sis, what do you want?'

The rest of them started at his words. They hadn't noticed me. I showed him the text.

'OK, I'll see you at home. You OK to get there yourself?'

Yes, I had a bus pass. I wouldn't have to speak to the driver so I was OK.

I met Josie at the bus station. 'Sorry!' she said brightly. 'I only found out about this today from the noticeboard in school and we have to go – it'll be so amazing.'

I shook my head in confusion.

'A face-painting workshop at the library! Like, they teach you how to do it. Don't you think that's the best thing ever to do after school on a horrible, wet Thursday afternoon?' She beamed at me. 'Come on! I've been looking forward to this all day!'

I chuckled to myself as I followed her. She really was nuts, in the best possible way.

Anarchy

noun

- a state of disorder due to absence or non-recognition of authority or other controlling systems
- absence of government and absolute freedom of the individual, regarded as a political ideal.

CHAPTER 9

'The funny thing is, Raf,' Silas said as he lounged on the sofa, staring out of the French windows on to our rain-swept garden, 'that nobody suspects it's me.'

Yes, I thought that was a bit odd too, but then I wasn't sure how many people realised that Silas knew Josie now. Lloyd might have seen him with her, but he had no idea of Silas's abilities. And Silas's friends weren't aware of the connection at all.

'Online is an anonymous world,' he said as the rain battered against the glass. 'Or it can be if you know how to make it that way. But too many people have thought that and got caught. You have to keep your guard up.'

I looked at him critically as he turned to face me.

'I *will* drop it all once Lloyd's learned his lesson. Just because I could do much worse stuff with the bots doesn't mean I intend to.'

I raised my eyebrows.

'Oh come on, don't look at me like that. I've always been able to do stuff like this, but I've never had reason to. Nothing's changed.' He laughed. 'What? You think I'm suddenly going to become some cyber-criminal mastermind and take over the world? In that case you need to get me a little white cat I can sit and stroke while I cackle maliciously as I execute my evil plans.'

My eyes rolled in disgust and he laughed again.

'Look, it'll work. Lloyd will leave Josie alone and he'll learn not to mess with people that way. It'll be good for him. I don't know what you're worrying about.'

I didn't think Silas had ever had a day's worry in his life. He practised the art of living in the moment to perfection. We were opposite poles, he and I: he repelled all the cares of life and I attracted them. Consequently nothing ever seemed to touch him that deeply. That's not to say he was superficial, but he never appeared to feel anything with the intensity that tore and ripped at me. 'Placid' my mother once called him, her nose wrinkling slightly in distaste because the job of the artist, she said, was to feel passionate intensity. She looked as if she didn't know how she'd come to have such a son. It was disloyal of me in that moment, but when I heard that I felt relief, because it wasn't just me who disappointed her.

But I didn't think Silas really cared about that either. He disregarded our mother's opinion on most things, perfectly content in the circle of himself, which opened only to allow me in.

His phone rang and he glanced at it. I saw the quick grimace and knew before asking what this was about. He looked up at me, knowing my eyes would be asking the question.

'Kirsty,' he said. 'I went on a few dates with her, but . . .'

He sighed. 'I managed to screw up again. I try to keep it light, nothing heavy, but it always goes wrong, Raf. You know, I don't get it. Toby manages to date without girls it getting so . . . *intense*. Why can't I do that? Maybe I should ask him how he manages it.'

He manages it by being Toby, I thought. No girl in her right mind would want to have him as a serious boyfriend. He was probably quite amusing from time to time, but you'd never get attached to anyone that, um, Toby-like!

I waved a finger at the phone.

Silas sighed more heavily. 'She says she's in love with me. Which is stupid. We've only been out four times. What is it with girls? Why are they like that?'

I couldn't help him there. He knew more girls than I did and knew them far better too. Though I could ask Josie. That might be an idea. I didn't have to tell her it was for Silas.

'I don't want anything that full-on with any of them. Raf, I just don't feel those things they seem to feel. Perhaps there's too much of Mum in me.' He stared at the raindrops on the window in a rare moment of uncertainty. 'Or Dad. They're both messed up when it comes to relationships, aren't they? One's a control freak and the other can't commit.'

I frowned.

'Dad split up with the latest girlfriend. I guess Mum didn't tell you that. You didn't hear it from me, OK?'

Nod.

'I'm going to have to tell Kirsty I don't feel the same way. And that I *won't* feel the same way. And it'd be better if we don't go out again.'

I texted him quickly. <Are you sure you might not get to like her more?>

Silas flashed a smile at the unexpected communication. 'I didn't think you were ever going to text me. I thought you might be saving it just for girly chats with Josie. Yeah, I'm sure. I'm beginning to think I'm not capable of being in love. Don't get me wrong, Raf, I like the girls I date. They're great. But that's it – it's just like.'

<Maybe it's different for boys.>

'No, that's just a myth passed around by girls who are sore they got ditched. Boys fall in love, sure they do. I've got mates who have. Like Sam.'

That was true. Sam was notoriously besotted with Cassie and had been since they first got together two years before.

'No, Raf. I think it's me. Like there's a bit of me missing that just can't make that jump.'

I'd never heard Silas sound so unsure, so doubting. It never occurred to me that he would ever think he was the one in the wrong.

He got up and flicked the TV on and stared moodily at that for a while. I guess it was less wearing than staring at rain.

'All the books, all the songs,' he said after a while in a quiet,

76

flat voice, 'the films – all about love. Like it's some amazing be-all and end-all. But what if there are people who just don't have that capacity, Rafi?'

I didn't know the answer to that, still trying to process this new side to my brother. But I couldn't believe it of him. If there were people who couldn't love in the way the poets and songwriters wrote about, then Silas couldn't be one of them, could he?

He flicked through channels and appeared to lose himself in the news reports.

This was Dad's fault. He should be here to talk to his son about male issues. He should be here setting an example, a role model for my brother, instead of being a dysfunctional mess who couldn't stick at anything or fight for anyone. Let's face it, he must know my mother wasn't going to be of much help to a seventeen-year-old boy confused about relationships. Since he left she had eschewed men (I loved that word eschew – it reminded me of Miss Havisham for some unaccountable reason) and devoted herself to 'her art'.

Silas sat forward, attracting my attention, and stared intently at the TV.

I crossed the room and tapped his shoulder in question as I sat down next to him.

'Shush!' he said.

I cast my eyes up at the ceiling. I knew what he meant, but oh, the irony!

The reporter on the TV said something about anarchists and a city riot. I was only half listening. The pictures showed the usual thing – teens and twenty-somethings all dressed in black, running around with masks on, throwing bricks at police and smashing windows.

Bunch of idiots. What was the point? They weren't going to achieve anything. Some of the ones at the back had banners with anti-government messages painted on them in red, with circled 'A's daubed in each corner. You could see in the pictures that they were checking mobile phones all the time and relaying instructions to each other.

But why was Silas so interested? I poked his shoulder again.

'They're protesting against government corruption,' he said. 'It's pretty fascinating how much dirt they've managed to dig up and leak to the media in the last few days. They're all over Twitter at the moment, spreading the word on who's done what.'

Corruption?

'A lot of dodgy stuff that the Cabinet has tried to sweep under the carpet. If you ask me, these guys aren't really that mad about it, but it gives them a stick to beat the government with and get the public more onside at the same time. But I reckon their main interest is just raising hell, whoever's in power.'

Yeah, whatever. I couldn't see the attraction at all. Like spraying graffiti tags on walls and smashing bus shelters – utterly useless and mindless. Anyone with half a brain wouldn't want to bother.

I made a drinking motion with my hand at Silas.

'Oh yeah, thanks. Coffee would be good please.'

I wandered off to the kitchen, leaving him to watch the losers on the news.

JOSIE'S PINTEREST BOARD

One day I may find my prince, but my dad will always be my king.

CHAPTER 10

Josie was waiting for us when we got off the school bus.

'You are not going to believe this.'

'Oh, I think I might,' Silas said under his breath. Only I heard him.

'Lloyd turned up outside school today and apologised to me in full view of EVERYONE! And . . .' She paused to check we were taking this in fully. 'And he said, so they could all hear it, that the photos of me weren't real and he'd faked them.'

'Wow,' said Silas, with a grin that bordered on smug. 'Result!'

She chuckled. 'Oh, and he added, very, very quietly, that would I please tell whoever it was on his back that he'd done *it* now and get them to leave him alone. Actually, his exact words were, "Now call off your pit bull!" Bless!'

'Yeah,' said Silas, kicking a pebble down the pavement as he walked, 'I'll take my teeth out of his neck now. As long as he keeps away. Hopefully he's learned his lesson and he's sussed that, when you try to be a player, you've got to face the possibility that there's someone who will play nastier than you.'

Certainly if Lloyd hadn't got that message by now then he must be really thick.

'I owe you massive thanks,' Josie said to him.

'No, you don't,' Silas replied. 'Not at all. You're hanging out with my sister and it's making her happy so you don't owe me a thing.'

He didn't see my face, but Josie did. I turned away abruptly and pretended to fiddle with something inside my bag. Silas walked on, but Josie shook her head at me as I followed slowly. 'Later,' she whispered.

My throat was tight and rough, as if sandpaper had been drawn down it. There was a scream waiting to come out. Of rage at Silas, that I didn't want a friend bought by his actions. I didn't want one on those terms. I wanted one like everybody else. One who liked me for me.

How did he not know that?

Josie invited me into her house as we got to the gate and I accepted gratefully. I didn't even want to see Silas right now.

'I honestly don't think he meant it how it sounded,' she said as we walked up her front path. 'I know how you interpreted it and I know why – he didn't phrase it well. But really all I think he meant was, "You're my sister's friend so I've got your back."'

I nodded, because it was expected of me, but she wasn't fooled.

'Now are you going to be so dumb that I have to tell you that is *so* not why we're friends? Please tell me you know that, right?'

I don't know. Maybe.

'I will get really mad with you if I have to explain that we're friends because we're just made to be. Because I totally thought you understood that already!'

Possibly . . .

'Oh, come on, Rafi!'

I forced myself to nod more certainly. Trust, right? That's what friends did.

She twitched her mouth from side to side, assessing me. Then she got her phone out and opened up her Pinterest page. 'See that?'

It was a quote by Emily Dickinson, written under a picture of an umbrella: 'I felt it shelter to speak to you.'

Ridiculously, tears welled up in my eyes.

'See, stoopid,' Josie said gruffly and hugged me. 'Now come in and I'll make us milkshakes with ice cream.'

Josie's house was a large Victorian villa with a double front. She pointed out a black VW Golf on the drive. 'My dad's old car. He's saving it for me when I learn to drive next year.' I looked suitably impressed.

We skirted round the path to the side of the house, through high, dense laurel hedges, to a side porch hidden from view from the road.

'We never use the front door,' she said, unlocking the porch and letting me into a big open-plan kitchen. It wasn't at all what I expected from the exterior, which was traditional decor framed by the standard period-style garden. But inside the walls had been ripped down to make a huge space painted stark white with glossy white kitchen units and a pale stone floor. The kitchen ran on into a living space with contemporary white sofas and a giant plasma TV screen mounted on the wall.

'This is where we mostly hang out,' she said.

We. She meant her and her dad of course. It seemed an awfully big space for the two of them. Come to think of it, it was a massive house for the two of them. I wondered if she had hoped to fill it with her friends before everything went wrong. Maybe two or three lounging around would make the room seem less barren.

She walked over to the island in the kitchen and began pulling glasses from a cupboard and throwing fruit and milk and ice cream into a blender. I watched, fascinated, from a high stool. This was not something I was familiar with. Silas might cook, but he didn't make fripperies like this. She whizzed the whole lot together and then decanted it into two tall glasses, added another scoop of vanilla ice cream to the top of each and stuck a straw in.

'Voilà!' she said, sliding a glass towards me and taking a deep, satisfied suck on her straw.

It tasted great: summer in a glass.

She caught my eye. 'Yeah, good, isn't it?'

The door opened and closed behind me and I turned nervously to find a man in a suit coming in. He was tall and broad-shouldered with a serious face. His skin was a darker shade of brown than Josie's and his hair was buzz-cut short.

'Hello,' he said to me and he had the deepest voice I'd ever heard. Rich too, a voice with many layers and tones, but most of all with a quiet and undeniable authority. This was not a man you argued with. I understood now why Toby said that day on the bus that Josie would never let her dad know what Lloyd had done. I'd tremble at having to confess anything to him.

And yet . . . he gave off this feeling that he'd keep you completely safe no matter what. Maybe she should have told him. He might have been mad at her, and his version of mad at you might be terribly difficult to take without crumbling to bits, but he'd have taken care of it. Of that I was sure.

Safe. Strong. That's what I got from him in the instant we weighed each other up. I wondered what he got from me.

'Dad, this is Rafi from down the street. You remember I told you she doesn't talk.'

I raised my hand in a polite little wave.

He smiled, a small, reserved thing, but oddly comforting. 'Yes. Hi, it's nice that Josie's made a friend here already. She's talked about you a lot. She says you're a very smart girl. And I can see that she's right.'

I felt the surprise express itself on my face.

He tapped the side of his head with one finger. 'Policeman's prerogative, summing a person up in a few seconds. And we have to be good at it.' He gave me a slow, serious wink and then walked towards the hall. 'I'm off to shower work away and get changed. Josie, why don't you cook something for your friend if she's hungry. She's welcome to stay for dinner.'

And in that moment how I wished he was my dad. Did Josie know how lucky she was? That calm, stable presence there at the end of every day for her. Expecting the best of her, but there to pick up the pieces when she failed.

'You want to stay for dinner?' Josie cocked her head at me hopefully.

Did dogs like bones? Yes, I wanted to stay. I wanted to drink in this atmosphere so I knew forever what normal was. Like an addict waiting for a hit, I wanted this sense of family vicariously over and over again.

Right then I was glad I had no words because I would not have wanted to have told my brother about this. It would have made me too sad.

I met a lady in the meads,

Full beautiful – a faery's child,

Her hair was long, her foot was light,

And her eyes were wild.

(John Keats – 'La Belle Dame Sans Merci')

CHAPTER 11

Josie and I settled into a rhythm of hanging out with each other most evenings and weekends. Despite my expectation that once the Lloyd business was over she would take up with her other friends again, that simply hadn't happened. It seemed that, like Mr Darcy, her good opinion once lost was lost forever. I ventured to say this to her, by text of course, and she laughed about it. Threw her head right back and laughed and laughed. 'Yeah, my sister, you're right about that.'

She called me that sometimes – my sister – and it made me happy.

My mother had an exhibition at a local gallery and insisted, in a rare moment of desire for familial solidarity, that we all went along one Saturday. Josie, never having had to suffer the exhibitions before, was fascinated and begged to come along. Silas didn't inflict it on any of his friends so there were just the three of us. There were a couple of other artists debuting in the exhibition, but my mother was the main attraction.

Silas and I looked politely over our mother's work, but really Josie was far more interested than we were. And then it would have been incredibly rude of us not to have given some time to the other artists so we trudged round their work too, listening to erudite types expounding on the merits of each piece. Or actually trying not to listen, but those people always have such loud voices that you can't shut them out.

We stopped in front of a sculpture and I had the first glimmer of genuine interest I'd had in the whole two hours we'd been here. At first glance it looked like a heap of twisted metal and no more, but look closer and you could see tiny creatures hiding within – a field mouse, a butterfly, a wren . . . I walked round it, looking for more. I heard Josie exclaim and I knew she'd begun to see too.

But Silas . . . Silas never did see it. Because just as he began to focus on the sculpture to see what had so attracted our attention, a girl stepped into his line of sight.

I caught her scent before I saw her, a subtle, warm waft of fruit and spices. She stood, one hand on her hip, one foot turned out in front of the other like a dancer. Silky black hair fell straight past her shoulders, framing a heart-shaped face with porcelain skin which appeared to be free of make-up. She was dressed entirely in black: black jeans, black T-shirt, black canvas parka with a fishtail back that reached her knees and black Converse sneakers. She was small, maybe five foot two, and slim enough to be jealous of, but with enough curves to be even more jealous of. I felt Josie draw in a breath of envy beside me as she spotted the girl.

Josie was pretty, yes, but this girl was in another league. It wasn't any one of her features individually that made her beautiful, but all put together she exuded *something* that even Josie and I could see.

Silas looked like he'd been sucker-punched.

'You like this one?' She spoke to me first, not to him.

Nod.

'Then you like hidden depths,' she said with a secretive smile. She turned to Silas. 'How about you?'

'Er . . . yeah . . . er . . .' Silas's cheeks had turned a faint pink.

Josie kissed her teeth and turned back to the sculpture.

The girl gave her a faintly amused glance and then proceeded to ignore her.

'I noticed you walking around.' I wasn't sure which of us she was talking to. 'Why do you come to an exhibition if you don't like it?'

Silas finally appeared to find words again. 'Oh, our mother's exhibiting so, you know, we've seen all her stuff before.'

'Clarissa Ramsey is your mother? Wow, that's amazing.' But she didn't say it as if she found it amazing. More like she was secretly laughing at us because that's how we expected her to react. She'd said what most people said when we told them who our mother was.

Josie wandered off to look at the next sculpture and I hesitated, caught between following her and worried about what would happen if I did. Silas was being highly weird with this girl.

'It's kind of more interesting for us to look at the other exhibitors,' he said, apparently not minding if she was laughing at him.

'Of course,' she said, swapping her feet round in that strange half-third position she was standing in. 'So what's your favourite work today?'

He opened his mouth to answer her and then stopped, flummoxed.

'Cat got your tongue?' she said, starting to look away across the gallery as if he was boring her.

Silas laughed, a hard, surprised snort. 'Looks like it,' he said.

She looked back at him, mild interest reviving. 'So do you have a favourite piece?'

'Not really.' He shrugged.

'Honesty,' she said thoughtfully, running her tongue over her teeth – small, white, even teeth. 'Finally.'

He gave a rueful smile and stared at his feet. I could tell he was thinking he'd blown something. Suddenly, passionately and desperately, I hoped he had.

'Lara,' she said abruptly, holding her hand out to shake in an oddly adult gesture. How old was she? Around eighteen?

My brother took her hand in a firm but gentle grip. 'Silas.'

She raised a perfectly arched eyebrow. 'Unusual.'

'Yes.'

At any other time, or with any other girl, it would be funny

91

to see him so at sea, but I had a strong feeling he was swimming way too far out from shore. I called him back in my head, for all the good that would do.

She straightened up. 'I should go. I have stuff to do.'

Silas's face fell. Yup, he'd blown it. And then inspiration struck him. 'Can I buy you a coffee? There's a café opposite here.'

She regarded him with an impenetrable expression. 'No, I don't think so, thank you. Goodbye.' And with that she walked off and didn't look back.

Silas stared after her like a dog whose bone has been taken away.

Josie reappeared by my shoulder. 'Hmmm . . .' she said, 'who on earth was she?'

I shrugged, perplexed.

'Loves herself for sure,' Josie said with a sniff.

But you would, wouldn't you, if you looked like her? To have that much power, to stop a boy in his tracks that way, so that even now he was staring after the place where you'd been, it was inconceivable to me. My head could not imagine inhabiting a world where that was my reality. And of course it never would be.

I wondered how it made Lara feel. Did she even notice how far removed she was from girls like me, the ones who slip through life without ever turning a head in the street? Or were we not worthy of her attention?

When my brother finally turned away from the spot where she'd last been, his eyes held a misty look, as if he was still not back with us, still somewhere trailing in her wake.

JOSIE'S PINTEREST BOARD

Love yourself enough to never lower your standards for anyone.

CHAPTER 12

I couldn't sleep so I pulled a hoody over my pyjamas and padded across the landing in bare feet to Silas's room. I didn't knock in case it woke my mother, but scratched quietly on his door instead.

'Come in,' was the whispered response.

I closed the door softly behind me and tapped a question on his shoulder.

He grinned briefly as he typed some mumbo-jumbo. 'Fixing the stuff I did to get Josie's loser to leave her alone.' He gestured to his bed and I curled up on there, pulling a corner of the duvet over my legs. 'But the crap I took down on that website stays taken down. Some of those comments! They were so far beyond out of order, they were in the stratosphere. I don't get guys like that – they say they like girls, but they don't or they wouldn't talk about them that way. Don't you ever go out with a boy who objectifies women that way!'

It was touching that he thought a boy would ever ask me to go out with him but there, that was classic Silas, forgetting how few people had the confidence not to follow and go with popular opinion.

'You're wrong – someone will,' he said. 'And it'll be someone special. You're lucky – the losers will leave you alone. You won't have to waste time with them, or with people who don't want you for who you really are.' He crossed over and stroked my hair. 'Don't regret the lack of quantity, Rafi. Don't ever do that because quantity means nothing. Quality is everything.'

Unaccountably I wanted to cry, in case he was right and there was hope. But no, Silas was a glass-half-full person and I just wasn't.

He went back to his computer, opened another screen and typed more nonsense.

Were all boys like him really? In the darkness after midnight, would they spill the secrets of their soul into the right ear? And would those secrets be beautiful?

I thought of Toby and snorted. No, it couldn't be that way with all boys. Not the ones who'd rather burp in your ear and fart on you than reveal a gossamer-thin thread of sensitivity, even if they actually possessed one. I was having a very hard time believing Toby and Lloyd had those threads at all.

I wanted to ask Silas because he might know. Maybe it was a boy secret after all and not to be revealed to girls. But even if I could have spoken, I didn't think I could have articulated the question – it was too much of a tangle of confused ideas and feelings in my head.

As a fourteen-year-old girl, finding a way to ask one of the great mysteries of life, like whether boys who think girls are just sex objects have feelings too, is completely impossible. I would've had to sit down and draft that question several times before I got it to make anything approaching sense.

Silas glanced over at me and then opened up an internet browser. 'I want to show you something, Rafi.'

I sat up and shuffled to the end of the bed. I didn't recognise the website he was on. He opened up what looked like a very long series of conversations, some of them with links to pictures.

'Read this.'

I scanned down the page and he scrolled as I read. After only a few posts, I wanted to turn away, uncomfortable at how these boys spoke to the girls.

'Read it,' said Silas.

I continued. They were trying to get the girls to post pictures, just like the kind Lloyd had taken of Josie. If they didn't post them, they'd be shunned and nobody on the site would want to speak to them. Some girls had obviously just left and not come back. Others did post, and then there were comments after discussing how they looked, some complimentary, some anything but. One of the girls got upset and they all laughed at her.

'Read enough now?' Silas asked.

Nod.

'Good. Remember that. And don't ever, ever let a boy treat you like that. If they try, you tell them where to go. Like Rachel — she takes no disrespect from any boy. You don't have to do stuff like that. No girl does. A boy who really likes you, he'll do whatever you want. A boy who tries to get you to do this stuff, he's got nothing you want. OK?'

Nod.

Silas nodded back, satisfied. 'Anyway, what's up? Can't sleep?'

Nod.

'You want to watch me kill stuff on here for a while?'

I thought about it. Probably wasn't the thing most guaranteed to send me off to sleep but I'd never watched him gaming before and I was quite fascinated to see him in action. This was a side of Silas I didn't know first-hand.

Nod.

He grinned. 'Tuck yourself up then.' He tilted the screen so I could see from my prone position on the bed and then he logged on to some war game and started.

And I learned that the look on his face when he made a kill was deadly.

RAFI'S TRUTH BOOK:

I have learned silence from the talkative,

tolerance from the intolerant, and

kindness from the unkind; yet strange,

I am ungrateful to these teachers.

(Kahlil Gibran)

CHAPTER 13

It was in morning break the next day, when I was thinking over what Silas said, that I remembered the girl in the gallery. Lara.

She wouldn't take that kind of thing from any guy, of that I was sure. She made me think of a quote Josie had posted on her page: 'I'm not a princess to need saving, I'm a queen and I've got this stuff handled.'

Yes, that was Lara. She walked out of that gallery like a queen leaving her subjects.

Even now I was wondering who she was, where she was from. Did Silas think about her? I was guessing yes.

I looked around me at the other girls milling about in the canteen. Not one of them seemed to have that air of completely self-contained assurance that she did. You could tell they worried if they were too fat or not pretty enough or too smart or their boobs were too small. Lara looked as if she'd never had such a thought in her life. On reflection, maybe she was the one who'd got it right.

It was as I looked around that it hit me just how much of a weirdo I was. I spent all day in this school alone, except for when I saw my brother, who hadn't appeared yet with his friends. All day I spent in silence, holed up in the solitariness of me. I hadn't wanted this, but it was a trap I'd sprung all by myself. The thing was, I didn't know how to get out of it now. Imagine if I came into school the next day suddenly speaking. Nobody, absolutely nobody, would shut up about it — it'd be all round the place in minutes. Hey, Silas's freak sister SPOKE!

The thought of that much attention made me want to curl up in a corner and die to escape notice. It was inescapable.

So this was my day . . . arrive here at school, sit in form room, go to lesson, sit through break, next lesson, then another, then lunch. Then more lessons. On and on. Day after day, without a word to anyone. Year after year. And no way out.

I was in tears at the back of the sports hall when Silas found me. One of his friends had seen me run out and had gone to get him.

'What's up?'

Everything.

'Was someone mean to you?'

No, nobody was anything to me. They never are.

'Rafi, you're worrying me. What's wrong?'

I want to know how to be normal. I can't be. I can't speak, I just can't. But I want to know how it's possible to get back even if I can't do it. I shook my head. It was nothing he could do anything about. He tried to give me a hug, but I shoved him away, ignoring the wounded look on his face.

Then his face hardened and he snatched my bag off me and

took my phone. I slapped out at him to try to get it back, but he held me off easily with one hand while he quickly texted with the other.

I wanted to scream at him . . . wanted it so badly . . . but . . . but . . . NOTHING came out. I kicked out at him in temper instead.

He handed me the phone back and I saw what he'd done.

It was a text to Josie. <Hey, this is Silas. R is really upset about something and won't tell me what. Can you come over later please?>

I stared at him, open-mouthed.

'If you won't tell me, tell her,' he said.

RAFI'S TRUTH BOOK

The heart has its reasons of which

reason knows nothing.

(Blaise Pascal)

CHAPTER 14

'Everyone needs someone, Rafi,' were Josie's first words to me when she came into my bedroom.

I shrugged. It wasn't true for me. I didn't need anyone. Even Silas. If I did, I wouldn't have shut them all out. Except, said a small voice in my head that sounded like my own the last time I heard it, it wasn't about shutting people out. That wasn't why I stopped speaking.

So many warped reasons in my head now that I used to justify why I didn't start talking. None of them bore any resemblance to why that little four-year-old me began to clam up.

I'd started writing the story when Josie asked me to. It wasn't very good or even very story-like at all. I wanted it to be something really good, strongly crafted, something read to be appreciated. But as usual I failed.

Josie spent a while trying to dig out of me what was wrong and, when that didn't work, she went in search of Silas, who presumably had let her in in the first place. They came back together.

'We're going to the library,' Silas announced, curtly I thought. 'I need to get a set of study notes for an essay I'm doing, Josie needs to get some stuff for her project and you can come with us instead of moping around here.'

I shook my head. I didn't want to go anywhere.

'Fine,' said Silas, and then in an act of utter betrayal, 'I'm telling Mum.'

I got my coat.

It was raining and we had to dodge puddles, huddled under umbrellas. The windows of the library were steamed up in a way that made the child in you want to draw pictures on them. Silas and Josie headed off in different directions to find what they needed. I wandered around the fiction shelves, collecting possibles to take out on loan.

I sat down with the books at a table near Silas, who was now scanning through his pile of books.

My phone blooped and when I checked it, it was my Twitter Feed. I sighed. I hadn't even wanted Twitter, but Silas and Josie had insisted on setting it up.

Silas Ramsey @silram99
@hottobyd In the library with @rafiram10 and @josiejjackson doing work stuff

A few moments later, another Tweet appeared.

Tobias the Man @hottobyd

@silram99 @rafiram10 @josiejjackson Coming over now! Need
to sort stuff for the weekend. You know Josie?

Over at his table, Silas groaned. 'I've got work, dumb-ass,'
he muttered. But he put his phone away and didn't send a
message back.

Josie came over and sat with me, shuffling books across the
table until she got them into some kind of order. I glanced at
them – history books. She got her pad out of her bag and began
writing down the titles and authors. Across from us, Silas had
buried his head in his books again.

'We lose marks if we just use Wikipedia,' Josie muttered. 'It's
not fair. Our history teacher is always going on about a range of
sources. Well, you can get a range off the internet, can't you?'
She sniffed. 'Anyway, Dad says they're going to close this library
soon. What are we supposed to do then? They'll have to let us
use the net.'

I shrugged. I couldn't see the problem.

'You don't get wet online!' Josie said, shivering as a drip ran
off her hair and down her neck. I grinned and shook my head,
going back to my book.

The next time I looked up, it was to find Josie with her
mouth open and my brother looking as if he'd just been shot in
the stomach. Toby was walking across the library towards us,

waving like the idiot he was, followed by . . . the girl from the exhibition.

The rain had made rats' tails of her black hair and her thin cotton parka was soaked through. But she still walked like she was treading on diamond dust while everyone else walked on coal.

'Hey,' said Toby, grinning and sitting down in front of Silas.

Silas tore his eyes away from Lara. 'Yeah,' he said dazedly.

Lara sat down next to Toby. There wasn't a flicker of recognition in her eyes.

'Woah,' Josie whispered in my ear. 'No way – is he going out with her?'

'This is Lara,' Toby said.

'Hi,' Silas said, his eyes already back on her like they were fixed with glue. 'We've met.'

She screwed her face up in confusion. If I did that, I would have looked like a pig or something. She still looked beautiful. 'Have we?'

'The art gallery . . . you probably don't remember . . . the exhibition . . . I saw you there . . .'

'Oh yeah. I remember you. The boy who didn't like anything.'

'Er, yeah, well, I guess I was in a mood with my mother and wasn't prepared to appreciate anything that day.'

Toby snorted. 'Si, I did not come here to talk about your mother. What are you up to this weekend?'

'No plans yet, why?'

He grinned. 'Jake's parents are away – last-minute break. He's got the place to himself. Party!'

Silas nodded. 'Could do.'

Toby looked around and nodded at Josie. 'Bring her if you want.'

'She's my sister's friend,' Silas replied, a little too quickly.

Toby shrugged, missing the point completely. Doh, Toby! 'Bring her as well then.'

'So are you into art?' Silas asked Lara.

Beside me, Josie raised an eyebrow. She was right: this was dangerous territory. If Lara was with Toby, then Silas shouldn't be showing an interest. It could have been an innocent question, but we could see the look in his eyes and it wasn't.

'I liked your mum's stuff,' Lara said. 'You might not, but I thought her work was pretty amazing.'

'I'm too used to it,' Silas said. 'Do you go to lots of exhibitions?'

She laughed. 'Busted! No, it was a one-off. I was bored that day. I like to do new things when I'm bored.'

Why had Toby brought her here? To show off to my brother?

She got up. 'Toby, I'm soaked through. I need to go home and get changed. No, it's OK – stay with your friends. The bus station is only round the corner. I'll see you at the party.'

I wasn't sure whether she said that last part to Toby or Silas or both.

She gave them a little wave as she went out of the door and disappeared into the rain again.

Silas sat back in his chair and looked at Toby. 'You kept her quiet,' he said.

Toby sniggered. 'Hot, isn't she? Like, on fire!'

Silas just stared at him.

'Yeah, well, I just met her so, you know, not running my mouth off to the lads about her and . . . you know . . .'

Next to me, Josie made a derisive noise. 'They're so not going out,' she said.

JOSIE'S PINTEREST BOARD

'Twere all one. That I should love a bright particular star.

(William Shakespeare)

CHAPTER 15

'So, you want to come to this party?' Silas asked Josie. 'Or are you going to hibernate for life after Lloyd?'

'With Rafi?'

'Yeah, why not? It'll do her good to mix.'

'She'll never agree to it.'

Excuse me, sitting right here on the sofa! I threw a cushion at them.

Silas caught it and laughed. 'Prove her wrong then,' he said with a wink.

'I dunno,' Josie said. 'There'll be loads of people there who saw all that stuff about me . . .'

'All the more reason to get back out there! And honestly it'll be pretty tame. Jake's parents would go mental if he had some big rowdy thing going on and trashed the place. He wouldn't dare, especially as he wants a car for his eighteenth. I wouldn't let Rafi go if it was going to be messy. I'll be surprised if anybody gets pissed enough to puke.'

Josie laughed. 'Oh, OK then. I guess you're right.'

And I was suddenly afflicted by my first ever party trauma . . . what *was* I going to wear?!

For someone with practically a social phobia – let's face it, lots of people think selective mutism is a kind of social phobia – the word party is bound to send them into a tailspin, which is pretty much where I was for the next few days. Josie managed to prise it out of me that I was freaking out over what to wear. So on Saturday she took me shopping and we bought new jeans and a top that was kind of cool and partyish but laid-back and not trying too hard all at once. Josie, I decided after a morning with her, was beyond awesome at shopping. She knew just where to look and just what to pick up to try on. She didn't amble around shops aimlessly like I saw other girls doing. No, she was more like a guided missile. Zoom in, scope the area, lock on target!

I enjoyed clothes shopping for the first time ever.

But the party was another matter. The closer it got to the time to leave, the sicker I felt in my stomach. I went over to Josie's and she put some make-up on me, just a little bit because she didn't use much herself. 'You don't need it,' she said, 'you've got good skin. And what looks right on my skin tone won't suit yours.' So she lined my eyes and gave me a slick of mascara, and I put on some lip-coloured lipstick. It felt a bit weird, but not too unlike myself. I'd worn the odd bit before to experiment – my mum bought me a kit last year for Christmas, but I pretended I wasn't interested. Actually, I just wasn't sure how to put it on.

We met Silas outside Josie's. Jake's house wasn't far so it was easy to walk. 'Good job,' said Silas. 'Mum's working. I stuck my head round the studio door to tell her I was going and she didn't even hear me.'

Josie laughed. 'Oh and I bet you never get like that when you're gaming?'

'Ouch!' Silas replied. 'Direct hit!'

'She's creative,' said Josie with a shrug. 'Aren't creative people often like that?'

'Probably. But living with it can get annoying.'

'You want to know annoying? My dad lines the tins up in the cupboard in straight lines. And they all have to be in exactly the right place. If you put beans with soup, he practically has a breakdown.'

'OK,' Silas said with a laugh. 'I get what you're saying. We're just not very alike, that's all.'

'Maybe you're more alike than you think. Both of you,' she said, looking at me. 'Oh, is this it?'

We went into Jake's house. I remembered coming round here to play when I was younger. Our mothers were vaguely friendly back then, though I think they'd drifted apart now as Mum never mentioned her these days. As Silas predicted, it wasn't wild. Just some loud music and people I recognised from school milling about, lounging on the sofas, filling the kitchen. Jake waved to Silas and chucked him a can of beer from across the hall. Silas pointed at us and Jake nodded, beckoning us through the crowd.

'This is Josie,' Silas said over the racket when we got to Jake in the kitchen.

'Hi, Josie,' Jake said. 'What do you want to drink?' Then he did a double take. '*That* Josie?'

Josie gritted her teeth and put her hands on her hips. 'Yeah, that Josie. Have you got a problem with that?'

Jake swallowed. He never was very good with angry girls. It was a standing joke that he was secretly scared stiff of Rachel. 'Um, no, absolutely not! Just didn't realise Silas knew you.' He shot Silas a betrayed glance.

'I'm a friend of Rafi's.'

'Oh, right.' He finally noticed me. 'What's she having, Si?'

Silas looked at me. 'Diet Coke? Yeah, thanks, Jake.'

'Me too,' Josie said.

'I need to stay sober,' she whispered to me as Jake went to grab our drinks. 'Too many people here who might say stuff about me and I don't want to be handling that even a little bit pissed.'

She steered me through the crowd in the hall into a sitting room without a TV, just lots of bookshelves. From the noise coming from a room opposite, the TV and stereo were in there. In this room, people were lounging around on the sofas, chilling. Rachel was there with her friends and when she saw us she moved up to make space.

'Hi,' she said, smiling at me. 'Silas said you were coming. And you must be Josie?'

'Yes.' I could see Josie waiting for the condemnation to appear in Rachel's eyes, the sneers, the little comments.

Rachel grinned at her. 'Please don't be offended, but your ex-boyfriend was a real dick! You can do WAY better, girl!'

Josie looked at her for a moment, astounded, and then burst out laughing. 'Ain't that the truth!' She high-fived Rachel and sat down.

It was only then we noticed Lara sitting quietly to the side of them. 'Hi, again,' she said.

'Oh, hi.' Josie gave her a guarded smile and I copied. I wasn't sure what to make of her yet, but if she was hanging out with Rachel and the others then she was probably OK. But then, if she was going out with Toby she maybe wasn't.

'Oh, have you met?' Rachel asked.

'Not really,' Lara said. 'We've bumped into each other a couple of times. I'm going to grab another drink. Anybody want one?'

When she'd gone, Josie looked around the others. 'I've got to ask,' she said, 'so I don't put my foot in it and offend her. Is she going out with Toby?'

They all burst out laughing. 'Hell, no!' Rachel's best friend, Clare, answered. 'But he wishes! No, she's just got a job in his mother's shop, and she doesn't know anyone round here. She only just moved into the area. So Toby has kind of adopted her — but don't worry, we already warned her.'

'They'd make a funny couple though,' one of the others said. 'Kind of like Gwyneth Paltrow dating Beaker from the Muppets.'

They were still laughing when Lara got back. She looked a

question around the group. 'Toby,' said Rachel in succinct explanation and Lara laughed and rolled her eyes. They were grey, I noticed, with long black lashes that didn't seem to have any mascara on them at all. She was dressed in a soft draping black T-shirt and slim-fitting black jeans and boots.

I wondered if she made the other girls feel overdressed and over-made-up.

Silas came through, followed by Jake and Toby. I knew the moment he spotted Lara, even though he tried not to show it.

The boys wandered over and sat down on the floor, Silas effectively outmanoeuvring Toby in getting to sit closest to Lara. Toby wore the kind of sullen expression that told us all he'd been busted and everyone now knew he and Lara were not an item.

I watched my brother as the conversation round me broke off into small pockets.

'Hi,' he said to Lara.

'Hi, boy who doesn't like art,' she said with a slight and private smile.

He laughed softly. 'It's Silas.'

'I'll try to remember,' she said, again with that self-contained smile.

'So if you're not into art, what are you into?'

She stared at him. Not like other girls did, not as if she was in any way trying to find an answer that pleased him. 'Politics,' she said finally, as if she was throwing down a gauntlet.

'Oh!' He looked as if that was the last thing he expected her to say. I know it took me by surprise.

'Didn't you think I had enough brain to be interested in something of importance?'

He gave her his most melting smile. 'It's obvious you have enough brain.'

But she thawed not even slightly, her only response a raised eyebrow. A challenge back.

'What are your political views then?'

She tossed her hair back and sat up straighter. 'You could sum them up as a belief that the state is immoral.'

Silas frowned. 'So that means any kind of government is wrong?'

'Yes.'

I noticed Josie watching them too, with a closed-down expression. Did she genuinely not like Lara or was she jealous? I knew the answer to that before I'd even finished asking myself.

'Isn't that anarchy?' Silas said.

Lara put her head on one side and looked at my brother with surprise. 'Yes, it's anarchy.'

Just then Toby leaned across my brother, shoving him to one side. 'What are you talking about that's so serious? Is he boring you, babe?'

'Ow, Toby, get off my foot!' Clare yelled as Toby tried to move over next to Lara. 'Clumsy idiot!'

'Oh, and I've got a big bone to pick with you, Si,' Toby growled. 'Me and Jake.'

'Yeah?' Silas said, shifting his arm from under a drunken Toby's shoulder.

'That thing with Lloyd, revenging on him — that was you, right? Come on, you can't hide it now. Not with her here.' He pointed at Josie.

Silas shrugged.

'What thing?' Lara asked as the girls all gasped in realisation.

'Josie's ex put porno shots — OW!' He stopped as Rachel slapped him. 'What was that for?'

'Toby, you are such a moron sometimes!'

'What? Well, he did. He put pictures of her all over the internet. Only Silas here went nuclear on his ass online and did this revenge thing on him. It was massive! People are still talking about it on the *Codes of War* forum. He hacked loads of people's machines and . . .' Toby paused as Lara was looking blank. 'Basically he did some very heavy stuff to him. And he pretended the whole time he didn't know a thing about it.' He reached over and punched Silas, not quite light enough for it to be entirely friendly. 'So me and Jake were freaking out about our machines being in this botnet and he didn't let on.'

'I cleaned them up for you, didn't I?' Silas asked, with ultimate unconcern.

'You could have told us!' Toby made another swing for him, which Silas held off easily.

Jake got up and grabbed Toby. 'Steady, tiger. Come on, let's get some air and calm down.'

'Was it really you?' Rachel asked as Toby was dragged away by Jake, muttering about 'that shit muscling in on his woman' which everyone pretended they hadn't heard.

Silas gave a non-committal shrug again. 'The guy needed stopping,' was all he said.

It was then I noticed Lara looking at Silas a little less coldly than before.

Silas was right. The party never did get wild. Toby threw up in the bushes outside and that was as bad as it got. Rachel and Josie got talking a bit about how the girls in Josie's school had reacted to Lloyd's stunt. Rachel wasn't impressed. 'I hate how some women behave towards each other,' she said. 'It's like they get a buzz from putting each other down, when there are enough guys queuing up to do that. We should be standing up for each other, not helping them keep us down.'

Lara nodded her agreement and I felt Josie warm to her a little. 'Like yesterday,' she said, 'I saw these two things in the news. One was about how this girl had been brutally murdered by a bunch of guys in South Africa and the other was about a woman getting bitched at online because her thighs met in the middle. So there's no comments on this first news article, but on the thigh gap thing — so many women lining up to slag her off about how fat she is. What the hell is that about?'

'Yes!' said Rachel, finally finding a kindred spirit. 'That is exactly what I mean!'

Silas leaned back and watched the two of them launch into a debate with a smile on his face.

RAFI'S TRUTH BOOK

Silence is become his mother tongue.

(Oliver Goldsmith)

CHAPTER 16

'So you still haven't talked to Josie either,' Silas said in a cross voice as we waited for the school bus.

I pulled a face at him.

'You know what I mean! And you know I wanted you to tell her what was upsetting you so much last week.'

I ignored him.

'Rafi, have you ever thought about getting some help with this? I know the counsellors you saw as a kid were worse than useless, but you're older now and it's not going away, sis. Don't you want it to stop?'

Silas practically never discussed this with me, mostly because it used to make me so upset when he tried to. Yes, the counsellors had been useless because how can you talk about not talking?

And the whole point was I didn't want to tell people, especially someone who was going to psychoanalyse everything I did. Imagine being married to one of *those* – you wouldn't be able to do anything without them scrutinising your every move and thought. Urgh! Creepy or what?

I gave him a half-hearted nod.

'Then you need to try. If you won't talk to a professional, you should be talking to your friends. Hell, Rafi, you should be making more friends. I'm pleased you've got Josie, but you need more. Not speaking doesn't mean you can't have friends. That's why I wanted you to come to the party. And you had fun, didn't you?'

I nodded sullenly. Yes, it had been good really, but I'd had Josie there, and him. And I knew everyone, except Lara of course.

'It's time to start talking, Rafi. I know you can do it. What I don't know is why you ever stopped, but I'm guessing if you could tell someone that you'd find it a lot easier to speak again.' He put his hands to his face and formed a bridge over his nose and blew out heavily. 'Please, please try to communicate with someone. I thought it'd be me you opened up to one day, but I was wrong . I dunno . . . you need a girl to talk to, not your dumb brother.'

But what I could never tell Silas was that he was part of the problem.

He looked hard at my shuttered face and then sighed. 'OK, I'll drop it. For now. But I want you to hang out with people more. Look, some of us are going to this meeting on Thursday night. Do you want to come? It's me and Rachel and Clare and Lara.'

Oh?

'Lara told Rachel about it at the party. It's some political thing. She thinks we might find it interesting. I don't think it'll be Josie's thing, but you might like it.'

I made a garland for her head,

And bracelets too, and fragrant zone;

She look'd at me as she did love,

And made sweet moan.

(John Keats – 'La Belle Dame Sans Merci')

CHAPTER 17

As it happened, Josie had a thing on with her dad on Thursday so couldn't make it anyway – some charity event for the families of police killed in action that she'd agreed to help at, looking after some of the little kids with party games and stuff.

Silas spent ages deciding what to wear to the meeting. My brother, who normally threw on whatever he felt like. In the end he dragged me in to give the seal of approval to jeans, some well-worn boots and a long-sleeved blue T-shirt. I understood the look he was going for: studenty and not trying too hard to impress. But I also understood that he'd picked that T-shirt because the colour suited him, and those jeans because he knew the shape made him look good.

We travelled into the city by train with Rachel and Clare and met Lara by the station. She wore what I was coming to recognise as her usual black and her face was clear of make-up again.

'Hi,' Silas said. 'Good week since I last saw you?'

'Fine. You?'

'Yes.' He hesitated. 'I've been looking forward to this.'

'Yeah, me too. This guy who's going to be speaking is excellent.'

I didn't think that was what he meant and I had a strong suspicion she knew that too, but Silas smiled and nodded. 'Hope so.'

'Let's go, this thing could get packed.'

She led us to a backstreet and a door painted black and red. We went in and up some stairs which opened out into a large room filled with chairs facing a lectern. The chairs were old and battered and the room smelt faintly of damp, but the seats were already filling with intense-faced twenty-somethings. I felt a growing sense of anticipation in the room as more and more people came in.

'Do you mind sitting at the front or does it make you feel like one of the nerdy kids at school?' Lara said with a laugh.

'The front is fine.' Rachel grinned at her.

She breezed through the people milling round and we followed her to our seats.

'So who is the speaker?' Rachel said as we sat down. Silas managed to wangle sitting next to Lara which did not go unnoticed by the girls, who exchanged meaningful, amused glances.

'He's an activist and a practising anarchist. Been campaigning for years, since he was a kid, mainly about the corruption of successive governments and he believes in direct action by the people for the people.'

That sounded suspiciously like running riot and breaking stuff up, but perhaps there was more to it. Rachel and Clare nodded and then tactfully began fiddling with their phones while Silas talked to Lara. Not quite sure what to do as I was sitting on his other side, I got my phone out too.

'I've never been to a meeting like this before,' he said.

'Have you never been involved in any kind of public protest?'

He shook his head.

She gave a little laugh, but it wasn't too unkind. 'Demo virgin! Yeah, we all have a first time. The important thing is to *have* a first time and not spend your life on the fence.'

'Getting splinters up your arse,' he added.

She laughed again, but this time with genuine amusement. 'I went on my first protest march when I was fourteen. I hopped on a bus and went down to London. They were all lined up on the Embankment with banners and whistles. I felt as if I came alive out there.'

'What was it about?'

'Student tuition fees.'

'I saw that on the news. It got nasty.'

She laughed. 'Yeah, it got a bit charged. The police got all heavy and tried to kettle us to keep control. So people got heavy back. They asked for it.'

'Were you in that part of the protest?'

She nodded, shifting closer to him as someone took the seat on the other side of her. 'I'd hooked up with some others while we were on the embankment. They saw I was on my own and took me under their wing. They were old hands at it so once it all kicked off, I was right in the middle with them. They looked after me.'

'You went down there on your own at fourteen and you didn't know anyone, and you'd never done it before.' He shook his head in amazement. 'That's kind of brave. I don't know any girls who would do that.'

'Yeah, I guess. But you have to believe in something, you know. Otherwise what is the point of you? You're just a sheep.'

'So that's what you believe in – the tuition fees issue?'

'That was just the start. That's what got me into politics. I was naive – I saw something that impacted directly on me and I reacted. It was only later when I got more savvy that I realised everything the establishment does impacts on me directly.' She gave a huff of disgust. 'It's like the government are always blathering on about how they want more young people involved in politics. Yeah, right! Their narrow, well-groomed little branch of "blinker the people" politics. They want us agreeing with them, not thinking for ourselves. They don't want me –' she waved her hand at the surrounding room '– they don't want these guys. They want us like the TV shows us to be: obsessed with drinking, drugs, getting laid. All about the party! And practically every dumb-ass kid out there falls for it and buys into that because they walk round with a blindfold over their eyes. Don't want to see the truth because they might have to use their little brain cells to think.'

'You're not like other girls,' Silas said. 'You're not like anyone I've ever met.'

'Yeah, well, you can keep those girls. The pink, frilly ones. Too busy with their make-up and hair straighteners and obsessing over losing a few kilos so they can get to size zero like some brain-rotted celebrity. Too busy with all that stuff to open their eyes and face that life isn't so pretty for most of this planet. The majority of women out there wake up worrying about how to get enough food so their children don't starve, and then there's the ones praying the soldiers or the rebel forces – doesn't matter which because they'll rape and kill just the same – that they don't come to their village. How the hell can you think about who some bimbo reality TV star is dating with that going on in your world, huh?'

'I don't know,' Silas said quietly.

She eyed him. 'I guess I ranted.'

'Maybe. But I liked listening to it.'

A movement at the front of the hall caught her eye.

'Yeah, well, we're not here to listen to me. We're here to listen to *him*.' She pointed to a man walking towards the lectern. He raised a hand to acknowledge the rush of applause that started as people saw him and then stood behind the lectern looking out on his audience.

Lara leaned over Silas to us and grinned. 'This'll be good. Promise!'

I have not loved the world, nor the world
  me;
I have not flatter'd its rank breath, nor
  bow'd
To its idolatries a patient knee –

(Lord Byron)

CHAPTER 18

The guy who stood behind the lectern was much younger than I'd expected, somewhere between twenty and twenty-three. He had a narrow face made narrower by a goatee beard and a mane of wavy muddy blond hair that fell to his shoulders. He looked more like a surfer dude than a political activist.

The applause stopped as he held up a hand to silence the audience.

'Thanks,' he said quietly and I was surprised at how softly spoken he was, with a vague Cornish burr to his voice. So that was where the surfer look came from.

'It's good to see so many of you here tonight,' he began and the audience listened all the harder because he didn't raise his voice. It was clear, and audible to everyone there, as long as you concentrated. I couldn't work out if it was a ruse of his or his natural tone. 'I want to talk to you about lies.'

An unexpected round of applause broke out again. At least, it was unexpected to me. The man at the lectern, however, seemed to take it in his stride. He smiled gently and held up his hand again. The audience fell quiet once more.

'We're fed them like mother's milk, aren't we?' he said conversationally. 'Expected to drink them down like obedient little boys and girls because really they're good for us. Better that the masses don't know the truth. That's reserved for the ones in Whitehall. Our elite! The ones, my friends, that the people of this country elected and put there, and the ones the people of this country employ through the extortionate and unfair taxation system that this government has forced on us.

'Today, only today, our elected representatives accepted an increase in their salaries just as foreign aid budgets are slashed. The aid that is designed to help the poorest and most vulnerable people on this planet. And the reason for this? That we need to attract high-calibre people into the role of MP. High-calibre people, my friends, high-calibre people.'

He paused and looked around them with that gentle smile.

'Let's take a few moments to explore what some of those high-calibre people have been up to recently. Because we need to know what we're paying for. We need to know why these high-calibre people are worth more than the life of a black child in Africa. We need to know so we can explain to the mother of one of those children dying from lack of anti-malarial drugs why it is that her child has to be sacrificed so we can keep our politicians in the manner to which they would like to become accustomed.'

There was a lot of noise from the audience in response. The speaker nodded and continued, moving on to talk about some of the recent scandals involving government ministers, both well known and ones I'd never heard of. The man was a compelling speaker, there was no doubt about it. He had his audience hanging on every word.

Lara sat a little forward in her seat, listening as intently as the rest. Maybe even more intently because she looked almost hypnotised. She really did believe passionately in all this stuff and it would be impossible for a boy to be with Lara without believing in it too. She cared too much to put up with someone who didn't. That was obvious.

The question was, did my brother believe in any of this?

Or did he want her so much that he'd fake it even if he didn't believe?

To be honest, some of what this guy was saying wasn't completely loony. He was making some powerful arguments, especially on the subject of capitalist greed and global poverty. The US, the speaker said, spent more on cosmetics than it would cost to give the entire world population a basic education. Water and sanitation for the world could be provided with less than what Europe spent on ice cream.

There was more, much more: nearly half the world's children lived in poverty; 22,000 children A DAY died due to poverty; 80 per cent of the world's population lived on less than 10 US dollars a day and around half lived on less than $2.50. And it went on and on. As you listened, you felt sick. That was the only human response to what he was saying because if you didn't feel sick and you didn't feel disgusted with yourself that you went from day to day with a level of privilege that the people quoted in those statistics could not imagine then what did that make you?

Silas leaned over and murmured in my ear. 'I paid a hundred and twenty quid for my last pair of trainers. At this precise moment I want to go and throw them in the river in shame.'

Lara glanced at him and he grimaced at her. She nodded her understanding.

'Remember, this is what they don't want us to hear,' she whispered. 'Capitalism thrives by trampling on the poor. For the big winners to make the bucks, there have to be big losers.'

The conclusion of the speech was a call to action. The man demanded they rise up in protest, take to the streets, show the government they could not get away with treating the poor like this. He talked about their duty to raise this issue over and over again until finally the powerful started to listen. And finally he spoke about how they must never give up, no matter how hopeless their cause seemed in the face of so much indifference.

'Remember, my friends, the words of Nelson Mandela in 1961. Right back in 1961 when ending apartheid was so far away it must have seemed like a pipe dream. And he said, "Only through hardship, sacrifice and militant action can freedom be won. The struggle is my life. I will continue fighting for freedom until the end of my days." A call to arms has never been said better. And that is what I put to you today: take a stand against indifference. Take a stand on the side of militant action and let's begin to make a change.'

He stopped and took a step back from the lectern. Deafening applause broke out as the audience got to their feet. We got up as Lara did, still stunned from listening to . . . well, what was that? I'd never heard anything like it. Beside me, Rachel and Clare clapped as hard as they could and whooped their appreciation.

How could you describe it? A call to anarchy? To protest? What exactly was this guy asking us to do?

The man made a motion to the side of the room and a few people came forward with leaflets and handed them out to the audience as they continued to applaud. Silas took one and looked down at it.

'Who are these people?' he asked Lara as the applause began to die down finally.

'ActionX,' she replied. 'A protest and pressure group who believe in taking an issue to the streets so it's slammed in the faces of the public and they can't ignore it. Neither can the government when they're out there getting their cause plastered all over TV screens.'

'Anarchists, yes?' Silas said.

'Yes. They're anarchists. They believe any government is inherently corrupt, but while there's one in power, it's their job to expose the stuff that is whitewashed and make the sheeple think about what's happening out there. What's really happening, not just whether there's another penny in tax on a bottle of wine or petrol has gone up. Which, if you watch the news reports on budget night, is all anyone in this country seems to care about. If it doesn't hit their pockets, stuff the rest of the world.'

The man turned away from the lectern and began to walk out of the hall.

'And who is he?

Lara gave a half-smile. 'Oh, him – his name's Dillon.'

There is a pleasure sure

In being mad which none but madmen

   know.

(John Dryden)

CHAPTER 19

Hey Dad,

I guess you'll never get this email, but I found myself needing to write it anyway. Maybe it's easier because I know you won't see it. I can't talk to Rafi about this. Odd, because I can talk to her about everything else, but for this I need to talk to a guy. I've no idea whether you'd understand or not – it's been so long since I've seen you that I don't know what you're like now. But I hope you would. I've sort of built it up in my head that you'd understand.

I've met someone. I wish I could talk to you about her because I've never met anyone like her. She's amazing. She has opinions on things I never even knew were happening. She knows so much. But most of all, she makes me *feel*. Really feel.

Her name's Lara. She took me to a meeting today, me and some friends and I took Rafi too. I know you'd be glad about that. I'm making her go out and do things like I know you'd want me to.

Lara sat next to me in the meeting and . . .

. . . there's no easy way to say this to your dad. It's hard for me to be grown up in front of you when the last time I saw you I was just a kid. But I know you'd get this. I think all guys would once they've been through it.

She sat next to me in the meeting. I looked down at her – she's only tiny – and my stomach did cartwheels at her closeness. Just a bit nearer and our arms would've been brushing. My face felt flushed and my fingers tingled at the thought of touching her skin. If I'd reached out, I could have traced the curve of her neck, touched the pale skin. I wanted so much to do that.

When she talks to me, it's like a challenge. It's never easy understanding what she means or what she wants to hear. I can't predict her.

If I could think straight about anything other than her, I would have been looking forward to tonight anyway, to be exposed to new ideas. But more than anything though, I wanted to please her. So she'd agree to see me again when I've worked out how to ask her on a real date. But even now, sitting here at the end of the night, how to please her is as elusive as ever. She's still a mystery. A beautiful, puzzling, complex mystery that I would do anything to solve.

I know so little about her, where she's from, why she moved here. What is it that draws her to these anarchists? She's just layer after layer of cool impenetrability.

I knew I needed to give this whole political scene a

chance. If I switched off from it now, I'd lose her. When she's talking about the things she's passionate about, she's more beautiful than ever. I could sit and watch and listen to her all day and still want to drink in more and more of her. I knew tonight that I'd do anything to make her laugh, anything to win that smile, the one that warms her eyes.

The chairs we were sitting on were so close together that her knee was only millimetres from mine. I could feel it pulling to mine like a magnet. I wanted to touch her so badly my hands were shaking.

So *this* is what it's like to really want someone.

Not that pale, feeble imitation I've felt with other girls where I've kissed them mostly because I knew I should. Just hormones and nothing more. This is so different. All-consuming. I didn't have the faintest idea what was going on in the room around us while we waited for the speech to start. All that mattered was that her skin was so close to mine. Nothing else. *Nothing*.

And this is what it's like to be in love. For it can't be anything else, this kind of madness. I wanted the whole world to go away and just leave the two of us so that I might find the courage to reach out and touch her. Even a finger brush. Anything. Anything just for my skin to touch hers.

Does she feel anything of what I feel? Even a faint shadow of it?

Did you ever feel this way about anyone, Dad? I wish you could tell me.

Silas

JOSIE'S PINTEREST BOARD

Love the people who saw you when you were invisible to everyone else.

CHAPTER 20

I relaxed on Josie's giant, squashy couch and shuffled through the choice of five DVDs she'd handed me. She'd announced it was Film Night and that apparently meant her dad was working so we had the place to ourselves and could have a film-watching marathon with plenty of snacks to support us. Josie was currently getting these ready. She took a packet of frankfurters from the microwave and replaced it with a bag of popcorn.

'Gotta love the hot dogs,' she said, ramming the frankfurters into buns and squirting mustard and ketchup on to them. 'Have you picked yet?'

I held up a romcom.

'Put it on, will you? This food's nearly ready and the trailers will run while I'm getting everything together. I never watch them – they do my head in.'

I put the film on, then helped her bring the food over and arrange it on the huge footstool that doubled as a coffee table.

Josie flopped on to the sofa beside me. 'Annnnddd PIG OUTTT!' she cried, grabbing a hot dog.

I didn't know how hungry I was until I started eating, or maybe it was because I was so relaxed there that my hunger let loose. I loved this room, loved chilling in it. I was going to have a room just like this when I was older.

Oh yes, I'd forgotten. Not much of a future out there for a basket case who won't talk. Not one that would finance a house and furniture like this anyway.

LOL. What did I think I was going to do? Live off Silas forever?

'What's up?' Josie said, pausing as she took a bite of hot dog.

I shook my head and she gave me her 'don't even try that on with me' look. She got up and took my phone off the arm of the sofa and dropped it into my lap.

I sighed. <I was thinking.>

'Doh, yes! About what?'

<About how life will be when I'm older.>

She gave me that hard stare again.

<If I don't start talking.>

She hit pause on the video. 'We can wait to watch this. So you do want to talk again?'

<YesNo.>

She laughed. 'You know I totally get what you mean by that. I don't understand why obviously, but that is so cool – YesNo. I love it!'

She won a smile from me.

'So let's do this! What is "Yes" about it?'

Even this was so hard. Couldn't we just watch the film?

'No, we can't just watch the film. Answer the question.'

How transparent was I?! Embarrassing!

Josie tapped her fingers expectantly on the arm of the couch. 'Any time now, you know, before the bread buns go mouldy . . .'

I stuck my tongue out at her and began to type. <Friends. Uni. Getting a job.>

She smirked. 'You forgot "Boyfriend". And don't look at me like that. You will so be having one. When you feel ready and there's no rush. Don't be dumb like me – wait for a good 'un. OK, so give me the "No".'

<Some people are mean, scary. Plus everyone will notice and talk about it. Don't want people saying stuff to me about it.>

'Yeah, that is going to be a bit of an issue. People are bound to make a big deal of it, there's no way round that. But we can get a plan together, you know, to cope with that part.' She passed me another hot dog. 'Come on, I can't eat all these on my own. Um, *can* you actually talk? You know, if you want to . . .'

I shook my head.

'So what stops you?'

<Don't know. Talking is like trying to breathe if there's no air. Just can't. Throat closes up.>

'And have you been to see people about this?'

<Ages ago. Don't go now. Don't like it.>

She frowned. 'When was the last time?'

<I was ten.>

'You are joking me,' she said with a gasp. 'You haven't been to

145

get help in all that time. What is your mum thinking of?'

I shrugged.

'Sorry, I shouldn't have said that. But why?'

<Mum thinks I do it on purpose so I can stop when I want. She doesn't think the people we saw were much good anyway. They didn't seem to understand the condition very well.>

'Silas said you had progressive mutism so obviously I looked that up. It said it's usually at school where kids clam up.'

Nod.

'But most of those kids still talk at home or they only stop for a short period, whereas with you it's been years.'

Nod.

'But this progressive mutism you have is where gradually someone stops talking to everyone?'

Nod.

'I read this blog by a dad whose daughter has had it for as long as you but he says most kids get over it much quicker.'

Yes, I was a freak, wasn't I? I knew this. I'd read all those internet articles myself, over and over. There was nothing googlable on mutism that I hadn't seen. Including how it used to be called elective mutism because the doctors, much like my mum now, believed at the time that we chose to be this way. I'd read about the treatment options available now, and how it had changed even in the years since I was tiny and first began to falter with speech. But I'd also read about how a lot of health professionals still didn't understand it and I didn't want to face more of that.

And the most infuriating part of those articles? The advice to parents on how they should act. Because it would never, never happen like that for me.

'So did this kick off when you started school? Is that where you first stopped talking?'

<No, I stopped at home first.>

Josie paused in taking a bite of her last hot dog. 'Really? I never read anything about that. They said it's a social phobia and usually kids can talk OK in the family, or at least more than they do outside it. I'm sure I read that they use the parent to get the child's answers to questions while the therapist is out of the room if that helps.'

Yes, I'd read that bit too. Ha!

'So who was the last person you spoke to?'

<Silas.>

'Yeah, I thought it might be.'

He'd been too young when I began to stop talking to be taken to therapy with me. I often wondered if they would have been able to halt the progression if he hadn't been. But no, I had to have Mum there as my attempt to have a voice. Which was kind of funny considering she was the one I stopped talking to first.

I never knew what that last therapist said to her that time she stormed out, dragging me back to the car by the arm and saying she'd never take me back there again. And she never did.

'Did you ever write that story, Rafi, the one I asked you to?'

Nod.

'You don't want me to see it yet, do you?'

Shake of head.

'OK. But you know why you stopped, don't you?'

Now it was a very strange thing but absolutely nobody had ever asked me that question, not even my brother. It's incredible how the most obvious things are the ones we overlook. *That's* a truth I kept in my notebook with the rest.

Nod. Because I really thought I did know. I thought in all these years I'd managed to suss it out.

Josie nodded back slowly. 'Then if you know that, I reckon one day when you're ready someone will be able to help you fix it. But you have to want it fixed. It has to come from you.' She sat up suddenly very straight as if a realisation had hit her. 'You control this. No one else. Maybe that's part of it. Having something to control when so much seems beyond control. You know?'

Yes, I knew. That wasn't how it started, but a journey takes us along many different paths from the one we began to walk on.

I grabbed the remote control from her and pressed play. Conversation over.

RAFI'S TRUTH BOOK

Expectation is the root of all heartache.

(William Shakespeare)

CHAPTER 21

I nearly didn't write about what happened to me next as, after all, this has always been about Silas and not me, but then I found I couldn't leave out my part, or Josie's, and have it still make sense. Our stories are so intertwined, like the three strands of a braid, that I have to tell it all.

It was, predictably, Silas that I gave the note to as soon as we got home from school. He glanced at it and then sat down on the couch. 'Why now? I'm pleased, of course. I think it's the right thing to do, have done for ages, but why now?'

I took the note back and scribbled on it. *Josie talked me into it*.

He sighed. 'I'm glad someone did. So you want me to tell Mum for you?'

More scribble. *She might listen to you*.

He made a huffing noise and raised his eyes to the ceiling. 'You think so? Never mind, I'll give it a go?'

When? my eyes asked.

'Tonight,' he said. 'As far as I know she's home tonight. I'll cook and then I'll drag her to the table. We'll talk about it then.'

My brother set the stage well. He laid the table and even chilled a bottle of white wine for our mother. She'd probably let him have a glass. He wasn't a big fan, but he'd sip it to be polite. 'Makes her think of me as more of an adult,' he said as he put a bowl of tossed salad on the table, 'which is not a bad thing for the purposes of this conversation.' He'd thrown together a bag of frozen seafood with some pasta sauce and cooked spaghetti. It would taste great, I could tell, from the smell wafting through the house. He made dessert too. 'Keep her at the table longer,' he said with a wink. 'Wear her down!' It was only a mango sorbet and ice-cream layer mix in some glasses, but it looked good.

Mum appeared at half six, just when we'd begun to think she wasn't coming back after all. Silas cleared his glower and bit his tongue until he could manage to say, 'Busy day?' with reasonable aplomb.

She showed us startled eyes, as if she hadn't fully realised we were there. Ghost children, that's what we were.

I'd always known that of myself, even from the earliest days before Dad left. I might as well have been a wraith around the house for she never saw me except to notice some misdemeanour. And as I tried so hard to stay out of trouble, in practice she seldom did see me.

'Not bad. I had a meeting with a broker who wants some pieces for an overseas client. It's a reasonably large commission but drearily dull, alas.'

'I cooked,' said Silas. 'It's ready if you want to sit down. So what does the drearily dull client want you to do?'

I laughed secretly at my brother getting what he really wanted in a sneaky sandwich with the commission talk. Funny and clever. But that was my brother.

He ushered Mum through to the dining room before she had time to process what he was up to. I zoomed through to the kitchen and appeared at his shoulder with the wine bottle just in time. 'Nice one,' he whispered out of our mother's earshot as he filled her glass.

'He's Icelandic, I understand. Wants me to do a series of paintings based on a theme of betrayal.'

Silas looked confused. 'That sounds quite open-ended. I would have thought it would be interesting. You know, it's not one of those "Give me a six-by-four canvas of a tree in winter" types.'

'Betrayal though,' she said with distaste, plucking a breadstick from the glass and nibbling delicately on it – I envied my mother that, the ability to nibble delicately. 'So . . . overdone at the moment. Mark Rackham's just exhibited with that as a theme, and then Judy Renfrew did a set of sculptures. Not to mention Clive Harding's show only last year.'

'So why didn't he go to them? He must like your work, I guess.' Silas waved at me to bring the food through from the kitchen while he kept her talking.

'Yes, he's a big fan apparently. And he thought nobody would convey betrayal more perfectly than me, or so his broker says.'

Silas laughed. 'Is this some personal thing for him, this theme of betrayal? Has he got dumped recently?'

Our mother winced. 'Silas, try to have some empathy.'

Ha! That was a joke coming from her!

'Yes, I understand he does want me to work on this theme for very particular reasons. I believe his marriage ended a few months ago.' She shook her head sadly. 'It's a painful time for him.'

Artistic people were allowed to feel pain. In fact, in my mother's eyes, it was only artistic people who felt true pain. The rest of us Philistines didn't have the temperament to suffer. I think she viewed us like cows – too placidly bovine to hurt much.

'Oh,' Silas replied, serving pasta on to the plates. 'Bummer. I guess he really loved her very badly if he's coughing up to pay you for a series. It's not like you're cheap.'

'You cannot set a price on art,' she answered with a pained expression.

Silas refrained from pointing out that no, actually, she set a hefty price tag on hers. Not that either of us minded. After all, her art paid for everything. It was the two-facedness of it that got on our nerves, but she would never see it like that.

She took a small bite of the pasta. My mother was one of those uber-annoying women who never got pasta sauce on her chin. Whereas I had to surreptitiously check over my face with my hand every few mouthfuls in case I was smeared with it. 'This is good,' she said. 'Did you cook it from scratch?'

'More or less,' Silas said, ignoring that the seafood came ready mixed in a bag from Waitrose and the sauce was out of a tub.

'Hmm, well done. You know, perhaps you have some ability as a chef. Have you considered exploring that as an avenue?'

To our mother, computing was not really an appropriate thing to be gifted in. You could tell she thought there was something terribly vulgar about it.

'It's something to think about,' Silas said, ducking the issue quickly before he got a lecture on how life without art was mere existence. Our sister Kerensa's maths genius was just allowable because everyone knew the link between maths and art and music. Look at Da Vinci: artist, sculptor, musician, mathematician.

Silas waited until her mouth was full and then added, 'Rafi has something she wants to ask you.'

'Rafi?' My mother forgot herself so far as to speak with her mouth full. And she sounded rather as if she'd forgotten who I was.

Silas's eyes flashed with annoyance and he looked away. 'Yes, she wants to go and see someone. I looked this stuff up and there's a choice – speech and language therapist or psychologist.'

My mother opened her mouth to give her views on that.

Silas cut in before she could get started. 'So I asked Rafi who she'd rather see, and she said the speech and language therapist because she hated the last psychologist she had.'

My mother ate another mouthful of spaghetti thoughtfully.

'Yes, I recall that one. Positively demonic! And no understanding of the condition either.' She looked at me as if I was an unusual variety of beetle found under a rock. 'Not that it's easy to understand at all. Heavens, nobody knows that better than we do. But one expects a professional to have some idea. I think this was the first case she'd ever come across in the flesh.' She tutted. 'And I doubt her textbook knowledge was up to much either.'

'So can you arrange it then? For her to see a therapist?'

She took a sip of wine. 'I suppose so. There may be a waiting list. There always seems to be a waiting list these days for any health issue, especially mental health. Margaret – you remember Margaret, did those sculptures with driftwood and steel that became fashionable a few years ago – told me she had to wait months to see someone to talk about her depression.'

Mental health. Thanks, Mum.

I hate that term 'mental health'. Nearly as much as I hate 'mentally ill'. Because everything mental comes from your brain or some other hormones acting on it. And your brain's an organ, just like your heart or your kidneys. You don't get people saying they are *cardiacally* ill and then have others make fun of it or shy away from them like it's catching. It's stupid! How is having something wrong with your brain different to having a broken leg or your pancreas not working properly?

'Well, if there's a long waiting list, can't she go to see a therapist privately?' Silas asked patiently.

My mother nodded. 'I would imagine that's possible. Though it may be a fearful waste of time and money if she behaves as she did last time and refuses to engage with them.'

'She won't. Because this time it's her choice. Rafi wants to go for herself, not because she's being made to or the school has said she has to. She wants to see if she can get better.'

The only word to describe the expression on my mother's face was astonished. And I realised that for years now she had never seriously considered the possibility that one day I might talk again.

Nice.

'Oh and there's one more thing,' Silas said.

'What's that?'

'She wants me to go with her, not you.'

I set her on my pacing steed,

And nothing else saw all day long,

For sidelong would she bend, and sing

A faery's song.

(John Keats – 'La Belle Dame Sans Merci')

CHAPTER 22

Dad, I finally did it!

I'll tell you the whole thing because I want you to see how amazing she is and, well, I'll have to tell you all of it for you to see that. Here goes: it's a bit like telling a story, I suppose, so I'll try to make it interesting for you.

My heart was pounding in my chest. She had said she'd be here, at the café opposite the bus station, waiting for the last bus home, but I still exploded inside like a cascade of fireworks when I saw her sitting there in the window seat.

I stopped for a moment to look at her before she saw me so I could drink in the sight of her. She'd answered my text when I'd asked if we could catch up with each other to say yes, here was where she'd be so come and find her. And I'd run there like an eager little puppy, but I didn't care. This could be risking everything because if she blew me out now I might never see her again. Or I'd see her only when she was hanging out with Rachel, Toby or the others, which would probably be worse.

She sipped her coffee, her small fingers curled round the cup, and it was unthinkable that I could lose her.

This had to work.

Her face didn't light up at the sight of me, but I can wait

for that if only it does one day. She isn't like the other girls, I need to remember that. I have to work to deserve her. I said hi and went to the counter to get another coffee for her and one for me.

She won't bring the kind of loving and being loved that my friend Sam describes, which sounds like sinking into a warm bath after a cold day with exhausted, aching muscles.

No, loving Lara . . .

. . . loving . . . I still can't quite believe I'm saying that to myself . . . *me* . . .

. . . loving Lara will be like standing out in a thunderstorm and, even if she never loves me back, being allowed near her is compensation enough.

Just so long as she doesn't already love someone else.

When I had that thought, I had a burst of jealousy so strong it made me take a step back from the counter.

She didn't, did she?

But I hardly knew anything about her. I liked that, liked the mystery. She didn't give everything away about herself in five minutes like some girls did, babbling on and on as if they couldn't shut up.

But Lara's more than a closed book; she's padlocked.

Another challenge then, to learn more about her.

I took the coffees back to the table. She made no move to start a conversation, but thanked me and swapped her finished cup with the full one. Then she watched through the window as an old woman at the bus stop berated two teenage boys for queue jumping.

'Our society has no respect for the old. It makes us poorer,' she said and took a sip of the fresh coffee.

I just watched her. It wasn't that I didn't agree. In some ways I find myself agreeing with everything she says. She makes me think about things I'd never considered before, look at the world in a new way.

Suddenly she stood up, pushed her chair back in a rush and ran out. Outside events had taken a turn for the worse. The two boys were yelling at the old woman and one of them had stepped forward menacingly. I got up and ran after Lara.

When I got out there, she was up in the faces of the two boys – or as up in their faces as someone of her height could be – standing between them and the old woman and yelling her head off. They looked startled for a moment, then their expressions turned ugly. As I arrived by her side, they'd broken out into the usual torrent of abuse dumb boys use when faced with a smart girl they feel threatened by.

This was going to get messy. The old woman had retreated further back, looking around for help. She was scared, but she wasn't giving way either.

I opened my mouth to intervene, fully expecting I could

end up getting my head kicked in, but what else was there to do? The smaller boy brought his fist up and swung at Lara's face. I went for him.

But I didn't react as fast as Lara. She brought her arm up to block the punch and simultaneously raised her leg to kick him in the stomach. The kid dropped to the ground screaming – it was like something from a martial arts film.

'It'll be your teeth next time,' Lara yelled. 'Weren't expecting that, were you? Think women can't look after themselves? Well, think again!'

We were attracting quite a lot of attention now. A group of men wearing the uniforms of the timber yard across the road came over to help.

'I'd get out of here if I were you,' I said to the boys. 'You're in way over your heads now.'

One of the men put his arm round the old woman, who he'd seen was upset even from where he'd been standing, and the others stood staring the boys out. The one on the ground hauled himself to his feet and his friend pulled him off into the road. They hobbled off together without another word.

Lara dropped her fighting stance and turned to me. 'Do you think the coffee's still hot?'

Back in the café, the coffee had not yet gone cold, so Lara sat down to finish it.

'Where did you learn to do that?' I asked her.

'The kick-boxing? I started doing it a few years ago. I got fed up with people like them trying to throw their weight about because I'm a girl and because I'm small.' She narrowed her eyes at me. 'In a world that's so violent towards women, we need to be able to protect ourselves.'

I would have protected you, I said silently to myself, but had to face facts that she'd probably done a better job than I could have. But this was a chance to dig for some information. 'So do you still take classes?'

'Occasionally, when I have time.' She'd thrown up a guarded expression as soon as I asked the question.

'What else do you do with your time? Do you go to college?'

'What is this? The Spanish Inquisition?'

'No, I just find you interesting, that's all.'

She raised an eyebrow. 'No, I don't go to college. I work full time in Toby's mum's shop. I used to go, but I dropped out a few months ago. Didn't like the course.'

'Don't you want to go to uni?'

'No.'

'So what will you do?'

'I want to spend a few years campaigning and travelling. Right now I'm working and saving money so I can go to Africa and do some volunteer work in the villages, building wells and helping improve the water supplies.'

I thought of how I want to go to Oxford to read computer science, but what's faffing around with code compared to getting out in the world and saving lives hands on by providing clean water? How many lives are lost each year according to that guy, Dillon, because people don't have access to it? I can't remember the exact figure, but it's a staggering amount.

'What do your parents think of that?' I asked. 'Will they be worried about you?'

She shook her head and shifted her eyes away from mine. 'We don't get on. They lead their lives and I lead mine. They give me an allowance and I accept it for now because it enables me to pay the rent on my flat and buy food, and that means everything I earn I can put towards travelling.' She looked back at me again. 'It's important to see what you're fighting for and really be part of that, otherwise you risk being nothing more than a sound bite.'

'Yeah, I guess.'

It scared me a little, just how far I'd have to shift my expectations to be with this girl, but to give up now would be unimaginable. I would, I realised, do anything.

Her lip curled. 'You guess?'

I shook my head at her. 'I know you think it sounds lame, but sometimes you . . . you rob me of words. I don't know what to say to you because my brain's frantically trying to process some new stuff you've thrown at me and my mouth can't keep up.'

She looked intrigued despite herself. 'What *do* you mean?'

'I mean you're not like anyone else I know and you make me think differently about stuff and that's great. Really great. More than great, it's amazing. But I want to pause and think about what you say. And you throw a grenade right out at me the second I don't give an answer exactly the way you think I should.'

'So what you mean is "shut up, Lara, sometimes, and let me just think", yes?' She laughed. 'OK, I'll concede that point – for now.'

She must have believed I was going to be around her or she wouldn't have said it. I whooped inside. But I had to keep it cool. She expected that and I had to deliver no matter how excited I secretly felt. 'That would be good, yeah.'

She laughed again. 'I can be full-on, I know that and I make no apologies for it. Without passion, life is grey and you may as well be one of the sheeple.'

Life would never be grey around her.

I'd ducked the issue long enough. 'So are you seeing anyone at the moment?'

She stared at me. 'No,' she said eventually. 'I'm not seeing anyone at the moment.'

'Are you completely opposed to the idea of seeing someone?'

Her eyes laughed. 'Not in principle. But it would take a lot to persuade me. I don't *need* a boyfriend.'

'I never for a second imagined you did.' Isn't that the truth! As if someone like her needs a guy. But I'd walk over hot coals to get her to see it could be good to have one around. As long as that one is me.

'Good,' she said. And added nothing more.

Either she'd just shut the conversation down or this was my opening. I had no idea which but I was going to win nothing by sitting there staring at her and not taking the biggest gamble of my life. 'So would you let me try to persuade you please?' I asked.

She made me wait for what seemed like forever, then . . .

'Yes, you can try to persuade me.' She laughed. 'But I make you no guarantees.'

It's 2 a.m. now and I need to sleep, Dad. I was too excited to sleep before I wrote this, but I guess talking to you worked and I'm going to crash now.

Silas

JOSIE'S PINTEREST BOARD

You can't start the next chapter of your life if you keep re-reading the last one.

CHAPTER 23

We sat in the waiting room, me trying to read a book and failing hopelessly as I stressed about what was through that door labelled Room 2, and Silas texting constantly.

This was my first appointment to tackle my problem in four years and I had no idea what was going to happen. Mum had made the appointment for me and she hadn't even attempted to get a regular one, but had paid for me to see this therapist for a full course of treatment, no matter how long it took. There had been a muttered late-night phone call to my father, which I clearly wasn't supposed to hear, where she told him he needed to pay half. 'After all, you probably caused this by what you did. She was fine before you walked out,' she said, quietly furious, into the phone. 'Some children stop talking because of trauma. They've never ruled it out as a possibility for her.'

But she was wrong. Dad leaving may not have helped, but it didn't strike me dumb on the spot.

She didn't tell me much about the appointment. Maybe she said more to Silas in private, but if she did he didn't share it with me. The only thing I knew is that the therapist had asked my mother to attend with me in the first instance, but on hearing that I wanted Silas instead she had agreed to that. Our mother had even offered to drive us and was going to hang around to collect us after. The woman's office was thirty miles from where we lived and that journey would have been a total pain by train, so I agreed to let her take us.

I looked around the waiting room for the fifty-third time as I couldn't concentrate on my book. I'd read the same paragraph over and over and it still didn't make sense. It was the kind of room I suppose I'd expected in that it had a warm, soothing feel. The walls were painted a soft lemon and around them were pictures of sea and countryside. My mother would hate them, but they were restful, which is exactly why I imagine they'd been picked.

The door to Room 2 opened and a woman in her thirties came out, carefully leading a small child by the hand. 'See you next week,' she said before closing the door behind her. She gave us a polite smile as she left.

My stomach clenched. We were next. I wasn't ready for this.

It was another minute before we were called and in that time I'd got up and run out of the waiting room ten times in my head.

The woman who came to the door and said, 'Rafaela Ramsey? Come in,' was younger than I'd thought she'd be. Around late twenties, she was plump with bobbed blonde hair. She looked as if nothing much ruffled her.

Silas got up and I followed on unwilling legs. Her office – clinic, whatever – was a twin of the waiting room. There was a small desk in the corner housing a computer, but she didn't sit at it, ushering us instead to low, soft chairs grouped round a coffee table in the middle of the room.

'Hi, Rafaela, I'm Andrea. And you're Silas?' she asked, turning from me to my brother.

'Yes,' he said, 'and everyone calls her Rafi.'

'Would you prefer that, for me to call you Rafi?' She turned back to me.

I looked to Silas in confusion. Hadn't he just told her that? Why was she asking me?

'Is it OK for you to nod or shake your head for me?'

Er . . . nod. But shouldn't she be talking to Silas to find out what was wrong with me so she knew how to fix me?

'So shall I call you Rafi?'

Nod.

She smiled. 'OK, so I'm going to ask you some questions in this first session. If it gets too much, just hold your hand up and I'll stop.' She put a tablet PC in front of me. 'No pressure, but if you want to share something, you can type on this.'

Silas looked at me. 'I think if it gets to that she'd prefer a pen and paper,' he said.

Andrea raised an eyebrow. 'Now that is unusual. Most people I see of your age prefer a computer. No problem though.' She whisked the tablet away and put a pad and a biro down on the table instead. 'Or you can draw if you like?'

I shook my head vehemently. God, no, I'd had enough of that in prep school with the speech and language woman they made me see there. I could still hear her voice in my head: 'Now draw me a little face to tell me if you're happy-smiley or sad today.'

'OK, so I'll go through your case details with you now, Rafi, so we can make sure you see it the same way. That's important. But first I need to tell you a bit about myself.'

Oh, I hadn't expected that.

'You probably know I'm a speech and language therapist. What you won't know is that I decided to go into this area because when I was very small I had a stammer and I was selectively mute at school for three years. So selective mutism is something I've always been really interested in and now I'm working as a therapist I specialise in cases of children who develop the condition. I don't come across many progressive mutes, because I'm sure you know that's much rarer, but I have treated a couple successfully in the past.'

I drew in a breath visibly.

'Is there something you'd like to ask?'

Nod, surprising myself at my courage.

She pushed the paper and pen over to me and smiled encouragingly.

I wrote: How many progressive mutes have you treated unsuccessfully?

She burst out laughing as she read it, and then looked at me for permission to show it to Silas. He laughed too.

'You're a smart cookie, aren't you? None,' she replied. 'I have treated exactly two people with your condition and in both cases we managed – and I say *we* because it takes hard work from the patient too – we managed to get them speaking again.' She cocked her head to one side as she looked at me. 'Does that make you feel better?'

Nod-shake.

'Because it's wonderful to think you might be able to talk again but terrifying too?'

I swallowed hard, now truly believing that she'd been mute too. Nod.

'It's the terror we need to work on, but we need to remember the wonderful too because that's what keeps us going. So today we're going to look at the past, but we're also going to begin to examine motives for change too.'

Silas was leaning back in his chair now, relaxed and watching us both.

'How old were you when you first began to struggle with speaking?'

I held up four fingers.

'And where did you first struggle – at school, at home, with strangers in new environments?'

I looked at Silas to answer for me – he knew this.

'It was at home,' he said.

'And you agree with that, Rafi?'

Nod.

'If your brother tells me something that isn't quite right, I need you to tell me.'

'I'm not going to do that,' Silas protested.

'No, not intentionally, but sometimes people with mutism can be quite secretive about their motives and it only comes out in a therapy situation. Rafi?'

Nod.

'OK, so you stopped talking at home first. To everyone?'

Shake of the head.

'Who did you first have trouble talking to?'

Now Silas didn't know this. I picked up the paper. *Carys.*

'And then?'

Mum.

Then Gideon.

'Was this before you had problems at school?'

Nod.

'Who was the last person you spoke to, Rafi?'

I pointed to Silas.

'Is that why you wanted your brother to come with you today?'

Shrug . . . nod.

'And how old were you then?'

I held up six fingers.

Silas interrupted us. 'She hadn't said much to me for ages

by that point. She occasionally whispered something, but then finally she stopped altogether.'

'What was Rafi like as a child?'

'How do you mean?'

'Was she outgoing, made friends easily, quiet, preferred her own company? What?'

'Yeah, quiet. She never did talk as much as the rest of us. And she hated getting in trouble. Used to cry a lot if she got told off. She was quiet when she went to school too. Played on her own a lot. Don't get me wrong, she did have some friends, but she always had this . . . solitary air about her too.'

Andrea turned back to me. 'Is that accurate, do you think?'

Nod. *Yes, I was always a weirdo.*

'And were you happy like that or did it bother you?'

I paused to work out how to answer that when, to my disgust and horror, a fat tear rolled down my cheek, followed by another.

Andrea got up and passed me a tissue. 'It bothered you,' she said gently.

Silas slipped an arm round my shoulders. 'Is there much more of this today?'

'I think we can leave the past there for now. I do want to spend a few minutes on motivation before we close. It's important to end on some positives. Rafi, can you think of one thing you'll enjoy when you talk, something you can't do now?'

I thought. It didn't take me long to come up with an answer.

Being able to talk to my friend Josie about things. I have to text her now if I want to tell her something.

'That's a good one. Have you been friends with Josie a long time?'

Shake of the head. No, only a couple of months.

'But she's a good friend?'

Nod. She talked me into seeing someone for help again.

Andrea smiled. 'Then she's a very good friend indeed. Can you think of any other positives?'

Again, it didn't take long. Speaking to my brother again.

'That's good – I can see you two are very close. Can I set this as an exercise for next time? I'd like you to come up with three more positives related to you beginning to speak again. We'll also look at some of your worries and explore what happened when you stopped talking. I'll set you some practical exercises at some point, but not this week.'

We closed the session, said polite goodbyes and left.

Once we were out in the street, Silas called Mum to come and get us. 'So what did you think?' he asked.

I gave him a surprised nod because actually it had been OK. Not how I thought it would go at all. I felt vaguely content instead of the sick, tummy-cramp sensations I'd expected from memory. Maybe Silas might get a normal sister one day after all.

War is when your government tells you who the enemy is. Revolution is when you figure it out for yourself.

(Anonymous)

CHAPTER 24

Hi Dad,

I feel a bit embarrassed telling you some of this stuff with Lara, but then I remember how you bought Mum a bunch of flowers home every Friday night, how you used to take her out for champagne cocktails whenever she landed a new commission just because she loves them so much. And how there's a tree at the bottom of our garden with both your initials carved into it, and the dates you first met, got engaged, got married. I don't know what went so wrong between you when you loved her once, but I think you of all people might get how I feel right now.

We went on a date. I wanted to take her on one not because I wanted to patronise her by treating her like any other girl – because I could see in her eyes that's what she was firing up to say (yes, I have got to know her a little bit now) – but because she was different to the others and that made her special. I wanted to show her how special.

I thought she'd be sarcastic about that, but she wasn't. She flushed a bit and wouldn't meet my eyes.

I spent three days searching for the perfect idea, rejecting so many possibilities before I found it, but it was more than worth the effort. I met her at the train station. She didn't ask me where we were going or what we were doing. She just walked beside me in silence. I wanted to take her hand, but I hadn't earned that right yet so I didn't try.

I gave her the window seat and she watched the trees flash past as the train raced through the countryside. The corners of her mouth were still curled upwards slightly and that was more than enough for me for now. When we got off the train at a tiny station in the middle of nowhere, she looked around, puzzled.

'It'll make sense soon,' I said.

We walked down a tarmacked road and then another and another, until we came to a narrow lane with the rough surface of a farm track. She followed me up it.

I've never felt so in love with a girl on a date before, but then, with the exception of Rafi of course, I've never known a girl who had less need to fill every second with noise. Lara was at ease without words and I loved that.

The countryside opened out as we reached the top of another hill and we could see below us the rolling contours of a country estate with a huge manor house in the centre. Lara stopped in her tracks to take a second look.

'This is where we're going?'

'Kind of,' I answered. 'Down there.'

I pointed to the right, down a track leading behind another

small hill. However, this one was carrying more traffic than would have been usual. There were battered Land Rovers making their way along it and a few people on foot, some trailing farm dogs at their heels.

'What is this?'

'You'll see.'

She didn't utter a word about how far we'd walked already or how much further it was. She paused to tighten a lace on her boot and then nodded at me to say she was ready to carry on. We trudged on down the hill and then took the path over to where the rest were heading. As we rounded a corner, we saw a large gathering of people and 4x4 vehicles blocking the lane.

'What's going on?' Lara demanded.

I beckoned her over to a nearby gate and then lifted her up to stand on top of it. 'What can you see?'

'A farm. This lot are blocking the entrance to a farm. They're spread out around the gate. They've got some placards on the ground, but I can't see what they say yet. It looks like they're all getting ready for something. Silas, what is this?'

I lifted her down again. There was a flush of excitement spreading across her cheeks as if she already had some idea what I was up to.

A man with a tatty waxed jacket and two spaniels at his heels passed us. 'Come to help?' he asked.

'Yes,' I replied.

'Come on down here then,' the man said. 'We're going to split up once we've got enough bodies. We need some to cover the back gate too. These devils are as sneaky as all hell.'

'We'll follow you then.'

'Aye, right.'

We fell in behind him.

'Silas, what is this?' Lara asked again, but her cheeks were bright now and her eyes more alive than I'd ever seen them.

I'd got it right, Dad. I'd actually got this right. And what I was thinking right then was let this be enough to make her give me a chance. Let this be enough for her to let me love her, even just a little.

You see, I knew you'd understand.

Silas

JOSIE'S PINTEREST BOARD

Do not regret growing older. It is a
privilege denied to many.

CHAPTER 25

On the morning that Silas took Lara on their first date, Josie spent some time hanging out with her dad. He felt like making a chocolate cake, he said, if she had nothing else planned. Josie understood this was code. Whenever her dad needed to talk to her about something big, he did it while they baked together. When he'd broken the news that her grandpa had died, he'd done it while they made cornflake cakes. So she knew that baking with chocolate meant really big news.

It was with an uncomfortable feeling in her stomach that she joined him in the kitchen. He was smiling, though. Which was unexpected, but she didn't drop her guard because his smile looked more forced than usual. Perhaps not awful news then, but certainly something important.

His voice was put-on cheery too as he got the ingredients out. 'We need the cocoa powder next,' he said consulting the cookbook as he weighed the flour.

Josie passed it to him silently and waited.

'We haven't done this for ages,' he said, as if they were having some lovely bonding experience that wasn't for any particular reason. But she knew better and marvelled that he didn't realise how transparent he was.

It wasn't until he'd weighed out everything and begun mixing that he finally got round to starting the conversation. Josie put the packets back in the cupboard as he beat the cake batter with a wooden spoon.

'I've got something to tell you,' he said, screwing his brow up with the effort he was putting into the mixing.

Yeah, he should just get on with it and tell her something she didn't know.

'OK,' she said as she put the remains of the butter back in the fridge. 'What?'

He looked at her. 'That's not a very encouraging tone of voice,' he remarked.

'I have a feeling you think it's something I'm not going to like.'

He sighed, stirring harder. 'Maybe not.'

'Go on then, what is it?' She felt in an odd way as if their roles were reversed here, like she was the parent waiting to hear what horrendous thing he'd done.

'I'm going out next week.'

She waited for the rest, but he didn't add anything.

'Yeah, Dad, come on – that's not it.'

He sighed more heavily and stirred still harder. 'To the cinema.'

'Great. And I need to know this because?'

It was ridiculous how nervous he looked as he met her eyes. 'On a date.'

'Oh!'

She was falling, that's how it felt. That plunging feeling, that lurch in the stomach that you get when a lift drops away too quickly and you wonder for a second if the pulley cord has broken.

Her father had a date.

Her father.

He watched her worriedly, waiting for her to respond.

But what could she say?

He hadn't been on a date since . . . well, since forever because Josie hadn't been around the last time for that had been with her mother. He'd never shown any interest in a woman since she died. He still had a photo of his wife by his bed and another on the wall of his study.

How could he be dating?

She opened her mouth to say something stupid about betraying her mother's memory, and didn't she mean anything to him, had he stopped loving her, and why, why, WHY?

But she stopped.

Two things stopped her. One was a Pinterest quote she'd snagged two days earlier that said: 'A part of those we love remains inside us, so be careful who you love because they will change you forever.' She'd pinned that as a warning, but it had occurred to her afterwards that it meant she carried a part of her mother inside her for always. And if that was true, then so did her dad.

The other was a memory. She was about ten and they were at the beach, in Devon she thought. She was playing on the sand and building a sandcastle with a moat around it while her father watched her. 'Do you need help?' he asked as she struggled over the sharp shale part of the beach in her bare feet with another bucket of water.

She looked at him in surprise. 'No, I want to do it so then I'll have made it all by myself.'

To her shock his eyes had filled with tears. She'd never seen her father cry, not that she could remember.

'Daddy?'

He dashed his hand over his face quickly. 'Sorry,' he said thickly, 'it's just that sometimes you remind me so much of your mum.'

And she remembered how proud she felt when he said that, but it was only now she realised how much love and loss there was in those words. So Josie didn't shout or rage at him about the date. She bit her lip and drew in a long breath, and then she sat on the kitchen stool and said, 'So tell me about it.'

RAFI'S TRUTH BOOK

Our lives begin to end the day we become

silent about things that matter.

(Martin Luther King, Jr)

CHAPTER 26

Hi again, Dad.

So I guess you want to know what happened after that. The next part was good. You'll want to hear this.

Lara took it all in – the scene by both gates, the placards saying 'Save the Symonds' and 'Where's your heart, Loxton?', the farmers and country people making a human barricade across the tracks in and out of the crumbling farmhouse. And the woman in the doorway of the farmhouse, her face lined with wrinkles from a life of hard work outdoors, now brushing away tears from her eyes as a man stood next to her and rubbed her arm before he went off to join the protesters at the front gate. As he reached them a cheer went up.

Lara looked so alive it was like a fire was burning inside her as she picked up one of the placards and held it high. 'Who are the Symonds?' she asked me.

'The farmers who live here. They rent the farm off the Loxton estate. Have done all their lives. Now Lord Loxton and his estate manager want to turn them out because they fell behind a couple of months with their rent while Mr Symonds was ill with pneumonia and couldn't work.

Basically they want them out so they can bring in some rich people who have horses and will pay a higher rent for the grazing than the Symonds can afford with their dairy cattle. So a lifetime's loyalty to the estate and they're out on their ears.'

'Scum,' Lara snapped. 'So how did you find out about this?'

'I did a bit of digging around for somewhere to take you and found an online protest against Loxton. Thought it was right up your street.' I could feel myself colouring up a bit and hoped she wouldn't notice, would think it was the wind or something. 'OK, it's not a conventional date, but I thought it might appeal to you more . . .'

For the first time I saw what her face looked like when a genuine, wholehearted smile warmed it. 'It's a perfect date. You were so right.'

Inside me, all kinds of mushy stuff happened. You know, birds burst into song, orchestras played triumphant marches and the sun burned the clouds away to shine in a clear blue sky. Lara had smiled. She really smiled. I had made her happy.

I never knew my happiness could depend so much on someone else's.

I picked up a placard too and took my place by her shoulder, and it felt like the only place in the entire universe that I wanted to be now.

Have you ever felt like that?

There's more, but I have to stop for a while. I've got work that has to be in tomorrow so I'll finish the rest another day.

Silas

RAFI'S TRUTH BOOK

Tis a fearful thing

To love what death can touch.

(Judah Halevi)

CHAPTER 27

The cake was in the oven, filling the kitchen with the delicious smell of baking and chocolate, and Josie's dad poured them some freshly made coffee.

'It's time,' he said. 'Your mother would tell me it's been long since time. She'd have no patience with me spending my life alone because I'd rather live with the memory of her than another woman.'

'Really?' It was so difficult to remember enough of her mother to know her. It was so long ago and Josie had been so little. She ate up others' memories of her as if she was starving, which she guessed she was really.

He nodded. 'She told me something just before she died. When she knew she was going and there was no fighting any longer. And that was right before the end, Josie, because she battled so hard to stay alive, as if she could scare the cancer away by how strong the fight in her was.'

'What did she say?'

He swallowed. The words were not easy to get out. 'When I said I'd love her forever, as much after death as in life, she told me I should find someone else to be with. I was angry with her. Didn't she understand? I couldn't love another woman like

190

her. There is no other woman like her.'

'So what did she say when you told her that?'

He laughed, one of those small, broken laughs people give when they remember something beautiful that's left them. 'She said don't be a damn fool. A ghost can't give you a hug after a bad day, and everyone needs a hug after a bad day.'

Josie felt the lump form in her throat instantly. 'You managed a long time on ghost hugs,' she said.

'I had you.' He reached over and hugged her. 'Ghost hugs and baby daughter hugs.'

'So why now?' she said when he let her go.

He kept hold of her hand. 'You'll be gone before I know it, sweetheart. To university and then on to your own life. And that's how it should be. How your mother and I wanted it to be for you. We wanted so much for you, you know. Wanted you to have every good thing we could think of. That was what upset her most at the end, that she'd not get to see you grow up.' He closed his eyes as if holding the memory tight to him.

'Who is she?'

'A colleague. She's new. Came up from the Met a couple of months ago.' He gave Josie a wry smile. 'She asked me out. A movie and a meal, she said. I got on with her fine, but I hadn't thought of her in that way. Then I thought about it, and you know I reckoned maybe I should. Just to see if it was possible to be with someone who isn't your mother.'

Josie felt as if she grew up in the moment between his words and her answer. 'Yeah, Dad, perhaps you should give it a go. Try it. You might have a good time.' She made a smile appear, even though she had to force it, because she had a feeling her mother would have told her to damn well do it.

She found me roots of relish sweet,

And honey wild, and manna-dew,

And sure in language strange she said –

'I love thee true.'

(John Keats – 'La Belle Dame Sans Merci')

CHAPTER 28

Dear Dad,

OK, this is the rest of it. And I swear to you, nothing happened that night, nothing!

The last train home was cancelled. I swore as I read the message on the screen at the deserted platform. There wasn't another going through until morning.

Lara's eyes were still shining from the battle. 'It doesn't matter,' she said.

'No, it does. I can't believe I didn't get us back on time for the 6.30, and then the 8.30 is cancelled!'

She shook her head. 'What we were doing was important. Much more important than making a train.'

'Did you enjoy it?'

For one beautiful, perfect moment, she leaned her head against my shoulder. 'Yes. I felt like I made a difference today. You know, we were there for those people and having their community come out for them like that, and having people travel miles to join in, that really meant something to them. And when the TV cameras turned up that was fantastic.'

'And what about the result?'

She tilted her head to look up. 'That was just the best

thing. When that agent from the Loxton estate turned up and said to the cameras it had all been a misunderstanding and they weren't going to be thrown out after all, and you could see it written all over his face that he was lying about the misunderstanding and had had to back down because of the bad press.'

'Yeah, that was pretty phenomenal. I get what you mean about this stuff now. I felt kind of high at that moment.'

'Me too.'

We stood in silence for a moment on the empty platform.

'So what do we do now?' I asked, and then wished I hadn't because I should be the one who had a solution.

'There's a shelter.' She pointed at the perspex tunnel further down the platform. 'There's a train at 7 a.m. It's a warm night. We'll sleep here.'

Every square millimetre of my skin began to tingle at the thought of sleeping beside her.

'There was a pub half a mile back down the lane,' I said. 'We could go and get some food first.'

She nodded. 'Sounds like a plan.'

We left the station and walked back the way we'd come. There was still plenty of light in the summer evening and the breeze blowing across our faces was warm. I sent a brief text to Mum as we walked, which she probably wouldn't even see until morning as half the time she never knows where her phone is or if it's charged. And I sent another to Rafi, who would be worried if I didn't show up.

When we got to the pub, lots of the other protesters were there and waved us over to sit with them. I watched Lara's face as she laughed with the wife of one of the local farmers – something about the pathetic statement given by Loxton. This was the real Lara. The stiff, defensive front she showed sometimes was totally dropped.

'So why did you come?' the woman asked her.

Lara grinned. 'I didn't know I was until today, but Silas knew I'd want to get involved.' She shrugged and gave a wry smile. 'I guess I'm just a scrapper, you know. I believe in people's rights and I believe we should fight for them when those rights are abused. But, you know, I just can't not fight. There's something inside me that has to.'

The woman laughed and Lara turned back to me.

'Well, it's true,' she said, flushing as I couldn't help laughing at her.

'Yeah, I know it is.'

She eyed me. 'There's something I've been meaning to ask you. That stunt you pulled with your sister's friend's guy – why did you do it?'

'Because he was a shit to her and he deserved taking down. Because I knew how to do it. Because nobody else was looking out for her. Because I thought, and I still think, it was the right thing to do. Because sometimes you have to stand up for people when they can't fight back.'

She leaned over and kissed me softly on the cheek. 'Yeah, you do.'

And after that I was flying, Dad. Totally flying. No drug could take you where I was.

As we were leaving after we'd eaten, the woman Lara had been talking to asked, 'How are you getting home?'

'I called my dad for a lift,' Lara said without a blink. 'He's picking us up by the station.'

'Why did you say that?' I asked her when we got outside.

'Because she'd have felt obliged to offer us a bed or find someone with a spare room otherwise.'

'Oh.'

So why hadn't she wanted that? Because we might have been put in the same room, or because she didn't want to feel obliged to them? Or did she really prefer to spend the night on a hard, cold train platform?

'How do you know that? It would never have occurred to me.'

'I grew up in a place a lot like this. That's how the people are.'

Now I didn't expect that, Dad. Not at all. My picture of her childhood is in some cool urban environment. It's impossible to tell where she's from by the way she speaks, but I'd never imagined it was some isolated rural spot.

We walked back to the station in silence. It was fully dark but Lara seemed comfortable to pick her way back down the lane by moonlight alone. The station was in darkness too, but the day's heat still lingered in the air and so I had some hope we wouldn't be miserably cold overnight.

Lara sat down under the shelter, leaning her back against the perspex wall and wriggling around, trying it out for comfort. 'No,' she said finally, 'I think sleeping on the ground will be more comfortable.' She scooted down and curled up on the tarmac floor with her head resting in the crook of her arm.

I didn't know where to position myself. Eventually I leaned back against the shelter. As she'd said, it wasn't comfortable, but it was much safer for the moment until I worked out exactly how to act around her right now.

My heart beat with a racing rhythm that said sleep was a long, long way away.

'So, Demo Virgin, what did you think of today?' said Lara through the darkness.

I rehearsed lots of explanations in my head before I realised that ultimately it was very simple.

'I get it,' I said. 'I get why you do it.'

There was a long, achingly long pause. And then, 'Why did you have to be the way you are?' She said it in the smallest voice I've ever heard her use, and there was something so sad in her tone. I didn't understand it.

'You don't like the way I am?' So hard to get those words out because I was so afraid of the answer.

She sighed heavily. 'I like the way you are. You shouldn't change.' And she turned over so she had her back to me and curled into a tighter ball. She didn't say goodnight, but I'd been dismissed from the conversation.

I crashed back down to earth with a bang.

I wish you could tell me what you think of it all. I really wish that badly. Never mind, it helps just to tell you.

Love, Silas

RAFI'S TRUTH BOOK

For I am caught between who I am

and who I want to be.

CHAPTER 29

I'd thought that I was feeling calmer about the whole speech therapist thing – until I was actually in the waiting room for my second appointment. She had given me a false sense of confidence last time for a little while, but of course I was still myself and the feeling of choking that I was so used to began to grow again in my throat as I waited. What if she tried to get me to speak today?

Silas was staring blankly at the wall in front, his phone in his hand. Obviously waiting for a message of some sort. He carried on staring at the wall and trying to pretend he wasn't checking his phone messages every few minutes until we were called through by Andrea.

'So how has it been since last time? Any thoughts you want to share?' She had the paper and pen at the ready for me this time.

I shook my head immediately, a reflex action. The relative easiness of our last session had disappeared and we were back to square one, except this time for some reason I felt even less like sharing. I shut down, like a hedgehog curling into a protective ball.

Nothing.

I had nothing to give.

'Did you manage to come up with more positive ideas about

what you can do once you start to talk again?'

There was no 'if' with Andrea. Last time I'd liked that. Today it felt like immeasurable pressure.

Still, I had to give her a crumb.

'Baby steps,' Silas urged, seeing my face.

Will be able to get a job, I wrote.

'Do you know what job you'd like to do when you're older?' Andrea asked.

Shake of the head. Not ready to share that. She might ask to see something I'd written and there was no way I could show her. Probably not ever.

I saw Silas cast me a sidelong glance, but he stayed silent. He knew about my writing, but as I wouldn't even show him he'd know I couldn't share it with Andrea.

'Thinking about some possibilities might be a good way forward then,' Andrea said.

I shook my head again.

She paused and examined my face, trying to read something there.

'OK, let's go back to the beginning and look at how this started for you again,' she said after a moment. 'I'd like you to tell me if there were times after you stopped talking when you wanted to try to speak and you couldn't.'

Nod.

'How exactly did that feel?'

I thought about it. Could I answer this? My pulse went up a bit, but nothing too bad. No, I didn't feel threatened by this question. She probably knew how it felt if she'd been mute too.

I wrote: Tight in my throat and sick in my tummy.

'And did you ever get pains in your tummy when you thought you might have to speak?'

Nod. Used to.

'But not now? What does it feel like now if you want to try to speak?'

Choking. Feel faint if it gets really bad.

'She stopped breathing once,' Silas said. 'It was at school when a new teacher tried to make her speak. The teacher kept shouting at her and she stopped breathing. She only started again when she passed out.'

Andrea compressed her lips. 'That must have been very frightening for you.'

It was. I thought I was going to die. I tried to forget about that incident and Silas knew it so he must have thought it was important to bring it up. I didn't listen to Silas explain what happened as Andrea prompted him for more information. I didn't need to listen – I remembered it all too well.

I was ten. We'd just got a new class teacher because our old one had left to go to another school halfway through the year. I wasn't sure what went wrong at the time, whether the teacher hadn't been told about my condition or if she just didn't believe in it. It turned out later that it was the latter, but we only found that out after Silas told my mum what had happened and she stormed into the school and went off like a nuclear bomb. I was mad with Silas for telling, but at least it meant I didn't have to be in the woman's class any more.

She'd looked annoyed when she read out the names from the register and I didn't answer but raised my hand instead. I cringed inside at her expression. I knew she was thinking what a nuisance I was. They all secretly thought that, even my last teacher who'd been one of the nicer ones. I was more work for them than the others. She didn't make any comment in registration though. It was later at reading time that the trouble began.

She was going round the class, telling people to read a page each from our books. I still remember the book: it was *Charlotte's Web*, which I loved up until then, but I've never been able to touch it since. She started with the person straight in front of her and then went down each row of desks and back up again. I must have had some sense of what was brewing because I recall that as it got closer and closer to what would have been my turn, I started to get a tummy ache. It wasn't that unusual for this to happen. I often got mild anxiety that a teacher would forget and try to make me read whenever we did this kind of thing, but this time it was bad. I held my stomach and tried to rub it without anyone noticing. Still, the moment she said, 'Rafaela, your turn,' it took me a second to process that my worst fear was really happening. It was so often a nightmare for me that I thought for a moment I was in a dream and tried to wake up.

Her voice came again, sharper this time. 'Rafaela! Stop daydreaming. Your turn to read!'

I stared at her helplessly.

'Don't look at me in that vacant way, child!' she snapped. 'Pay attention. Page 83, begin at the top.'

Another girl put her hand up, looking at me nervously. She was ignored as the teacher got up and began to come over.

'Please, Miss,' the girl said hesitantly, 'Rafi can't talk.'

The teacher whirled round. 'And who asked for your opinion, young lady?'

The girl fell silent and put her head down.

My throat was tightening painfully, a tightness that was spreading down into my chest as the woman got closer.

I remember her shoes: black patent court shoes with a scuff on one toe. I remember I focused on the scuff as I tried to breathe. *One in, one out*, I told myself, attempting to count so I didn't forget how to do it. *One in, one out*.

She stabbed her finger at the page. 'From here! Now read!'

One in, one out.

She bent over me. 'I will not tolerate this nonsense. Begin reading now!'

One in . . .

But the breath wouldn't come in. My chest was too tight.

She was angry. Her face was reddening as her frustration with me built.

I couldn't do it, I couldn't.

I shook my head.

And that was when she really exploded.

'How DARE you shake your head at me?' she shouted. 'I don't know who you think you are, young lady, but I do not accept behaviour like that from anyone in my class. Now, I have given you an instruction and you had better do as you are told.'

Silas said to me after that she'd probably gone so far by this point that she couldn't have backed down even if she could see it wasn't working or she'd lose face in front of the other kids.

'You WILL do as you are told,' she yelled as I still didn't begin reading.

I couldn't breathe in or out by this time. I heard the other kids talking about it the following week when I returned to school and apparently I went purple.

'If you don't do as you are told, we will all sit here until you do read. And if this whole class has to miss their break and playtime at lunch because you won't do as you are told, then it will be very much the worse for you, madam, won't it?'

My stomach cramped so badly that I fell forward on to the desk.

'READ!'

I couldn't hear her any more. The ringing in my ears got too loud. They said I fainted and fell to the floor. They said she thought I was faking it at first and carried on shouting at me to get up and stop being so silly, but then a teacher came in from another class to see what all the fuss was about. She called for the Headmistress, who had me taken to the sickroom where they kept me for the rest of the day. The school nurse stayed with me, but nobody called my mum. Silas said with disgust that they were probably hoping to cover it up. After all, *I* wouldn't talk. But one of the little girls in my class, I think the one who had tried to speak up, went over to the netting that separated the prep department from the senior school and got someone to find Silas. She told him what had happened.

When I look back on that now, she could have become a friend, if I'd had the courage to realise it. It wasn't until I made friends with Josie that I began to recognise signs of friendship, but that girl did two nice things for me that day. If I'd tried to be friends with her after that, maybe my time in the prep would have been different.

Andrea stood up. 'I think I'll make us a drink and get the biscuits out,' she said. Her cheeks were flushed.

'It's OK,' Silas whispered as she switched the kettle on and rummaged in a drawer. 'She's not mad with you, just with that stupid woman.'

Andrea made us tea and handed the biscuits round. There were chocolate digestives. She smiled as I took one. 'If I was on a desert island,' she said, 'and could take only one kind of biscuit, I'd take chocolate digestives.'

I frowned and grabbed the writing pad. *They'd melt*.

Andrea laughed. 'You are far too sharp not to speak, Rafi, and too funny.'

Nice try, Andrea, but that wasn't how I saw it.

'So that was a very negative memory associated with not speaking,' she said as I munched my way through biscuit number two. 'Can you think of any more positives to balance that out?'

To be honest, right at that point my view on co-operation changed. I might have felt like shutting down at the start of the session, but now I genuinely did want to think of some positives because that memory was just so depressing.

Make more friends.

Because, you know, perhaps I could. If I was a braver, speaking person, I could talk to Rachel. She was Silas's friend, but I liked her and she was interesting. I would like to be able to tell her that.

In another world, on another planet, I might talk again. In this one, right now, I couldn't really see it happening.

'You seem to have lost some confidence since last time we met,' Andrea said, proffering the biscuits again. 'That's a shame because you need to stay focused if we're going to do this and that means you need to keep believing you *can*. Because you can, you know. There's no physical reason for not speaking so that means it *is* possible, no matter how hard it may seem to you at the moment.'

She sat back in the chair and looked at me. Her face was calm, but Silas's was a mass of frustration.

'I thought she really wanted to do it this time,' he said.

I do . . . don't . . . do . . . Oh, how can I want to when I don't even know how it feels to talk any more?

'I think she does or she wouldn't be sitting here now,' Andrea replied. 'But it's been a long time and there are some very big barriers to overcome first. Rome wasn't built in a day and Rafi won't be cured in one either! You have to be patient.'

He gave her a rueful smile. 'I guess.'

'You often see a backward slide before an improvement.' She was talking to me as well as him. 'It's as if, when the sufferer begins to see there's a real possibility of the mutism being over, when that starts to become tangible, they panic and retreat. But it's a very important part of the process. It may look like moving backwards, but in fact it's a giant step forward. Now, Rafi, I want you to take another step. I want you to think of one thing associated with you becoming mute that I don't know about, and maybe even Silas doesn't. And I want you to tell us. Can you try, please?'

One very obvious thing occurred to me. The thing I'd lied about last time. I was ashamed that first time, ashamed of what it would reveal about my family.

But something else had happened as Silas dragged up that prep school memory. At the time I was horrified about my mother going into the school to complain. I'd heard her shout so often. What if she did that in the school? I'd *die*. Better not to make a fuss. I stood in the hall as she was leaving me with Kerensa so she could go and raise hell with the Head – her description not mine. I stared and stared at her with tears falling down my face, willing her to understand, but she didn't even look at me. It had to be her way of course. I hated her for doing that.

Now, looking back years later, I saw something different in that memory. I saw her anger at her child being hurt, and I saw her going all out to protect me.

A lump formed in my throat.

I'd never seen it that way before.

She was outside somewhere now, sitting in her car, waiting for us.

The lump in my throat pressed more painfully and my eyes stung with some unshed tears. Maybe a tiny bit of her did care about me.

I took hold of the pen again. It might be important to tell this. It might help me get better.

I didn't tell the truth last time I was here. It wasn't Carys I stopped talking to first. It was Mum. But she didn't notice.

Andrea read what I'd written with her usual careful therapist's give-nothing-away face, but Silas winced.

'Why did you say it was Carys?'

She was the first one to realise. I did stop talking to her

210

eventually, but Carys realised it before Mum did.

Could anyone blame me for thinking Mum didn't care after that?

But she was here now. And she was waiting for me. Had I got it wrong back then? What if she cared more than I'd thought?

To love is so startling it leaves little time for anything else.

(Emily Dickinson)

CHAPTER 30

A new coffee shop had opened on the high street and Josie and I went to try it out on Friday after school. It wasn't one of the big chains but a rip-off looky-like. But the coffee was just as good, and the cookies. Plus it was right on our doorstep and not much was. It got our seal of approval all right.

Josie was telling me about a fantastic plan she'd come up with for us for the weekend. We were going to the zoo tomorrow. I had never been to the zoo before, not even on a school trip. This was another thing I loved about Josie. Out of nowhere, she would come up with something exciting to do.

'Always try to do something awesome at least once a month, that's my motto!' she said, as I grinned and waved my hands about in a general effort to show my appreciation of her efforts. 'Life is too short to waste.'

I guess many people didn't know the truth of that as well as she did.

Rachel, Toby and the group from sixth form came in. Rachel and the girls waved at us while they queued.

'Your brother not with them?' Josie asked.

That was odd. He'd told me he had something on with his friends after school. I shrugged.

Once they'd got their orders, they came over to sit at the table next to us.

'Any good?' Clare asked Josie, gesturing at her coffee mug.

'Actually, yeah, very,' Josie said. 'We're impressed.'

'What've you done with Silas?' Toby asked. 'I thought he was hanging out with you guys tonight.'

I shook my head and pointed at them. They looked puzzled.

'She thought he was with you,' Josie explained.

'No,' Rachel said. 'He hasn't been out with us for a while. We pretty much only see him in school these days.'

Josie frowned, remembering as I was all the times Silas said he was with them . . . or rather, he hadn't exactly said that, but he must have known that was what we thought.

So where was he?

'Hmm,' Rachel said, with a conspiratorial glance at Clare. 'I think someone is seeing someone, don't you?'

Toby glowered and sank down in his chair. Clare laughed. 'I think so too.'

'Aww, it's nice,' Rachel said. 'I like her. She'll be good for him, not like all those "yes, Silas, no, Silas" types he usually ends up with.'

Clare rolled her eyes. 'He always ends up with them because they engineer it. I don't think he's ever actually asked one of them out properly on a date.'

So they all thought he was probably out with Lara. But why was he keeping it so quiet? Toby's sullen face might be a clue to that.

'Do you think he was with her that night he texted you to say he wasn't coming home?' Josie asked when we were on our way back to her place.

That stopped me in my tracks. Perhaps he had been. But if he was so into her, why hadn't he told me? He'd always talked to me about things like that before.

I felt jealousy bite with jagged teeth.

The news was on when we got to Josie's house and her dad was watching it while he was getting ready to go out to work, hastily eating a bowl of stir-fry at the kitchen counter.

'Police from across the Home Counties have been drafted in to support the Metropolitan Police in managing tomorrow's protest in the capital,' the news reporter announced. 'The anticipated protests by various groups about the level of profits made by the global multinationals have been causing concern. While many of the groups involved have made it clear they expect the protests to be peaceful, a significant minority are said to be preparing for the kind of disturbances London saw in the student riots. Angry at what they say is the exploitation of people in developing countries at the expense of the fat-cat West, their leaders have been using social media sites to whip up support for vandalism and occupation of premises tomorrow. London braces itself for disruption, and the police brace themselves for a difficult day.'

'Are you involved in that?' Josie asked.

'Yeah, I've been pulled in. We all have.' Her dad shook his head at the TV and carried on speed-eating his dinner.

'I was going to ask him for a lift to the zoo,' Josie whispered glumly. 'Do you think your mum will drop us off and pick us up?'

I almost laughed. Of course she wouldn't.

'You could try,' Josie said pleadingly.

I nodded. If she wanted me to do that, I'd better go home and ask now in case Mum was going out.

I was in luck. Mum was eating her dinner too. I scribbled a note: *Josie's dad was going to drop us off at the zoo tomorrow, but now he has to work. Could you take us and then pick us up please?*

She stopped eating and looked at me. I felt her judge me again — *why can you not ask me this with your* voice? I always felt her judgement when she looked at me, always had done and I guess I always would.

'Yes,' she said, and my head almost fell off in shock. 'What time do you want to go?'

RAFI'S TRUTH BOOK

Give me somewhere to

stand and I will move

the earch.

(Archimedes)

CHAPTER 31

Dear Dad,

It's been the longest day and I can't tell you all of it now, but I'll tell you some of it while it's still fresh in my mind.

I was scared Lara was going to be distant with me after our date, as it didn't end at all according to plan. But she hasn't. We've been hanging out together more, mostly in the library or the new coffee shop in town. Just half an hour here and there when she has time. But on our own more, like she's happy to be alone with me now without Rachel and Toby and all the others around. I told her I wanted to see more of her and was that OK, and she said yes, but she was busy. She was a bit cagey about telling me why, but eventually I got it out of her. She's been doing some campaigning for those people who ran the meeting she took me to, ActionX. Said they were doing some good work at the moment and she wanted to give some support. Then she told me about a march in London and asked me if I wanted to come with her.

I felt like it was a test. Obviously, Dad, you know I had to pass it. And when she told me what it was about, well, they've got a point. Someone should be stopping this stuff from going on.

She met me at the train station. She had this little smile when she saw me, this little smile that totally slayed me. My heart leaped so high I wondered how it could still be in my chest. It was . . . *trusting* of me in a way I'd never seen from her before. With it, and with every move, every word, more and more, she reels me in and I don't care how fast I'm caught.

'Hey,' she said. 'So are you still up for this?'

'Completely.'

'You know it could get heavy?'

'I know.'

She grinned. The platform announcer called the train. 'Let's do this then,' she said.

There was evidence of what was coming even at the station when we got off the train in London. I could see it in a grimness around the eyes and the mouths of some of the people making their way down to the Embankment where the march was scheduled to start. Professional protesters, all looking like the ActionX people, a sameness to how they dressed and, yes, a sameness to their expressions on a day like this. I glanced at Lara – I could see it in her face too, that strange elation and a sort of deadliness.

I've never felt anything like the vibes from the crowd as they gathered on the Embankment. The noise was deafening; the rattles and whistles and chanting made my ears ring until I could no longer hear what Lara said as she read instructions from her phone. Her eyes were shining with battle-joy though and she mimed directions to me. We broke off from the crowd and headed down the side of the route towards a pub, where we met a group I recognised from the night of the meeting. They were the ones leafleting after the talk. Even if I hadn't seen the faces before I would have known them by their clothes and a look of oneness about them.

And in the middle of them, Dillon. He had a certain presence even off the podium.

'Hey, Lara,' one of the younger guys said.

'Hi, Tyler.' She smiled at an older girl. 'Hi, Katrin.'

The girl looked at us with a strange expression. I couldn't make it out. For a second it looked like disgust, but she masked it quickly. 'New recruit?' She nodded towards me.

'Yeah, he's up for it. He knows what to expect.'

'First demo?'

'No, we've been out on one together before.'

Dillon was watching me with curiosity, and something else I couldn't put my finger on. What was it with these guys? Did they go to some special training camp for impenetrability?

'I'm Katrin,' the older girl said. 'I'm directing things on the ground so if I tell you to do something –'

'Then I do as you tell me.' I sensed the faster they

understood I wasn't going to go maverick on them under pressure, the better.

She thawed a bit and almost smiled. 'Yes. Speaking of directing things, Dillon, shouldn't you be out of here by now?'

'Yeah. Now everyone's here and we're ready to roll, I'll get gone.' He slipped off through the crowd a lot more easily than I'd found it to get through.

'Does he know the codes?' Katrin asked Lara. Lara shook her head. 'Stay close to her then,' she said to me. 'If we have to use the phones to keep in touch, Lara knows what to do.'

A sudden roar from the crowd alerted us to the people starting to move. The march was finally beginning.

It wasn't what I expected. I'd seen the news. I'd been on the Loxton protest with Lara. I thought I knew what I was in for.

By 4 p.m. I knew I was a naive fool.

It was around noon when we started to march and it seemed good-natured. We made our way slowly down the Embankment, too many people for us to do more than move at a crawl. And then we turned into Westminster. That's when I started to notice things, like the groups of skinny, black-clothed people sitting around on steps drinking cans of Special Brew, with animal face masks pushed just far back enough to allow them to drink, but not far enough for the CCTV to identify their faces.

'They're not with us,' Lara mouthed when she saw me staring.

'Do you know them?'

She shrugged. 'Ish. They're OK. Not bad to have around when it gets nasty.'

I wasn't scared, Dad, but I wasn't at all easy with it either.

As we passed Portcullis House, I had to laugh at the policemen on the steps guarding the entrance to Parliament. Their bombproof gear of densely padded puffy trousers made them stand with their legs splayed out. 'Gangsta!' I said to Lara and her face lit up with laughter.

I loved seeing her like this, so alive.

The chanting and shouting and whistling reached fever pitch outside the House of Commons and the crowd slowed to a halt. We stood together as one body, shouting at the top of our lungs. It must have been as audible inside as it was out there. I was light-headed, elated . . . it really felt like we were doing something important here. It felt like someone MUST listen.

I looked around and saw the banners, hundreds of words all shouting for the same thing – for fair treatment of workers in the Third World, for no more exploitation, for no more obscene profits at the expense of the poor.

The government had the power to stop this, right?

They had to listen to this, didn't they?

The noise, the pulse sounding in my ears like the banging of the drum a guy was playing across the street, the smell of diesel fumes mixed with hope . . . I can still feel it all now. I looked down at Lara and knew she felt the same. I got it. I totally and utterly got it. There was nothing like this feeling. No wonder it was such a big deal for her. A professional difference-maker, that's what Lara is. And it felt like a good thing to be right then.

The march set off again, down past the Cenotaph and on into the heart of the London shopping area. The masked people were beginning to move around along the sides of the march. Then Lara got a text.

'OK, we're on.' I could hear her now the noise had dropped as the crowd thinned out.

She pulled a soft black mask out of her pocket and slipped it over her face, then handed one to me.

'Hurry up, before the CCTV picks us up!'

I dragged the mask on hurriedly.

'Ready?'

'Yes.'

'Follow me.'

She jogged up the side of the crowd. People began to glance at us as we passed and Lara called out to them,

'Stand up against injustice and show this government how you really feel. Direct action!'

I saw someone on the other side of the crowd beginning to do the same thing, and another further up the street.

'Come on – join us!' Lara yelled as she ran.

A wave of noise followed us. There were some jeers about stupid kids from some of the protesters, but I also heard some yelling encouragement. As we got further up the street, I even saw a couple of people begin to follow us, pulling scarves up over their faces.

I still didn't have any idea what I was getting into. I knew there'd be trouble, but nothing like the scale of what was to come.

RAFI'S TRUTH BOOK

If life had a second edition,

how I would correct the proofs.

(John Clare)

CHAPTER 32

Mum dropped us off at the zoo and told me to call an hour before I wanted picking up. I held my hand up to say thanks as she drove off.

When we looked at the map, we realised how enormous the zoo was so we had to prioritise what we really wanted to see in case we didn't get round all of it.

'Elephants, obviously.'

Of course. That was a given.

'And the lions.'

Oh yes.

But first we walked through the grassy areas looking at the animals they had roaming loose, funny things that looked like big rabbits – maras, the map said they were called. And then on past the bison and moose. After that was a large, mainly grassed enclosure. We peered in through the netting, scanning around until Josie pointed in excitement.

'There!'

And there they were. Six ghostly grey-white shapes flitting up and down on the far side of the enclosure: the wolves.

We watched them in silence as they stalked round each other in circles, a stiff-legged dance showing how aware they were of us. I could feel how they didn't want us there. We had invaded their privacy. The desire for isolation, to run free and unseen in immense open spaces, was almost tangible.

I understood them perfectly; that terrified me.

My bubble of elation burst and I grabbed Josie's sleeve to pull her away. She was taken aback at my sudden urgency to move on, but she didn't object.

'What freaked you out about them?' she said once we'd moved on to look at the much safer option of reindeer.

<They are so sad.>

She thought about teasing me, I could see it in her face, but then she changed her mind.

'I think you may be the most sensitive person I've ever met,' she said quietly as we leaned on the fence and looked at the reindeer serenely eating grass. 'As in you practically absorb other people's feelings into yourself and translate them before that person even knows what they are themselves.'

I thought about it and shrugged.

'I think that's what makes it so hard for you to deal with people. You see what they don't even know they're showing. You see things they never intended you to see. If we could all do that, Raf, I think we'd go crazy.'

Did she mean I was crazy then?

'Seriously, with all that going on in your head, not talking is like the mildest reaction. I'd be in bits.'

Lucky me.

'I can't take it when people think badly of me.' Josie sniffed. 'I'll correct that — I didn't *used* to be able to until I got a crash course in coping, courtesy of Lloyd.'

We left the reindeer pen and walked slowly up the path to where the white rhinos were also busy chomping grass. Josie scuffed the ground with her toe as she walked.

'It was horrible,' she said. 'I've never felt so awful in my whole entire life. And it just hit out of nowhere. At first I didn't even know what Lloyd had done. I knew he was mad at me, but I walked into school that day and people in the corridors were pointing at me and laughing. You know, I thought I had something on my hair, like a bird had pooped on me or something like that, so I went into the toilets. And no, there was nothing on me, but this girl I sort of knew just looked at me and said, "Tramp!" and walked out.'

I could feel my nerves tingling in sympathy for her, scared for what would happen next.

'I knew then it was something bad, from the look on that girl's face and from how everyone was acting. When I got to form it was worse. My friends all stopped talking when I came in. I said "Hi" and went over, but they just *looked* at me. Then Alice sniggered and after that they all started. I asked them what was going on, but Alice just said, "Oh come on, Josie. We all know." And I honestly didn't have a clue. So I ignored them and sat down at my desk because the teacher was coming in.'

We stopped by the rhinos and sat on a bench. Josie paused to 'aww' at a cute little baby rhino and then she went on.

'And it went on like that all through registration. My so-called friends just kept looking at me with these shocked and disgusted expressions. I worked out it must be something to do with Lloyd because he'd been so mad at me when I told him we were over. It was too coincidental for this to be nothing to do with him. Eventually, when the bell went, I managed to get Chrissie on her own in the toilets and she told me what he'd done. I could see she believed his lies. After all, he had photos so why wouldn't she?'

Josie's face crumpled and she buried her head in her hands. I stroked her hair. It seemed like a good thing to do for an upset person.

'It was so awful, Rafi. I went from being a normal person with friends to someone who no one would speak to, except to say mean stuff. And Chrissie said some *really* mean stuff about how she didn't want to hang out with a slapper like me. I have never felt so alone as I did then. I don't know how I would have coped if it had gone on any longer. Boys started yelling stuff at me in the corridors and everywhere I went people were –'

She stopped and sat herself upright, making herself back into the Josie I knew.

'I never thought someone like me could be bullied, never

imagined it would happen. Not that I was Miss Uber-Popular Prom Queen, but I had plenty of friends. Or so I thought. I know how wrong I was now. I'm OK at lessons. I'm not clever like your brother, but if I work really hard I could get to uni. There was nothing about me for anyone to pick on. But in one day I went from average to hated. That's all it took and that's kind of terrifying. One mistake and . . .' She shook her head.

'Every day after that, until your brother stopped it, my life was completely miserable. And I thought it was never going to end. Every day it seemed to get worse. That day we first met, a girl I didn't even know walked up to me in the corridor and slapped me round the face. All her friends stood there and laughed. These were girls I'd never done anything to in my life. And it was OK to hit me and yell names because Lloyd posted those pictures. I mean, even if I had done what he said, why did that make it OK to bully me?'

<It didn't.>

Josie gave a huge sniff and hugged me. 'I love you, you know that? Because you would never treat anyone that way. I wish you would stop thinking you should be something more than you are because what you are is great. So what if all your family are like some mega-brains? You don't have to be like them. You don't have to be like anyone other than you.'

By the time we got to the lion enclosure, we'd both cheered

up. In fact we were helpless with laughter because on a hillock next to the fence, a group of very discontented lions were sitting watching a herd of antelope skipping about in the next enclosure. Their expressions clearly said 'prospective DINNER!' The antelope on the other hand were practically taunting them in a 'can't get me' way as they pranced up and down by the wire, perfectly safe and they knew it.

'Whoever decided to put those lions there is just evil,' Josie gasped, her eyes beginning to cry with laughter. 'Look at their faces.'

As if to emphasise her point, one of the lionesses got up and began to stalk towards the fence. The antelope, completely unconcerned, presented its bum to her and started to eat grass. The lioness sat down in a huff.

When I could stop laughing again, I checked my phone. Nothing from Silas. I'd texted him earlier with a friendly <What're you up to today?> because he'd left the house that morning before I'd been up. Which was odd.

'You know, if he's with Lara, he's not going to want to lose face texting his little sis to say where he is,' Josie said, watching me.

Silas wouldn't have cared about that once.

'Has he ever brought her home?'

Actually, no, he hadn't.

'Hmm.'

What did that mean? I drew a question mark in the air.

'Do you think Rachel and Clare are right? Is he really seeing her? And if so, why does she never come round yours? I saw her getting on a bus to go out of town a couple of days ago, and it was late. Dad was driving me back home from swimming practice because it was raining so hard he came to get me, and there she was getting on a bus heading for London. At that time of night, on her own, in the rain. That's odd, isn't it?'

OK, that was kind of weird.

'I get why she'd like your brother. He's a good guy and he's not been beaten with the ugly stick in any way.'

So Josie liked my brother and thought he was cute – hmm.

'And I know she's mega pretty, but . . .' Josie frowned. 'She's . . . oh, I don't know . . . it's probably nothing. We don't know they're even together, so it doesn't matter. Come on, where next?'

A riot is at bottom the language of the
unheard.

(Martin Luther King, Jr)

CHAPTER 33

By the time we reached Oxford Street, we'd broken off from the main body of the demonstration. The police tried to close us down as soon as they realised what was happening. I saw the TV footage streaming on to Lara's phone – from above you could see the real picture, not just a splinter group from the centre of the demo where we were, but others from the top end, and the rear, all heading into Oxford Street down different routes. And from other points in the city, small huddles of masked demonstrators suddenly springing into visibility and making their way to the same points. From the helicopter in the sky, it looked like a starburst collapsing inwards on itself.

It was the number of people that shocked me as we ran through the ranks of protesters. From a few people breaking off here and there in the march, and others following them to join in, they'd grown to a huge crowd. For the first time I understood how planned and co-ordinated this thing was. The police looked hopelessly outnumbered, the majority of them still left on the main route with the thousands of passive protesters.

A small group of police in riot gear had got separated from the main body trying to stem the flow of demonstrators further down the street. They were surrounded by black-clad figures waving metal bars. One of them went down in the scuffle and, for a sickening moment, I thought I was going to witness the man being battered bloody. But Katrin's team were too well disciplined for that, and it *was* them – I could see the X logos on their shoulders. Instead they grabbed for the riot shields and batons of the officer who went down and the ones trying to help him. Once they had what they wanted they let the officers go and the men ran full pelt back to their colleagues, stripped of all their protection.

Katrin's crew wielded their trophies in the air and the crowd around them roared. I was still catching my breath with relief that they hadn't attacked the policeman, but I cheered too, my head spinning with the noise and the just-too-much-to-bear-energy that had enveloped us as soon as we'd arrived.

And then there was a sharp, acrid stench that made my nostrils wrinkle up. From further down the street came more cheering, and I could see strange flashes of light through the cloud.

'What is it?' I asked Lara.

'They're petrol-bombing the shops.'

That tiny middle-class pocket within me gave a shudder of horror. *This is wrong*, it said.

I told it to shut up. I drowned out its voice by gazing into her eyes as anarchy unfolded around us. This was what the girl I love lives for. If anyone had ever doubted that, one look at her face now would show them the truth of it.

If she was ever to love me, I had to learn to love this too. There's no compromise with Lara. She's the most implacable person I've ever met. As I watched her pick up a pole from the ground and charge at a window to smash it through, as I heard the CRAASSHHH of breaking glass, I felt prouder of her than I'd ever felt of anyone in my whole life. She was so totally and utterly herself and it was the most beautiful, rare thing.

'Grab the barrier,' she yelled as she hauled a metal gate up. I hurried to get the other side and we pulled it up between us.

She gave me a mad grin. 'CHARRRGGGGGE!'

And we ran together towards the next window, breaking off at the last minute and hurling the gate through the glass. A petrol bomb soared over our heads to smash in a burst of flames inside the shop. Lara leaped up and punched the air and, as she turned to me, I burst out laughing like I really was one of them.

She grabbed my arm and pulled me towards her. I realised what she was going to do only a fraction of a second before her lips met mine. And in that fraction of a second, I thought I'd explode from the anticipation, nerves, desperation . . .

. . . and then she was kissing me to the stench of burning petrol and the sound of breaking glass.

RAFI'S TRUTH BOOK

How great is the distance between two people who share the same blood, but not the same understanding.

CHAPTER 34

Back home at dinner time, I lounged on the sofa with a bowl of pasta, watching the news. It was mostly about the protest in London: another riot, shops smashed up, crazies dressed in black hurling things at the police. One idiot hurled a metal gate at the riot officers. I winced as I saw a policeman – no, a woman – knocked to the floor and kicked.

What was the point of this?

Morons. How did hurting the police help to stop big companies making money off the poor?

The footage rolled back to show the march at the start . . . peaceful, loads of people all coming together to make a point.

And then this.

You could see the moment it started. Masked people suddenly started to burst out from the anonymity of the crowd and . . . and yes, this looked co-ordinated. They said that on the TV, that it was well planned. And that the police would be seeking to find out who was behind this and make arrests.

Mum came in with a glass of wine and sat down on the sofa beside me. 'Sometimes, Rafaela, you look at me as if you think I've let you down.'

I looked up at her, shocked.

'And sometimes, Rafaela, I think perhaps I have.'

OK, this was very uncomfortable. Why couldn't Silas be here if she was going to be like this? He could have headed her off.

'I am aware that we are not only not on the same page, but not even in the same library, yet . . .'

She glugged the rest of the glass down and I so wished I could speak so I could say I had to go to the toilet or something.

'. . . I am still your mother.'

I could feel her eyes on me as I stared at my feet. Feel the tension stiffen my spine. Feel that hated tight sensation grab me by the throat.

'When you were tiny, I fed you and carried you. I held you up for your first steps.' My mother's voice shook. 'Your first word was Mama, did you know that? And now you won't even say my name, let alone speak to me. Do you have any idea, Rafaela, how that feels? My own daughter will not speak to me.'

Do you know how it feels not to be able to do that?

'I know you think it's my fault. I can see it in your eyes. What I don't understand is why. All of those so-called experts I took you to see, they all told me how terribly unusual it was for you not to speak to me. Normally, they said, a child of that age would talk to her mother if no one else. But not you, Rafaela, not you.' Her face changed, contorted. 'Why? WHY? What did I do? Why won't you TELL me?'

I began to shake. I wanted to cry. I wanted her to stop. To leave me alone. To stop judging me. To . . . to . . . love me for who I was.

But that was impossible. Like wanting the moon.

I wanted to shout out what was inside, but it was stuck there, useless, like it always was.

Well, I might not be able to tell her, but I could show her! For the first time in my life I would not give in and be invisible. I threw my bowl to the floor so hard that it smashed even on the thick carpet, then I got up and stamped out, crashed up the stairs and slammed my bedroom door behind me.

I made noise. And it felt good.

Revolution requires extensive and widespread destruction . . . since in this way and only in this way are new worlds born.

(Mikhail Bakunin)

CHAPTER 35

There's more, Dad.

I suppose I should tell you all of it. Even the parts that don't make us look too good. Shades of grey though, right? Nothing is ever black and white.

The fires had taken over at least two of the shops. The police helicopter circled constantly overhead. We found ourselves increasingly surrounded, but by now it didn't matter, Katrin said. Our objectives had been achieved. All that remained was to cause as much disruption for as long as possible and then escape before we were closed down any further. As night fell, the mood of the other demonstrators turned darker too. Police reinforcements backed up the thin lines of the original officers and there were now pitched battles raging between the protesters and the police as each group tried to force the other back.

Somehow the noise seemed louder in the night; my head was aching now. Me and Lara sat in a quieter pocket of the street, warmed by the flames from a burning clothes store. The smell made me feel sick and I wondered if these people would ever get tired of the yelling and fighting. The ActionX people mostly had their masks off now. They were well back from police lines and it was too dark for the camera on the helicopter to pick their faces out. Mostly they were just sitting about like us. It was the others battling the police, the ones I'd seen earlier sitting around drinking.

Lara leaned against my shoulder. Her near frenzy earlier had had burnt itself out. Her eyes looked heavy and drowsy, as mine felt. I just wanted to go home now. To get some food, to sleep. But I didn't want to leave her.

My nausea grew stronger. I didn't know if it was the smoke from the burning shops or that I was so hungry. I hadn't eaten since the train.

A pair of black trainers appeared in front of me.

Katrin.

'We're ready to get out of here,' she said. 'It's about to get heavy and Dillon doesn't want any more losses.' She nodded down the street to where – and I wanted to retch as I saw it – some of the animal mask lot had breached police defences and were raining petrol bombs and street debris down on injured officers on the ground. I saw one man kick a wounded policeman in the head and had to look away before I really was sick.

Lara sprang to her feet, suddenly alert again. I dragged myself up slowly, aching in places I didn't know could ache.

'You know where to go?' Katrin asked, the others already beginning to melt off out of sight into the darkness.

Lara grinned. 'See you back at HQ.'

I looked around. I didn't have a clue how we were going to get out. It seemed as if we were surrounded on all sides.

Lara tugged my arm. 'Let's go.'

I nodded gratefully, but a moment later my relief was shattered. She slipped off away from the crowd with me following . . . straight towards one of the burning shops. 'There's a back exit,' she said.

'Are you completely insane? We are not going in there. We could be killed!'

She rolled her eyes. 'We won't be killed. It's fine. It's all planned.'

'Planned? Walking through a burning building is planned? No! Absolutely no way. I'd rather be arrested than dead.'

Lara put her hand on my arm and, despite everything, my skin felt a thrill at the pressure of her fingers through my sleeve. 'Me too, but we won't be dead or arrested. It'll be OK. Katrin had this whole thing sorted from the start.'

'Oh really, and Katrin is an expert on fire safety, is she? Works for the fire brigade?'

Lara sighed. 'Look, Katrin plans everything to the last letter. If she has this down as a safe exit route, it is. Now I'm going. You can come . . . or not.'

And with that she walked past the front doors of the shop, where flames licked out, taunting me as I watched, and she hopped over a low ledge into the shop through a smashed window.

What could I do? I couldn't let her go alone. I ran in pursuit.

Inside the shop the smoke masked us from the outside. I coughed, peering around to find Lara, my eyes smarting. And then she was in front of me, face masked, her hand pulling my own mask up over my face. I realised I could breathe better then. She took my hand and led me through the smoke.

We wove in and out of counters full of expensive handbags and perfume, stepping over burning debris on the floor, but I realised that although the smoke was eye-stingingly thick and I could only see a couple of metres in front of me, we were nowhere near the flames. The fire was concentrated at the front of the store where the clothing racks blazed. Over here to the side of the shop the sprinkler system had doused everything enough to stop the fire spreading to us . . . for now. I also realised just how narrow our window of escape was. It wouldn't take long before the whole place was burning.

Our silent walk through the store seemed to go on forever, though it could only have taken five minutes. Lara route-marched me along until suddenly the smoke cleared and miraculously I was out in the cold, fresh air. I pulled my mask away and breathed in great gulps of it.

Lara didn't let me linger there long. She broke into a jog and I forced aching, exhausted muscles to follow her. There were no police back here in the tangle of narrow streets she led me through. 'Katrin knew they'd never think anyone would come this way.'

'Why wasn't the back door locked after they evacuated the shops?'

'They almost never do that because looters do more damage breaking in. But Jez, Katrin's guy, was responsible for making sure all the escape routes were clear so if it had been locked, he would have busted it open. Jez is bombproof on jobs like this.'

Lara took us out on to a wide street. I didn't recognise it, but we were well clear of the riot now. When I turned back, I could see the red light in the sky from the fires and hear the din from the clash of rioters and police.

When I looked at Lara, her eyes were bright and clear and a grin spread across her face. She laughed. 'London's burning!'

She took me to a road of terraced houses. 'This is HQ,' Lara said, opening the front door of one of them.

I followed her on and off a series of Tube trains, until I had no odea where we were, except it was somewhere on the outskirts of London. The rows of houses didn't look like much, certainly not as if one of them hid the headquarters of what at that moment I was beginning to suspect was a terrorist cell. And if they hadn't quite got that far yet, I didn't think they had miles to go.

I said as much to Lara. Obviously she wouldn't agree, but I wanted to see her reaction, even if it did make her hate me. There was something about what I'd seen tonight that made me feel dirty.

She shrugged. 'What's the saying? "One man's terrorist is another man's freedom fighter." So, yeah, whatever.'

I was too tired to argue.

The kitchen and what would normally have been the sitting room of the house were packed with activists like us, freshly returned from the riot. The sitting room didn't have sofas. In fact it was empty apart from piles of sleeping bags that people were sitting on, some of them starting to curl up and bed down in the corners. Most of the ones who were awake nodded to Lara as we passed through to a room at the back, where we found Dillon and Katrin and the others. Jez and Tyler she called two of them, but the rest I didn't pay too much attention to for, like me, they looked exhausted and ready to drop. Katrin was still buzzing like Lara, discharging invisible sparks of energy as she came down from her battle high. The one Lara called Jez was calm and relaxed, leaning against the wall as his girlfriend filled Dillon in on the details with waving hands and flashing eyes. Tyler watched a lot, but didn't say much. Mostly he watched Lara. Was he jealous?

Lara didn't say much herself, except to respond, 'Yeah, fine, no issues,' to Katrin's question about whether we got out of there without incident.

There was an empty sofa in this room. Lara led me over to it and pulled me down to join her. She tucked her feet up under herself and curled into my side, her head resting on my shoulder. Her hair was cool against my cheek and I could smell the smoke lingering in it. Her soft skin caressed my neck as her cheek snuggled against me. I wanted to coil round her, envelop her within me so she could never leave.

My skin never wanted to be without her again.

Katrin was staring at me, hard and hostile. Tyler was still watching me with that odd look too. Jez's expression was completely blank and the others looked carefully away. I didn't know what was going on. Did they think they owned her or something? Did they not trust me – was that it?

Only Dillon seemed normal, sitting down on a chair opposite us. 'All right, Lara? Cool. So you're Silas, right? How did your first time go? Enjoy it?'

I felt a pressure I've never felt before – to agree, to fit in.

No, not even for her would I do that.

'Yes and no.'

Dillon nodded. 'Tell me.'

Lara didn't flinch or stiffen. In fact, she felt utterly relaxed, no hint that she might be embarrassed by my reaction.

'At first it was great,' I said, looking Dillon straight in the eye. 'I felt good. We were marching and I felt like I was doing something worthwhile for possibly the first time in my life. I understood why you guys do it.'

'But?' Dillon prompted.

'But then it changed – and I could live with the destruction even. I could see *why*. But then there was the violence. I didn't like the violence.'

Dillon's face split into a wide grin. 'Me neither,' he said. He reached out and shook my hand. 'Welcome to ActionX, brother.'

By my side, Lara looked up at me with a soft, sleepy smile that made my insides molten.

Dillon nodded seriously. 'I want to find another way. That's what I've been working on. No violence. But hit right where it gets only the people at the top, the ones who deserve it. Absolutely no collateral damage and no bloodshed.' He pinned me with that intense gaze he'd used on his audience from the podium. 'You interested in that?'

I grinned. 'Oh yeah! I'm interested in *that*.'

. . . And that's it, Dad. All of it. I know you'll never get this email, but I'd like you to understand why I did it. It is about Lara of course. But it's more. I felt something out there.

Something that matters. The world won't ever change if we all sit safe inside our own houses and don't try, will it? I hope you'd be proud of me for trying.

Love, Silas

JOSIE'S PINTEREST BOARD

When you can't control the winds, adjust your sails.

CHAPTER 36

Even though Silas closed the front door extra quietly, it woke me up. I glanced at the alarm clock. It was four in the morning. I got up and padded out with bare feet on to the landing. Silas was walking up the stairs as if every bone and muscle hurt. He had deep dark circles under his eyes that I could see even in the moonlight shining in from the window.

I grabbed his arm. Where have you been?

He shook his head at me. 'Not now, Rafi. Too tired.' He opened the door of his bedroom. 'I need to sleep.'

I sniffed. He smelt funny. I couldn't put my finger on it for a second.

He went inside the bedroom and closed the door.

As I climbed slowly back into bed, I realised what the smell was. It was smoke.

In the morning, I texted Josie. It was time. I didn't know why now, I just knew it was. <Got something I need you to read.>

She texted back a few minutes later. <Want to come round here?>

<Yes.>

It was easier to do this away from my family. Too much of it was about them for me to feel comfortable exposing this to view in my own house.

I walked round to Josie's. It was still sunny even though the afternoon was almost over. I could smell the smoke from a barbecue wafting through from a back garden and with it the scent of something spicy cooking . . . Mmm, chilli and lime maybe. As I got closer to Josie's house I discovered the cooking smell was coming from her place. I headed round the back to find her dad standing over the barbecue with a bottle of beer in his hand. Josie was flopped in a garden chair, one leg dangling over the arm.

'Rafi,' he said in that rich, deep, safe voice, 'yeah! Good you came over. Food's nearly ready and I cooked too much again.'

Josie laughed. 'Dad always gets carried away with a barbecue and cooks too much. We end up eating leftovers the next day every single time.'

I sniffed the air. Was that coconut with the lime? He had some chicken skewers on the barbecue. I could see from the colour they'd been marinated in something. Whatever it was it smelt delicious and my mouth was watering.

Josie's dad tapped the side of his nose when he saw me sniffing. 'Old Caribbean recipe,' he said. 'My mother taught it to me.'

Josie nodded. 'Grandma cooks like a dream. Whenever she comes to stay I end up putting a ton of weight on.' She patted the chair beside her. Come and sit down.' As I did, she whispered,

'We'll go up to the gazebo after this and you can show me whatever it is.' She pointed up the garden to a large painted gazebo carefully positioned to catch the last of the evening sun.

Her dad motioned to her to pass him a plate and he put one of the chicken skewers on it for me. 'You try that and see what you think. But watch it – it'll be hot.' He chuckled and I guessed he meant more than it had just come off the barbecue.

I blew on the skewer vigorously as Josie helped her dad serve the food on to three plates. There was a table and chairs further up the garden, but nobody could be bothered to walk up there so we lounged on our chairs with cold drinks by our feet. I bit into the chicken and an explosion of flavours hit my tongue and I gasped. It was so rare for me to make any kind of noise that Josie jumped. Her dad clapped his hands together and punched the air. I grinned. He was right, it was fantastic. Lime and coconut and a massive chilli kick that was just the right side of mouth-burning. The chicken was juicy and tender and almost melted off the skewer on to my tongue. It was too good to wolf down, but far too good to nibble. I compromised by eating it in large bites with my eyes shut to savour the flavour while Josie's dad laughed at my face.

'Have another,' he said, topping my plate up. 'Josie doesn't bring so many friends round these days so I've lost my appreciative audience!'

Had he asked why, I wondered, and how had she got out of that one? In a normal family if friends stopped coming round, a parent noticed things like that. It was only in the weird world of the Ramseys that they didn't.

Josie's dad sat with us and chatted in a way I wasn't used to. I suppose it was regular, normal stuff like what exams were coming up at school and was Josie still struggling with her A-level choices for next year or had she made her mind up. Was there anything particular we wanted to do over the long summer break? And then he was thinking of renting a holiday cottage in the Lakes for a week or so and would I like to come along?

'Oh, say yes, Rafi. It'll be fun,' Josie pleaded and I nodded without thinking it through because I felt so relaxed around these two. It was as if it didn't matter whether I spoke or not. It was OK either way.

There was no danger of Mum taking me and Silas on holiday. She might book an artists' retreat for herself for a few days, but family holidays were another thing we didn't do. I'm not sure it had ever occurred to her to take us on one. I couldn't remember if we had ever been when Dad was there – though Silas might know.

Josie's dad said we didn't have to help clear up when we'd eaten; he was just going to throw everything in the dishwasher anyway so to go off and do our own thing. Josie poured us a couple more glasses of juice and we headed to the gazebo. I felt a flutter of butterflies in my stomach as it got closer to the time when I'd have to hand my story over.

I took a gulp of juice and held the notebook up.

'Is this what I think it is?' Josie asked and her mouth hung open in shock.

Nod.

'Oh. My. God. Hang on, let me get comfortable.' She shifted about on the wooden bench so her feet were up and her back was leaning against the plank wall.

There was no need. It wasn't a very long story. She'd be disappointed. I was sure she was hoping for something more than my pathetic little paragraphs. It wasn't even a story. Just rambling, repeating myself, trying to find words for why there were no words. Trying to make sense of the senseless.

I handed her the notebook and leaned my head against the wall to let the nausea and panic wash through me as she read. If I tried hard enough I might get them to not only wash through me but right out of me again.

I didn't watch Josie as she read. I closed my eyes and saw my words swim in front of my face.

Once upon not very long ago in a place not very far away, there lived a girl who just wanted everything to be nice. She hated rows and raised voices. She hated feeling stupid. And most of all she hated not being as special as the rest of her family.

When she went to school, the other children there were more normal than her family was but she still felt like a boring oddball because she couldn't join in with their games. She didn't understand them and she didn't know how to talk to the other children. At home, everybody talked about terribly important things, things she didn't understand much about. They used big words and she struggled to follow what they were saying and no one had time to explain it to her. When she did try to join in, it seemed as if they were impatient for her to finish so they could get back to talking properly in their clever way.

But the children at school weren't like that at all. They said strange things like 'You stink!' to each other, which all of them seemed to find massively funny and she couldn't see why it was funny at all because a) they didn't stink and b) if they did, that wouldn't be funny, would it? So the other children would give her strange looks when she didn't laugh and she didn't think they liked to play with her much.

The teachers scared her. They would ask her questions and look very hard at her when she was supposed to give an answer. And when that happened all the other children in the class looked at her too. She realised she didn't like being looked at so much.

As she got a little bit older, she saw more and more how special her brothers and sisters were and how different she was. They were all so talented in different ways and so intelligent. They didn't have any trouble understanding the complicated things that were talked about around the dinner table. Even the brother nearest to her in age could keep up with ease whereas she struggled to know what to say at all. And again, when she joined in, it wasn't as good as the things they said and they often didn't listen to her the way they listened to each other. From this she knew that she wasn't very good at talking.

Gradually she stopped trying. Also, if she didn't talk, she realised she got told off less because people didn't notice her so much. It was a little bit like being a ghost. At the dinner table she practised being very, very quiet and it worked – nobody noticed she was there. Except the brother closest to her in age, but she learned that if she pulled funny faces at him when nobody was looking, he laughed, but he didn't expect her to speak either.

She decided life was easier when nobody noticed her.

One day, when she was trying to answer a question her mother asked her about what she wanted for lunch, and she very badly wanted tomato soup, she realised that even though Mummy asked her what she wanted, she wasn't listening at all to her answer. She began to stammer 'T-t-t-tom-' but the words wouldn't come out and Mummy didn't care. She felt her throat lock up as she understood that what she said didn't matter to Mummy. After that, whenever she tried to talk to Mummy the same thing happened – her throat got so tight she couldn't speak.

But Mummy didn't even notice.

When she sat at the table with her family and they all talked about their interesting and important things, she came to understand that she wasn't interesting or important at all. Not like them. And when she realised that, it got even harder to talk to them until, one by one, the choking thing in her throat happened when she tried to speak to any of them.

Once she stopped talking at home, except to the brother closest to her in age to whom she still managed to whisper, it became harder to talk in school and then she found she couldn't speak to anyone there either. They did look at her in school when she spoke, but in a scary way and that was very hard to bear. At home no one listened, but at school they paid too much attention. She knew how useless she was because she couldn't bear either.

And it got worse and worse. The more people realised she didn't speak and tried to make her, the more attention was on her. Even Mummy paid attention now, but Mummy's attention was the scariest of all because it was angry. She could see how frustrated Mummy was with her all the time. Mummy must be sorry she was ever born - that's how it felt.

And then one day she couldn't talk at all. Even to Silas.

'Rafi,' Josie said with a wobble in her voice.

I looked up.

'It's not true, you know. I understand how it must have seemed that way, but you're every bit as special a person as any of them. You've got to try to get over this. You can't spend your life feeling this way. It's not right. Does anyone else know?'

I shook my head.

'You need to show your therapist.'

Vigorous head-shake.

'No because you've written it or no because of what it says?'

I shrugged. Both probably.

'What if I came with you next time and told her why it started. Then you wouldn't have to let her read it.'

That was a possibility, but . . .

I shook my head again.

'Don't you want Silas to know?' And she looked like she understood exactly why I didn't want Silas to know. 'That's it, isn't it? Then don't take him to that session. Take me instead. I'll talk to him about it if you want.'

If she could get him to let me go with her . . . and if she could get him to let Mum let me go with her . . .

Could Andrea help me if she knew the truth? Did I have the courage to let her know?

Nearly all men can stand adversity, but if you want to test a man's character, give him power.

(Abraham Lincoln)

CHAPTER 37

Dear Dad,

It's OK. Everything's fine.

Today we went over to Dillon's HQ. They were planning something big. Everyone said Dillon had been very secretive about it until now, but he'd invited a bunch of them around for the big reveal. From how excited Lara was, it didn't look like she got asked into ActionX's inner circle that much and this was a really big deal for her, so I couldn't say no. Even when what I really wanted was to just hang out, just her and me. Isolation from the world, like we were the only two people on the planet and had forever to get to know each other.

Everyone had congregated in the room they'd used for the sleepover last time. It was still empty, but there were cushions thrown on the floor to sit on. Lara sat close and leaned into me again. She didn't speak much to the others. Just quiet hellos. Was she intimidated by them? I found that hard to believe, but if she really did want in to their leadership clique then perhaps she was overawed by what they did. Certainly she did seem impressed by Katrin and her uber-planning on the night of the riot.

Tyler brought mugs of herbal tea and coffee around for everyone. Dillon was nowhere in sight at this point. Katrin was chattering animatedly to some guys I hadn't seen before, though from what she was saying they'd been very active in the riot.

Jez came and sat by us. 'So,' he said and smiled and nodded.

I waited, but that seemed to be it.

Lara smiled back at Jez so I decided that was the expected response and followed suit. This had to be the most laid-back guy on the planet. What did Katrin, who's more than a bit manic, see in him?

Dillon entered and the room quietened in a moment. Something about that irritated me, but if I'm honest it scared me a bit too. To have that kind of power over people . . .

Dillon looked round and smiled. 'You're all here. Very cool. OK, let's get on with it.' He sat down on a floor cushion against the back wall, everyone else seated round him like he was some guru or something. But at the time I found myself sucked into hanging on Dillon's every word like all the rest.

'Some of you know I've been planning a direction change for ActionX. Since we lost Deef, I've been re-evaluating what we've been doing. And you know, guys, there are things about what we've done and how we've done it that don't sit well with me.'

It was as if the whole room leaned forward to hear as his voice fell lower.

'There are things we've done I'm ashamed of. Oh, I know when you're caught up in the moment that it all seems OK, but is it really?' He looked round them, one by one in turn, his face serious. 'Is it really OK at 2 a.m. when you think about who got hurt and how? A lot of you here have got good reason to hate the police after the way you've been treated on demos. Even in the street you're picked up for stop and searches. But what we need to remember – and I think I've forgotten this at times too – is that the police are not who we are fighting. They're simply the instruments of the people we're doing battle with. The people in power are the ones we want to hit and they hide behind the riot squads like they hide behind the armies they send out to be butchered for them.' He leaned back against the wall. 'We're hitting the wrong target.'

There was complete silence and then a wave of agreement spread round the room, some vocalised, some nodded. I nodded too because wasn't that more or less what I'd been thinking after the riot?

'So where I've got to with this,' Dillon continued, 'is that we need a change of plan badly. We're still at war here, my friends, but we're taking our battle out into a new arena. And this is where I need your help.'

Again everyone listened intently.

'Let's fight where there are no casualties. Let's cause maximum disruption and economic loss, but no loss of blood. I'm talking war, my friends, but I'm talking cyberwar.'

The hairs on the back of my neck stood on end.

Dillon reached over and slung his arm round Tyler's neck. 'Now most of you know Tyler has some mad skills with computers, and he's given me a lot of advice over the last few weeks. But the scale of the hit I want to make and keep on making is not something he can do – he's told me that. He knows all about where to hit, but the how is where we're stuck. This is why I've asked you guys round today, partly to talk to you about this change in focus, but also to ask for your help. Do any of you know of anyone who'd be sympathetic to our cause who could team up with Tyler on this stuff? It needs some seriously crazy technical skill –'

He broke off and looked across the room . . . to where I'd raised my hand.

I don't know now why I did it, Dad. There're things about Dillon I like, but there're things I don't. Maybe you think it was to impress Lara. Maybe it was a bit, but that's not all of it. I think most of it was because I believe in a lot of what they do.

It'll be fine though, Dad. Really. If there's one place I understand totally what I'm doing, it's out there in cyberspace. Wish me luck!

Love, Silas

JOSIE'S PINTEREST BOARD

Love is composed of a single soul inhabiting two bodies.

(Aristotle)

CHAPTER 38

'So how did it go?'

Josie met her dad in the hall, one hand on her hip and an expectant expression on her face. He laughed and gently scooted her to one side and came through to the kitchen.

I had been flopped on their big sofa, idly watching TV with Josie, and I quickly got up to go. If they were about to have a frank father–daughter conversation then I should leave. Immediately.

Josie shook her head at me vehemently and I shrank back down on the sofa. Oh God, they weren't going to row, were they? From what Josie had said before about their 'Dad dating' chats, it hadn't sounded bad, but if she was going to get huffy about it now I didn't want to be caught up in the middle of it.

It was hard to think of anything I'd hate more, short of obvious things like Silas dying or something.

Her dad sat on a kitchen stool. 'Make me a coffee, please, Baby D. I've had too much wine.'

Josie didn't show a shred of embarrassment over the pet name. I liked this about her.

Instead she looked at him, narrow-eyed and assessing. 'That good then?'

He laughed and waved her to get into the kitchen. 'Coffee first!'

She grinned and started the machine up. They had one of those huge coffee makers that looked as if it would be more at home in a café, but their kitchen was so vast that they got away with it. It confused me with its dials and levers, but Josie seemed to be able to get it to do anything she wanted — espresso, latte, cappuccino . . . it did the works.

She made me a cappuccino with extra froth without asking, just a wink, and her dad a long, strong Americano. Her regular hit was latte with a dose of hazelnut syrup and she made hers as she began her dad's interrogation.

'So come on, give! How did it go?'

Her dad sipped the coffee and closed his eyes and sighed. 'Oh, that's good!'

'DAD!'

He shook his head, eyes still closed. 'Peace, child. Everything in good time.'

She growled. 'You are so infuriating sometimes.'

I laughed inside as she sat down on the stool opposite him and pulled it close. She was right up in his face.

He laughed too when he opened his eyes, but out loud.

'Baby D, you have no patience, this is your trouble.'

She tapped the counter, nails clicking on the granite. 'I think I've been very patient, Daddy. Now do you think you can get round to telling me before my eighteenth birthday?'

I cowered against the sofa cushions, trying to be invisible. I would never dare speak to my mother that way. Not that I dared speak to my mother at all.

To my surprise, Josie's dad – despite his formidable reputation according to Silas's friend Toby – didn't seem to care at all, even though I was there to hear it. Or did he forget I could hear, in the way that people did?

'OK.' He set his coffee down on the counter. 'We went to see the film. It wasn't bad. Maybe wouldn't want to see it again if it came on TV, but, you know, watchable. I think the lead guy is overrated though –'

'DAD!'

He laughed. 'Yeah, all right. We went to see the film and then we got dinner at this fancy Japanese place that's just opened. Now *that* was good – I'll take you sometime.'

I was momentarily stunned. I'd read about fathers taking their daughters to dinner, about whole families going to dinner together too, but I suppose I thought it was something that just happened in books, having no experience of it myself. I had a sudden picture of me and my mother sitting together in a hypothetical Japanese restaurant. It was just too absurd for the image to last more than a few seconds. I tried to picture it with my father instead and then realised I couldn't remember what he looked like well enough any more.

'What about her?' Josie asked. 'Angelica.'

She hadn't told me the woman's name before. I tried to

visualise what an Angelica might look like. Tall, I decided. It was definitely a tall person's name. But I couldn't decide if she'd be black or white. Hmm, either . . .

'Well, it wasn't the worst time ever. You know, we talk easy enough. But . . .' He shrugged. 'I don't think we'll be more than friends.'

For a second I wanted to laugh. Most inappropriately. But really the way he was getting round to where he was really going with this reminded me so much of Silas and those conversations about the girls pre-Lara.

I stifled the urge.

Josie could have been either immensely relieved or slightly regretful. It was difficult to say, and looking at her I couldn't guess which feeling was winning.

'Dad, have you really given her a chance?'

It cost her to ask that, but she did anyway.

He sipped the coffee slowly and thought. I liked this about him, the time he took to give an answer. It made me think there'd be truth and importance in his words when he did speak them.

'I think so. It's like this, Baby D, and I guess we haven't talked much about this stuff . . . we should have because your mum would have had these talks with you and I should have tried . . . but that kind of attraction you get to someone you want to carry on dating . . .' He gave a little shake of his head as he tried to find the right words. 'It can't be created from nothing. It's there or it's not. And with Angelica, I told you I hadn't thought of her like that. Maybe if we weren't at work, a different environment, then that *something* might have sparked a little. That's what I thought. I should have known better, but it's been a long time for me. And it was so different with your mother anyway.'

Josie bit her lip. 'How was it different with Mum?'

There's something about the smile people get when they remember the dead – so happy and heart-shattered all at once that it hurts your soul to see it. But they're the lucky ones – lucky to have known someone so wonderful that it still lights them up like a match has been struck within them and their memory-lamp burns with a bright flare.

'When you meet someone like that, the one you know you're meant to be with, you don't wonder if you like them. You know. It's in every tingle of your skin when you're with them, in how your stomach wobbles when you know you're about to see them, how they fill your thoughts every waking second, and your sleeping ones too.'

'Can't that be fake though?' Josie asked with a shake in her voice. 'Can't you feel all that when it isn't real?'

He paused to think. 'Yes, you can get a crush on someone. I guess it feels a lot like that when you do. And everyone gets a crush sometime or other, especially at your age. But the real thing, Josie, that's different.'

'How?'

'It's stronger, so much stronger. You might think you're in love with a crush but the real thing blows that right out of the water. And the other thing with it is . . . it's . . . well . . .' His forehead creased with effort. 'It's *nicer*.'

'Nicer?' Josie's face screwed up to match his.

'Yeah, nicer.' He grinned, pleased with himself. 'That's exactly it. You can relax with her, be yourself. It's never hard work being around her.'

Josie looked astonished. 'Really?'

'Yes, really. Even when you go through tough times together, your tough times are easier with her than they'd be with anyone else.'

I'd never heard a grown man in real life talk about love before. If I had words, I'd have fallen silent with shock. He'd been drinking wine of course. Maybe he couldn't have spoken that way if he was completely sober. Maybe that was why he said it in front of me.

'And that's how it was with Mum?'

He gave that smile again. 'That's how it was.'

'But what about *Wuthering Heights*?'

'What?' Josie's father looked confused.

'*Wuthering Heights*. Heathcliff and Cathy. Um, ultimate passion. You know, love being all-consuming and –'

Josie's dad let out a peal of laughter. He looked up at her and saw her serious, cross face and he burst out laughing again, slapping at the counter he laughed so hard.

'What?' she said angrily.

'Oh precious, you don't want to be loving like that. It might sound like the best way in a book, all that sad stuff, but who wants that in their life? It's all just misery and tearing yourself up.'

He took hold of her hand and became more serious. 'Now you listen to me, girl, because this is important. There's a kind of love which isn't about all that tortured romance stuff women seem to like in books. It's the love that means there's a hot dinner waiting for you on the table when you've had a bad day at work. The love that means a wife never has to ask her husband to put the bins out. The kind that bursts a man's heart when he sees how his wife takes care of her child. And if you ask me, that love's worth so much more than the other kind that it's not even worth bothering about what's in those books.'

He leaned forward and kissed her forehead. 'You wait for a man who loves you like that.' And then he winked at her. 'To be honest, Baby D, if you bring home a man who doesn't love you like that, he's gonna have to get past me.'

Josie burst out laughing then, but behind that I could see the cogs of her brain whirring furiously, as mine were, trying to process what he'd said.

Because I thought I might just have heard the biggest truth ever for my collection.

She took me to her Elfin grot,

And there she wept, and sigh'd full sore,

And there I shut her wild wild eyes

With kisses four.

(John Keats – 'La Belle Dame Sans Merci')

CHAPTER 39

Dear Dad,

I'm still not entirely sure what had possessed me when I raised my hand and volunteered my services to Dillon. Perhaps I was swept away by the moment – Dillon is persuasive. Or it could have been all about showing Lara I can be useful too. Because, in this area, none of them could touch me.

For a moment there in that room, she looked at me with admiration. She looked up at me, as they all turned to see what I had to say. I told Dillon I could do it, not bragging, just genuine. And she looked proud of me.

I might have hacked into the Pentagon to see that.

Which, I guess, is how I came to be sitting with Dillon and Tyler in an upstairs room while Tyler briefed me.

'We want a big hit, something to get us noticed.'

'Like who? The companies you went after on the demo?'

Tyler shook his head. 'It'd make sense to hit them, make them sit up and think about what they're doing. But no, we're going for maximum attention on this so we're going after the government.'

A shudder ran through him. It could have been fear or

excitement or both. So this wasn't some piddly little messing up of a store's website then. They really were serious when they said they needed some brainpower behind it. Could I do it? Was I that good? It was a challenge. And not much challenged me so, hell, yes, I was doing this thing because the buzz if I managed it – that would be insane.

'Full-scale Denial of Service attack. Can you do that?' Dillon asked in his quiet voice.

'On who?'

'I want it as big as you can get it. I don't know how good you are. Can you take down something like the Parliament site? The Home Office? The Ministry of Defence?'

I shrugged. 'Probably. Is that what you want hit – their public websites? Or do you want me to bring their networks down?'

Dillon's eyes sparked like I'd seen Lara's eyes spark when she went into battle. 'You can do that? Then I want you to hit the lot.'

I leaned back in the chair. It was interesting how the balance of power had suddenly shifted here. A little bit of me liked that – Dillon, who everyone viewed with such adulation, looking at me like I was something special. It was a part of me I wasn't proud of, but nevertheless there it was.

I thought through it while Dillon and Tyler waited.

'I've got an idea,' I said eventually. 'But I need to play

around for a while.'

'What's the idea?' Tyler asked.

'Not yet. I'll tell you when I know I can do it.'

'Leave him in peace,' Dillon said. 'We'll go downstairs. Let us know when you're ready.'

'Tell Lara I could be a while.'

'She won't mind. She's chatting to Katrin.'

I nodded and turned back to the computer, the cogs of my brain whirring already. And I began typing.

It was much, much later when I finally went downstairs. My eyes were heavy from too long in front of the screen. I half expected Lara to have given up and gone, but she was still there, talking to Dillon now as Katrin appeared to have left. I could hear Tyler crashing about in the kitchen and he came through as he heard me arrive downstairs.

'How's it going? You need coffee?'

'Yeah, that'd be good.'

'Wait one minute. The kettle's boiled and I don't want to miss this.' He shot off.

I sank down on to a floor cushion.

'You OK?' Lara asked, moving to sit by me.

'Yeah, I'm good. Just tired.' And I was, but inside I felt like Lara in her battle mode.

Tyler came back with the coffee. I like Tyler. There's something simple and uncomplicated about the guy, even if he does appear to be jealous of me and Lara because he was looking at us in that strange way again. Or rather, *not* looking at us, as if he didn't ever want to see us together in the same frame.

'So tell us the plan,' Tyler said eagerly, sitting down too.

'Think of a house of cards,' I replied. 'You topple one card and then the rest fall one after the other, gathering momentum until the whole lot collapses.'

Dillon shifted. 'Yeah, so what're you thinking?'

'I'm thinking first I take down the public websites, one by one, the unimportant ones first. And I replace what's there with our own messages.'

Our . . . it felt strange to say that.

'And then the bigger ones get hit. Then their infrastructure – take down their networks. Total Denial of Service. I want them to see the small attacks and be running around trying to stop those, then the second-wave DoS hits and they don't have a clue that was on its way.'

'And how long are you thinking of spreading these out over?'

'A couple of days.'

Tyler choked on his coffee. 'A couple of days? Man, I thought you were going to say months or something.'

'No, that gives them the chance to respond and protect. It needs to be fast.'

'Yeah, I get that! I just thought it'd take you months to do it.'

'It needs setting up in advance so it can go quickly, in a wave, from one stage to another to another.'

'How long for the set-up?' Dillon asked.

'I did some digging around tonight. I've got a week off from school soon for half term so I reckon in the next few weeks. Certainly this month.'

All three of them looked awestruck. I felt like a god, I can't deny it. This must be how Dillon feels when he has all those people hanging on his every word, believing in him like a messiah.

I knew it was wrong. But I liked it.

I left with Lara not long after that. We walked back through lamplit streets to the train station.

'I'll get off at your stop and walk you home,' I said.

'That's not necessary. If I need help, I'll ask for it.'

'I didn't say you needed help. Just . . . it's not safe this late on your own. And before you start bristling up at me about that, I didn't make the world this way, did I? But it's my fault we're so late and I don't want anything happening to you.'

'I can protect myself. You've seen that.'

I sighed. The train was pulling into the station. 'But if there are two of us then you're less likely to need to. You can't deny that.'

'And what about you, walking home alone afterwards?'

There was a horrible sneer on her face as she said it and momentarily I was sick of her attitude.

But I know, Dad, it would drive me crazy to be a girl and have to put up with restrictions like that so I sort of understood. I just wished she wouldn't take it out on me.

We got on the train and found a seat. She stared out of the window even though it was too dark to see a thing.

'Is it because you don't want me to see your flat?'

'What?' She didn't turn and kept looking right out of that window.

'Your flat. You told me your parents pay for it for you.'

'Yeah, they do.'

'And is that why you don't want me to walk you home? You don't want me at your flat.' I had a sudden flash of inspiration. 'I wasn't going to try it on! I really was just going to walk you home and then get the next train.'

She finally looked at me. 'No, it's not that. I'm quite capable of telling you to get lost if you get pushy –'

'Yes, I know that.'

'I really don't like this concept that I have to be looked after. I need to be free.'

'OK.' I gave up.

We journeyed on a while longer in silence.

'Lara?'

'Yes?'

'What are we? Are we . . . together?'

And there she was staring out of the window again. 'I don't want to be owned by anyone,' she said.

'I don't want to own you. I want to know what we are.'

'This,' she said, and she grabbed my face between her hands and pulled it to her. She kissed me, urgently, intensely, like it mattered more than breathing.

And I didn't care very much about breathing when she kissed me.

'This is what we are,' she said when she finally pulled away, leaving me dazed and drunk.

When the train pulled in at her station, she got off alone.

So what is this, Dad? Do you know? Because I sure as hell don't.

Love, Silas

JOSIE'S PINTEREST BOARD

We know what we are, but know not what we may be.

(William Shakespeare)

CHAPTER 40

Josie somehow worked some magic on Silas. He had a face like a wet Monday morning when she appeared at our front door the next day. From the way he was snapping at everyone, I thought he'd probably had a bust-up with Lara, especially as he kept looking at his phone and I never once heard the message tone go off.

But Josie whisked into our hall and ignored his grim face. 'I want to speak to you,' she announced and she grabbed him by the sleeve and pulled him into the empty sitting room, closing the door firmly behind her.

When he came out a few minutes later, he shrugged at me. 'I'll sort it with Mum then,' he said in a bemused way as if he wasn't entirely sure what was going on, but it was easier to give in than argue.

So at my next appointment, it was Josie sitting with me in the waiting room. Mum had apparently pre-warned Andrea, who said it was OK. She certainly showed no surprise when she called us in.

Josie wasted no time on pleasantries. 'Rafi said I could tell you about what happened when she stopped talking. That's why I've come with her.'

Now at that Andrea did show her shock. 'And Rafi shared this with you?'

'Yes, she wrote it down for me. She doesn't want you to see because she isn't happy about people reading what she's written in general, although I think she's a really good writer. But she said I could tell you.'

'Her mother and brother aren't aware of this, are they?'

'Nope. She didn't want them to know. It'll be obvious why when I explain.' And with that she launched into her edited version of my story.

She did very well. She explained how it all came about and how I felt as it happened. I didn't know if the tears that started to flow down my face when she got halfway through were from hearing it all spoken about, or because it was clear from her retelling that she understood so well how it had been for me.

She paused when she realised I was crying, but Andrea said gently, 'I think it might be better to carry on and get it over with,' so she did.

At the end, and it didn't take long, Andrea sighed. 'It's a pity this didn't come out at the start because a therapist could certainly have helped you deal with those feelings.'

'How?' Josie demanded.

I couldn't help smiling at that. Ever practical and moving forward, that was her.

Andrea adopted a careful expression. 'It depends how Rafi

feels, but one way would be to bring the whole family together and discuss it —'

I flew to my feet, shaking my head furiously. *No, no, NO!*

'I thought you might feel like that,' Andrea said. 'It could be very effective, but only when you're ready for it. I do want you to think about it though, for the future.'

'If she doesn't want that, what else can you do?' Josie demanded.

'We can obviously work on restoring her self-confidence and building up her self-esteem. And most importantly, making her feel worth listening to! The fear of being looked at when she speaks is very common. But there are some practical exercises we can try too, so that when she's ready to speak, she finds it easier to begin. To use your voice after so many years is difficult.'

'Not like riding a bike then?' Josie asked.

Andrea laughed and so did I, though my version was silent. 'It is in a way. Once you get going it comes back to you, but getting started again can be hard . . . wobbly.'

'How can I help?'

Just with that question Josie helped more than she could possibly know. Just by wanting to.

'You can give her someone to practise in front of. I was going to suggest she practise the first exercise alone at home, but she may find it easier to do it with you. See which she prefers and go with that in the first instance.'

'What does she have to do?'

'It's a technique called shaping. What I want you to do, Rafi, is pick a sound, like a hum. And I want you to try to make that sound. To keep practising it until you feel comfortable with it. When you are, we try another sound. Eventually we attempt something that sounds more like speech, like the sound of a letter. But first we start with something non-threatening like a hum.'

'OK,' said Josie with enthusiasm. 'I get it. Maybe she could move on to humming a little tune or something.'

'That would be fantastic.'

'We'll work on it,' Josie said, beaming. 'By the next time she's sees you, we'll have it nailed!'

O what can ail thee, knight-at-arms,
Alone and palely loitering?
The sedge has wither'd from the lake,
And no birds sing.

(John Keats – 'La Belle Dame Sans Merci')

CHAPTER 41

Dear Dad,

I wish I could say things had got less confusing, but I can't. Why do girls have to be so complicated? I finally got Lara to text me back and agree to meet me after days of silence. We met in the coffee shop in town and I asked her why she wouldn't answer my texts.

'I was busy.' Her eyes were threatening.

'Too busy to text me? Or too mad with me?'

'I told you – you don't own me.'

'And that's why you didn't text me – to show me that.'

'I told you. I was busy.' She slammed her empty cup down on the table.

'Doing what? Saving the world?' I regretted it as soon as the words left my mouth.

'I thought that's what you wanted too. I thought that's why you were helping us. Or is that just one big fake?'

I sank my head in my hands because she was partly right. In some ways I am just one big fake. But if I told her that I'd lose her forever. And just when I'd started to believe there might be some point in what ActionX was doing.

'I don't understand why we can't hang out together normally.'

'I'm not *normal*.' She practically spat it at me.

'No and that's why I . . . like you. But I don't know if you like me. You never invite me to yours and you never want to come to my house either. I've met your friends, but you're not interested in mine. And you got on with them, didn't you? When we first met.'

She stared back at me with an unreadable expression, or rather several because so many changes flitted across her face I had no idea what I was seeing.

And then she got up. 'OK, so let's go to your house.'

'What? Now?'

'Yes, right now. Why not?'

And so we came home. Mum was out, but Rafi was in, watching a box set on DVD in the sitting room.

'Hi, Rafi,' Lara said and then there was a long pause as she took in the enormity of trying to have a conversation with someone who didn't speak.

Rafi gave Lara a slight smile. I knew what that smile meant. It meant, 'Don't bother.'

'I'll make coffee,' I said and escaped to the kitchen. When I came back they were watching the DVD in silence. I was a bit annoyed with Lara for that. She could have tried to make an effort with Rafi. I know she's not easy to deal with, but

Lara could have made some attempt. If she likes me, she would have — that's what I was thinking. So perhaps she doesn't really.

Why had she come round then?

Perhaps to her I was like all the girls before her had been to me — she just wasn't that into me.

I was relieved when Josie showed up. At least Lara could talk to her.

I don't know, Dad. I really thought she was beginning to like me. Now it feels that I was wrong. Has it ever been like this for you? I wish you could tell me.

Love, Silas

You have witchcraft in your lips.

(William Shakespeare)

CHAPTER 42

I was so pleased when Josie turned up. My peaceful afternoon had been shattered when Silas appeared with Lara and then left me alone with her, like I was meant to entertain her or something.

Not that she made any effort. She smiled distantly and then sat back to watch the DVD. I should have been glad, I suppose, because I didn't have to attempt to communicate back, but really it all just felt a bit rude.

Silas had gone to make coffee and after a minute Lara's phone rang. She answered it.

'Hey, what's up?'

'You're not supposed to call me though?'

'No, he's not here at this moment, but . . .'

My ears pricked up. She was talking quietly, but I could hear her quite clearly even over the TV. I pretended to be totally focused on what I was watching.

'Yeah, he'll be ready to do it . . . No, we haven't talked about it . . . What do you mean, how do I know then? He'll be ready all right!'

From the corner of my eye, I saw her sneak a look at me.

'Look, I have to go. This isn't a good time. No, I'm not going to screw it up now! I'll call you later.'

She rang off and I kept my face as perfectly blank as if I'd heard nothing at all. I'd had years of practice at that after all.

I could feel her looking at me, but I didn't even blink out of turn and after a moment she relaxed and went back to watching the TV. Did she think I was really that deaf or stupid? It was hard to imagine what went through people's heads when they acted like I couldn't hear. I should be used to it by now, but it still took me by surprise.

But what was that all about? I didn't like the sound of it. Not one bit, although there was nothing specific she'd said that I could have identified as disturbing. She could have been talking about anything. So why did I think Silas was involved?

My brother came back into the room with coffee and then the doorbell rang. He went to answer it. Josie was back from her visit to her grandmother. I could have hugged her with relief.

Silas disappeared off again to make her coffee.

'Hi,' Josie said to Lara. 'Haven't seen you about much lately.'

'No, I've been busy.' There was something supercilious about the way she said it, sitting on our sofa with her silk-shiny hair and her perfect, perfect little features. Something neutral inside me crystallised into dislike.

'Are you in love with him?' Josie asked, obnoxiously bright.

Even I didn't know where that came from! What was she up to?

Lara's face sharpened with displeasure. 'That's a bit heavy.

We've only just started seeing each other and we're not . . . you know . . . not . . .'

No, I didn't know and neither did Josie.

'Well, love is for further on than we are . . .' She stopped and took a breath, not quite as together as she liked to pretend she was. 'Look, Silas is great and I like him a lot, but I don't fall in love that easily. It takes time, you know.'

Josie flinched as if she thought that was aimed at her for the Lloyd situation. Then her eyes narrowed. 'Silas doesn't talk about you much. So do you live and what do you do?'

Lara sighed in an exasperated way. I sensed her dismissive attitude was actually staged to put us off. She shifted in her seat, edgy and uncomfortable – her face was sharp with it.

'I live in Graycombe, for what it's worth.' That was the town near here. 'And at the moment I work in a shop because I'm saving up to go travelling. Any more questions?' Her Ice Queen chill was designed to shut Josie down, that much was clear.

'It's cute that you guys are together though.'

'Yeah,' Lara replied in an anything-but-cute voice. Actually, it could have frozen icicles in a summer heatwave.

'What you up to today then?' Josie grinned at her like she hadn't noticed the chill factor.

'Just hanging out.'

'Aw, and he brought you home to meet the family. That's so sweet. Has he met yours yet?'

'No.'

'Why not?' Josie dropped the cutesy façade and eyeballed her. 'And how come you never let him hang out with his friends any more?'

Lara made a sound of disgust. 'He can do what he wants. And why do you care? Jealous?'

Josie didn't miss a blink. 'Nope. He did me a favour and I owe him, that's all.'

'You're jealous,' Lara said with a humourless laugh and she got up and walked to the window where she stood and looked out.

I would have thought that I'd have wished to be like Lara – beautiful and tough, delicate and imposing all at once. But I didn't. There was something just too remote about her. Something too out there for me to want to copy.

Silas came back in with Josie's coffee. Lara turned at the sound.

'Let's get out of here,' she said.

He nodded. Of course. And followed her from the room.

'He looks a bit pale, your brother. Has he been ill?' Josie asked.

No – I shook my head – Silas hadn't been ill, but he had been spending a lot of time cooped up in his bedroom messing with his computer. I thought it was because he wasn't seeing Lara and he was moping around up there, and texted that to Josie.

'Hmm,' she replied. I followed her gaze to the garden outside where Lara was walking down the path with Silas. When they got to the apple tree, she turned and pulled my brother's head down.

She kissed him hard, and long, like I'd only ever seen people kiss in films. But what did I know of kissing?

Josie knew more though. She shook her head at the pair of them wrapped round each other. 'That was a show for us,' she said. 'You know what? I really don't like that girl.'

JOSIE'S PINTEREST BOARD

Listen has the same letters as silent.

CHAPTER 43

When Josie had told Andrea we were going to work on the shaping techniques, she wasn't kidding. Every day after school she dragged me into her bedroom, shut the window so I couldn't obsess over people passing outside and hearing me, and she pretty much made me hum.

I'd never responded to pressure well, but this was pressure Josie-style so it came with a bounce and a big grin and lots of confidence that of course I could and would do it. For the first ten days, I couldn't make a sound. By day five, I was in tears as she encouraged me to hum. I couldn't do it . . . nothing came out. I tried, and tried, and tried, but it just wouldn't happen, and the more I tried the more I began to panic.

Can't do it, useless, stupid failure. Can't even hum, let alone speak.

Josie pulled me into a bear hug. 'Like riding a bike, remember? Lots of wobbles at the start. And not being able to take your feet off the pedals. But it's OK. You'll do it.' She pulled back and studied my face. 'Yes, you will. You will, Rafi. I believe you can even if you don't.' She grew stern. 'And you know what? Someone in your gifted but massively lacking-in-common-sense family should have made you believe in yourself years ago.'

Silas had quite a lot of common sense. I didn't credit the others with much, but he did.

'And I include your brother in that. I know you think he's the best thing ever, and I owe him hugely myself so I don't like dissing him, but from what I've seen of the way he's mooning around after that girl, even he gets it wrong sometimes.'

Lara had accused Josie of being jealous; was she?

She shook her head. 'Anyway, forget Ice Queen. Let's try again. Make a little sound, any sound, anything at all. Forget the hum if it helps, just do a noise.'

I gathered myself in a huge effort and managed . . . an 'ERRRRR!' of frustration.

'YAY!' Josie leaped up and punched the air. 'You did it! You actually did it!'

But it wasn't a hum.

'Do it again, anything!'

I tried once more. 'EH . . .' came out loudly, louder than I'd thought possible.

It was as Andrea said – I had no control. The sounds I made were loud, then quiet, and never what I wanted them to be. But they were sounds. And Josie's wild cheering was infectious.

Despite myself, a small grin of triumph curled at the corners of my mouth.

I was still on a high from my victory the next day at school, until lunchtime when my good mood came crashing down. I did my usual thing of hiding out in the library. Rachel and Clare were sitting in there, browsing through newspapers for an essay on General Studies they said, as they invited me to sit at their table. I nodded my thanks and took a seat at the top corner out of the way of all their spread-out paper and files.

I was reading my book when I heard Rachel exclaim, 'OMG, look at this!'

Clare leaned over and read the newspaper article Rachel was looking at. 'ActionX? Aren't they the people Lara took us to see?'

'Yeah, but I thought they were OK. I never realised they were like this.'

'Glad we didn't really get involved now, aren't you?'

'Totally. Hey, you don't think Silas —'

And then they stopped as if they'd remembered I was there. I pretended I hadn't heard, but during next lesson I faked feeling ill with a bit of dramatic clutching at my mouth and stomach so I could go out to the toilet. Only I went to the library instead and picked up the paper Rachel had been reading. The librarian was on her lunch break. It didn't take me long to find the article.

David Armstrong, known to associates as 'Deef', was today refused bail after violent incidents at the court. Armstrong was being charged with incitement to riot, violent affray and assault on a police officer. The court was told how on entering the court building, he had briefly escaped custody and attacked two police constables in the process. Both officers required hospital treatment. Armstrong has been told to expect a custodial sentence for his part in the London riots several weeks ago. He was dragged from the court screaming abusive language at the court officials. Armstrong is a member of the anarchist group ActionX, who were again implicated in violent demonstrations in London last week where police were attacked, shops looted and burned, and one civilian was hospitalised with head injuries sustained when he was accidentally caught up in the protest.

I sat back in the chair, my heart racing. Silas had come back smelling of smoke the night of those last lot of riots. Not the one this Deef had been arrested for, but the one after that. ActionX were there . . .

What on earth had my brother got himself into?

I have so much of you in my heart.

(John Keats)

CHAPTER 44

Dear Dad,

I'm feeling better about it all now. You might not like what I've got to tell you, but part of me hopes you'd be a little bit proud of me for fighting for something I believe in.

I began for real today. Lara and I went over to Dillon's. We didn't waste any time – we went straight upstairs into Dillon's inner cyber-sanctum where Tyler was waiting for us.

'Dude, I am so stoked about this. I cannot wait,' Tyler said, practically bouncing up and down in his chair. 'I've never been part of a hit this big. This is like something Anonymous would do. I've only ever read about this stuff.'

Lara smiled and a shiver ran along my spine as I thought of how she'd grabbed me and kissed me under the apple tree. How the next day when I met her at the bus station, after she'd texted me to say she needed to see me, she'd told me, eyes melting as she looked up at me in a way I'd never seen her look at me before, that she knew she was difficult and that she could be cold. But what she needed me to know was that I wasn't like any guy she knew. She could see I was different and could I just give her time to – and this was the part I replayed over and over again wondering what it meant and how I could help her because she had totally slayed me with this bit – could I just give her time to get over her demons.

Give her time?

I would have waited an eternity for her.

As I sat down in the chair to make the attack, I knew all Dillon's speeches, all Katrin's battle fervour, were nothing to me. When it really came down to it, ActionX's pull for me was totally down to Lara, not them. Because it mattered to her, and what mattered to her mattered to me. Beyond that nothing much did any more. A levels, university – all the stuff that had seemed so important just a few weeks ago, all gone away. And now there was only her . . . her eyes looking into mine . . . her lips on my mouth. She was everything.

Tyler was wildly excited about this attack. Dillon, when he came in, was jittery with anticipation too. I was as calm as a general orchestrating his umpteenth battle.

I nodded at them as they sat round in a circle to watch the opening of what they all hoped would be a legendary assault. And then I hit the keys.

I was barely conscious of time passing . . .

. . . the others came and went . . .

. . . coffee and food appeared at my elbow and I hardly noticed them go down . . .

. . . Lara went off to sleep for a while at some point and

returned, her hair mussed up, yawning hugely . . .

Finally I rolled my chair back and turned to them. 'It's done.'

Tyler pushed past me and opened the web browser. He typed rapidly for a moment and then . . .

'Oh my God! You did it!'

They crowded round. The UK Parliament website was now a black screen with a message in red letters stamped across it:

ACTIONX EXPOSES THE UK GOVERNMENT

20% of the world's population live in extreme poverty. Our government makes noise to say they want to end this, but 1 in 10 British-registered FTSE 100 multinationals fails to disclose tax havens. Poor countries lose more money to tax havens in a year than they receive in aid. Tax havens are one of the biggest barriers to ending global poverty. AND THE UK GOVERNMENT REFUSES TO ENFORCE TAX HAVEN TRANSPARENCY LAWS FOR ITS BIG COMPANIES. THEY PROMISE TO TACKLE THIS IN THE G8 THEN BREAK THEIR PROMISE AT HOME. LIARS!!!

This information was brought to you by ActionX – fighting for a world free from poverty and corruption.

Dillon clapped his hands. 'Well done, my friend.'

Tyler surfed frantically around the net, pulling up page after page of government websites, all bearing the same message.

I pushed him aside gently and logged into the Ministry of Defence's internal network. The same message came up.

Dillon whistled. 'TOTAL Denial of Service!'

Tyler's mouth hung open. 'This is the biggest thing I've ever seen. Dude, you are a genius. You, like, pwned the whole government.'

Lara just smiled at me. But that smile said everything I had ever dreamed it would say.

Love, Silas

JOSIE'S PINTEREST BOARD

Be yourself; everyone else is already taken.

(Oscar Wilde)

CHAPTER 45

'Progress is progress,' said Andrea, smiling hugely at our next appointment, with Josie nodding vigorously in agreement.

I was less sure.

'It doesn't matter that it's not the sound I asked you to make,' said Andrea firmly, correctly interpreting my expression. 'What matters is that for the first time in years you've been able to make some sounds in front of someone else. And you've been able to do it several times.'

It hadn't always worked. On some days after my initial success, I'd tried for an hour and still not been able to make anything come out, but on other days, yes, I had. Still no humming though. It was as if my brain resisted that because it was the noise I'd been set. Did that mean that there was something wrong with me? Was my mother right and I was just oppositional by nature?

No, I hated being shouted at so that couldn't be it.

Unless I *was* oppositional, but didn't have the courage to do it properly so this was my weak attempt at it, not talking.

Very brave. What an amazing specimen I was.

'What are you thinking now?' Andrea asked sharply. More sharply than I'd heard her speak before.

Must have given away more than I intended. I shrugged, but she wasn't fooled.

'It's important we're honest with each other,' she said, holding my gaze. 'And I'm going to be honest with you. I think you are having some very negative thoughts at this moment. Is that true?'

Were they negative if they were correct?

'Rafi, are you having thoughts about yourself that I wouldn't want you to have?' she persisted.

Shamefaced, I nodded slowly. Josie moved to the chair next to me and held my hand.

'I want you to tell me what those thoughts are,' Andrea said. 'I know you don't want to, but I also know you wouldn't be here if you didn't want to get better so you're going to have to trust me on this one.' She pushed the pen and pad towards me.

I picked them up reluctantly and then hesitated. I couldn't do this.

'Go on,' Josie urged.

So I wrote down what I was thinking.

Andrea read it without comment and then got up and walked over to the window. She looked out at the street below for a long minute.

'Being mute is not defiance,' she said. 'I've never believed that for a second. I know that's what the professionals used to think, but in none of the numerous cases I've seen, selective and progressive mutes, have I ever come across one who's been doing it out of defiance. And I certainly don't think that of you. You're reacting to the pressure of expectation. That's why you can't make the sound that I set you. It's a classic response.'

Andrea wouldn't lie to me about that, which left two possibilities: a) she was right about me, or b) she had it totally wrong and I was the exception to the rule.

And it all came down to this: I wasn't exceptional in anything, was I? So that meant she had to be right.

I slumped back in the chair and sobbed while Josie hugged me and clucked over me and tried to mop my eyes with a tissue.

'One thing I don't understand,' Josie said, 'is how she can write so well, but not talk.'

'It's hard to come to terms with when you first come across someone with selective mutism, but it's like this: Rafi isn't bad at communicating; she afraid of it. And, specifically for Rafi, it seems she's afraid of being bad at it. With writing, there's less pressure. Fewer people will wait for her to write something down – only the people who really care what she's saying. So that takes the pressure off her.'

'So she wants to express herself,' Josie said slowly, 'but she kind of freezes up when she tries to speak?'

I nodded as Andrea said simultaneously, 'Yes, that's it exactly. One thing we do with our younger patients is to get them to draw how they feel, or use plastic letters to spell out words that are important to them, to encourage them to keep communicating in other ways. Your mum said they tried that with you, Rafi.'

Yes, they'd done a lot of that in school when it first started. But I didn't like the attention.

'She said it didn't work, that you seemed to shut down even more. One thing I've found with those little ones is not to look at them too much, not to put them under any pressure to answer.' She smiled at me. 'I call them my most delicate flowers – they wilt from too much time in direct sunlight. They need a little shade to flourish.'

I looked at her with my mouth open, really made eye contact in a way I seldom wanted to do. If she'd been my therapist when I was that young . . .

I burst into tears again.

'Sometimes,' Andrea said, taking my hand, 'the hardest thing to face in life is yourself.'

And even through my tears, I recognised that as a truth I had to collect.

Josie and I spent some time just chilling together in my room that evening. Silas was out. Mum stayed in. When we got home, she'd handed me some cold cucumber slices from the fridge for my tear-swollen eyes, but she'd made no comment. She was different though – she made me and Josie dinner. It wasn't great – her cooking never was – but it was one of those small Mum-things that she never normally did.

And it's the small things that matter most. At least it is to me.

I'd told Josie about the ActionX article already and she'd said she'd do some digging around.

'I came up with something, but I didn't want to tell you until after the session with Andrea,' she said. 'There's some major stuff going on with this ActionX at the moment.' She got me to log on to my laptop. 'Have you seen all the stuff in the news about this cyber-attack on the government?'

I'd vaguely heard something, but hadn't paid any attention to it because it didn't interest me.

Josie opened up the BBC news website. 'Read that. It was ActionX.'

Love is too young to know what
conscience is.

(William Shakespeare)

CHAPTER 46

Dear Dad,

They'd come after me, I knew that. But I'd covered my tracks. I was confident. And I might have been in and out of their systems at home for weeks while I prepared the attack, but when it came to the hit I'd done it from Dillon's place. They'd find it harder to trace it back to me that way.

It took them a full day to get everything back to normal, which was frankly incompetence. In that time, millions had seen the ActionX message. It had been blasted all over the TV and radio. Irate government representatives – blustering ones, and the genuinely clueless – all had been dragged out and paraded in front of a media dying to know how and why this had happened.

I watched it all with a smile. ActionX threw a party at Dillon's and the lesser ranks spoke to me in the reverential tones they used to Dillon, like I was a god. But I didn't care about any of that. I cared that Lara led me upstairs, away from all the noise, and told me she loved me.

She loves me. The world began and ended with that moment.

I've tried to come up with so many descriptions of how it

feels: that it's like being on another planet, just me and her, that we're on an island bounded by sea that buffers us from the rest of the world, that everything and everyone in the world is silent and painted in black and white while we're in stereo-sound Technicolor. But in the end there were no words for it. It was her, it was me and that was all.

We'd stood in Dillon's cyber-base, surrounded by dirty coffee cups, and Lara had touched my face. A brush of her fingers down my cheek. A gesture of affection, unmistakable. 'I love you,' she whispered, her eyes locked with mine, and everything became worthwhile. All the time it had taken me to plan this, not seeing my friends for weeks, not even really seeing my sister . . . all worth it to hear those three words.

'I love you,' I said back, raw-voiced. I didn't care how stupid I sounded. I wanted her to know she was everything. No games between us.

Kissing her was the most perfect chaos. I fell to pieces when her lips were on mine. I could spin away into a billion tiny shards scattered throughout the universe, every one engraved with her name.

I understand now why poets described love as akin to madness.

Love, Silas

JOSIE'S PINTEREST BOARD

Fall seven times.

Stand up eight.

CHAPTER 47

Andrea hadn't set me any more homework after the last session. Josie had, in her bulldozering way, told her we'd keep trying with the humming until we really had nailed it.

And so that's just what we did. We kept to the routine. Night after night I'd sit in her room and see what noises I could stand to make. Because that's what it was. It was all about how much fear I felt when making them.

And then one day, out of nowhere, I did it. We weren't officially practising. It was Saturday and we were relaxing in Josie's garden while her dad was mowing the lawn. She had the radio on beside us and there was a song I really liked on the radio. Josie was singing along to it and then she suddenly froze and sat bolt upright, staring at me.

'You did it!' she exclaimed, but in a hushed voice.

Did what?

'You hummed. Just then. You hummed along to the song.'

And I didn't even know I'd done it. I'd hummed in my head, but it had leaked out. I wondered how many times that had happened before when there was nobody around to hear.

Maybe never. But maybe a few.

I could feel the fizzles of excitement building up inside me. I'd done something *right*.

Josie stopped looking stunned and leaped up, whooping. She pulled me to my feet. 'Come on, we're celebrating!' and she danced me round and round the garden while her dad looked on indulgently, like he was used to two crazy girls prancing over his cut grass.

Was this the first and tiniest of steps on a long road to recovery? Or was it nothing but a fluke? I didn't know either way, but it felt good to celebrate and be happy and have hope for once.

Silas brought Lara home again that evening. They hung out in front of the TV, wrapped in each other and round each other on the sofa. I noticed Toby texted him to see if he wanted to meet up, but Silas ignored it. And Lara said nothing about that at all. And I could not understand why he wanted to drop everyone for her. Even when they weren't together, which they seemed to be much more lately, he didn't see the others, but stayed burrowed upstairs, glued to his computer.

Lara acted like she loved him, but she'd said she didn't. Had she changed her mind?

I wanted to leave the room really, leave them alone because they gave off exclusion vibes as strongly as a slap in the face. But I wouldn't. I needed to see Lara with him. I needed to understand what this thing between them was.

What did she have that made him change so much? Made him perhaps commit the crime that the news agencies were still talking about. Because from the moment I'd seen that stuff about ActionX, there was no doubt in my mind – my brother was in on it. Maybe not on his own, maybe he had help, but he was involved.

It scared me to even think about what might happen if anyone found out. I wanted to talk to him about it, but for the first time with Silas, I didn't know how to start when I had no voice.

I couldn't sleep that night. The heat was oppressive and my bedroom stuffy even though I'd left the window wide open. There was no breeze to stir the curtains; the air was dead and heavy. I almost drifted off a dozen times, but then would wake, sweating and kicking around on the bed in a vain attempt to find a cooler spot.

In the end I got up and peeked out on to the landing. A chink of faint light shone from under Silas's door – his computer screen. I debated going to see him, but in the end went and sat back on my bed, scared of what I might find him doing.

I hated myself for that act of cowardice. My brother could be in there getting himself into even more trouble. If I could speak, I could go in there and ask him! And then somehow the idea came into my head that I should try to make a sound while I was by myself. The thought came to me quite suddenly as I sat cross-legged on the bed: *Try to do it on your own.*

So I sat there and tried to do again what I'd done at Josie's, to make any kind of sound at all. For over half an hour, I tried and tried to make *something* happen, but it wouldn't. I willed my throat to open and work, but it remained stubbornly frozen. I fought back tears of frustration, hearing Andrea's and Josie's words in my head, hearing their voices of encouragement and trying to hold on to belief. But still there was nothing.

And finally I had to face facts. It wasn't going to happen. If I couldn't do it here in the silence and dark of my own familiar room, how could I possibly have imagined I'd ever be able to speak whole sentences out there in the world?

No. This was my life – silence. I should just accept that and stop torturing myself with visions of what could but would never be.

I lay down again, the cotton pillowcase cool against my frustration-flushed cheek. Even my brother had given up on me. He didn't care any more. Never asked how therapy had gone. It would be no surprise to my mother that I'd failed. And Josie would learn that's what I was – a failure.

I saw the letters in front of me, giant and red, like graffiti painted in blood.

FAILURE

I closed my eyes and cried until sleep came to release me again.

JOSIE'S PINTEREST BOARD

I will make better mistakes
tomorrow.

CHAPTER 48

'What do you mean you're giving up?' Josie's face was furious.
'You are not! We are going to see this thing through.' She
stormed past me and past Silas making his way from the stairs
to the sitting room, still half asleep. 'Excuse me!' she snapped at
him as they crashed into each other in the doorway.

'Sorry,' Silas mumbled, trying not to yawn.

She stopped and fronted up to him. 'Have you spoken to your
sister recently?'

'Eh?'

'Rafi has just texted me to say she's giving up on counselling
and that she can't do it any longer.'

I trailed into the sitting room after them, shrinking inside. If
I'd known it was going to cause all this trouble . . .

'Oh.'

'Is that all you can say? Are you so wrapped up in your silly
girlfriend that you don't care about how Rafi is doing now?'

Silas's face turned from bemused to furious. 'What's with the
insults? You leave Lara out of this.'

Josie rolled her eyes.

'She hasn't done anything to you, you spiteful –'

'Who's calling names now?'

I wanted the feeling inside me to explode into noise, but of course it couldn't, so instead I picked up the TV remote and threw it against the wall.

It smashed, sending shards of black plastic around the room. One hit Silas on the cheek and left a trail of blood running down his face.

I swallowed, nausea building as I saw the scarlet streak on my brother's face. But they stopped screaming at each other. I ran out of the room and upstairs and locked my bedroom door.

Later, Josie told me what happened next.

'She can't give up now,' Josie said, sitting down on the arm of the sofa wearily as if she'd run a long way. 'Has she told you about how well she's been doing?'

'No,' said Silas, leaning against the door and feeling his cheek. He stared at the blood on his fingers. 'She hasn't told me anything at all.'

'Would you have been there to listen if she had?'

Silas glowered at her. 'Maybe not. For once I was having a life that doesn't involve my sister, but that doesn't mean I don't care.'

Josie stood up and set her hands on her hips. 'At this point, I'm going to give you some unasked-for advice about your girlfriend. I've been there with the whole "obsessively wanting to see them all the time" business. Shutting your friends out for them. It took me a while to realise, but that's probably why my so-called friends dumped me so easily when Lloyd started trashing me. I bet they secretly thought I deserved it for being such a useless friend. And that's one mistake I'll never make again.'

Silas folded his arms in front of him. 'What are you trying to say?'

'That you're doing the selfsame stupid thing I did. You're cutting everyone else out so she's all you've got. And I'm telling you because I know – it's a really dumb-ass thing to do. Let's just hope that's the only dumb-ass thing you're doing!'

Silas was so furious he missed the meaning of her last point. 'Yeah, well, somehow I doubt she's going to post naked photos of me over the internet.'

Josie drew in a breath. 'That was low!'

'Maybe. But I didn't ask for your advice or your criticism.'

'Yeah, I know that, but someone needs to say it to you. And Rafi can't!'

'Obviously.' Silas huffed out his breath angrily.

'When was the last time you saw your friends?' she demanded.

Silas ran his hand through his hair and didn't answer.

'See?'

'Shut up.' But when he looked at Josie again he was calmer. 'OK, so you said Rafi was doing well . . . so now I'm listening – fill me in.'

Josie told him about my last few appointments and how I'd made progress, how I'd started to make noises, and then about the hum.

'So why's she giving up now?' Silas asked, frowning.

'I don't know. I was trying to get her to tell me when . . .'

'When I got in the way?'

'I was hoping you were going to help.'

He thumped the doorframe with his fist. 'I should have sat her down with you and talked to her. I know that. I don't know why I didn't.'

'I told you,' Josie said. 'You're too wrapped up in that girl.'

Silas stared back at her miserably. 'I *want* to argue with you.'

'But you know I'm right.' Her voice softened. 'Look, it happens. I know that better than anyone. But that doesn't make it good for you or her or anyone around you. I swear to God, the next time I go out with a boy, it's not going to be like that. I'm gonna keep it balanced.' She frowned. 'I'm gonna keep *myself*. You know?'

'Yes,' Silas said in a small voice.

Josie eyed him, not quite sure if he was agreeing with her to shut her up or because he meant it. She went with the latter in the end simply because he looked so deflated she decided he must be genuine. Deflated was pretty much how you felt when you realised you were making a complete loser of yourself over another person. She didn't say that to him of course, but she added in her head: 'And one who doesn't love you nearly as much as you love them either'.

She expected him to mooch off and think about it. Or

perhaps get angry again. Boys could be unpredictable like that, frustration blowing out of them in raised voices and smashed things unexpectedly just when you thought they'd calmed down. Not like her dad. Her dad's anger was slow to flame, but so much more terrible because it was a fire more difficult to extinguish. There was no shouting at her and never anything broken, but the part that was hardest to bear was the look of disappointment that came with it. Thank God . . . no, thank Silas really . . . that he'd never found out about Lloyd. She wished she'd never lied to him about it now because Lloyd was in no way worth it, but it had been a season of temporary insanity, her love for him.

'It wasn't really love,' Josie said slowly. And it must have been to Silas for there was no one else there to hear her. 'I don't think love is really like that. Do you?'

'I don't know,' he said finally, 'but I do know I wouldn't waste another second of my time thinking about that moron.'

She nodded.

'Do you think we should go and speak to Rafi?' he suggested. 'Present a united front?'

Josie nodded again.

'Come on.'

He knocked on my door. 'Rafi, open it, please. We want to talk to you.'

It wasn't opened instantly. I was busy and it took a little more persuasion than that, but eventually I unlocked it and they walked into my room.

Silas stared, his mouth open, shock written plainly on his face. 'Rafi, what are you doing?'

RAFI'S TRUTH WALL

If you don't understand
my silence, how will you ever
understand my words?

CHAPTER 49

I clicked the lid back on the permanent black marker as Silas stared at the white wall on the other side of my bedroom, now disfigured with black scrawl.

'If you don't understand my silence, how will you ever understand my words?' he read aloud in a dazed voice.

Josie raised an eyebrow at me, and then marched forward and grabbed the pen. She uncapped it, selected a fresh bit of wall and wrote in her own distinctive scrolling hand:

Courage is fear that didn't give up.

Tears welled up in my eyes.

'What? What is going on?' my brother asked.

Josie understood my silence. Better than anyone ever had.

'It's Rafi's truth wall,' Josie replied.

Silas walked over and sat on my bed. 'Look, I don't get any of this. Can someone please tell me what is going on?'

Josie went and sat next to him. 'It's Rafi's thing – she collects quotes. Things that are like the big truths in life. She's very into that stuff. She keeps them in a book. We swap our favourites.'

'You do it too?'

'Kind of. I have a thing for Pinterest. You know, ten minutes where I'm bored and there's nothing doing, I get my phone out and scroll through the quotes page on there. Pin my favourites. So when I found out Rafi liked that stuff, we started swapping.'

Silas pointed to the wall. 'So what is this?'

Josie grinned at me. 'This is Rafi shouting, that's what this is.'

I stumbled towards her and hugged her. I hugged her for knowing.

She spoke to Silas over the top of my head. 'Rafi doesn't shout enough. That's her problem. She lets herself disappear and not be heard. If you ask me, this here –' and she nodded to the wall '– is one hell of a good thing.'

'Right.' Silas still sounded more than half confused but I heard the lid on the marker pop again and he got up.

When I looked round, he was writing on the wall too:

One word spoken by you is more important than a thousand from others.

He capped the pen and tossed it back to me. 'I love you,' he said.

'Who said that?' Josie asked, pointing at his writing.

He looked me straight in the eyes. 'Me,' he replied, and then he went out and closed the door gently behind him.

Josie shook her head slowly. 'You know, there've been moments when I've thought your brother is practically a saint, and others where I've thought that he's a whole new level of dumb. But right now, I totally get why you think he's a genius.'

And there she lullèd me asleep,
And there I dream'd – Ah! Woe betide!
The latest dream I ever dream'd
On the cold hill's side.

(John Keats – 'La Belle Dame Sans Merci')

CHAPTER 50

Dear Dad,

I don't know how to make sense of anything any more. Just when you think you have it all sussed out, then . . .

Rafi. And Josie.

So this morning, Josie goes crazy at me for neglecting Rafi when she needs me. I got mad because I know she's right. There was no need for her to be bitchy about Lara though – it's not her fault.

But Josie asked me this question about her and her dick of an ex. She asked me if what she felt for him, what I feel for Lara, is really love. Now how would you answer that?

Anything with half the intensity of what I feel with Lara can't be anything other than love. Josie's thing with Lloyd might have been a crush. My thing isn't. It's like that garbage poetry they make you read in school – two souls entwined, all of that. Maybe that stuff isn't as much garbage as I thought when they made me study it.

But I can't understand why Josie wanted to confide this in me. She sounded . . . sad . . . in a way I haven't seen her be since just after the Lloyd incident. I haven't really told you much about Josie. I've never spoken much to her in depth, just regular 'heys' and 'how are yous' unless it's about Rafi. But I've got used to her face around the place. She smiles a lot. She laughs a lot. I hadn't realised until just then, when I saw her so far from smiling as she remembered that jerk that it made me unhappy too. She's like a weather forecast, Josie – mainly sunshine with the occasional shower. It's only when the showers come that you know you miss the sunshine.

And then, weirder than all that, just before we went upstairs to see Rafi, I gave her a quick, one-armed, friendly hug. I just wanted to take her sadness away. I would have thought it would feel like hugging Rafi. But it didn't.

I keep trying to block it out, how she fitted perfectly into my shoulder, that she was so warm and soft, that she smelt ever so faintly of peach or mango or something else I couldn't identify. On another girl it might have been sickly, but on her it just smelt right. I just don't understand why I noticed that stuff at all.

I want Lara. Only Lara.

Would you know? I guess you would. You left Mum for another woman after all. This will sound horrible, but I don't want to be like that, Dad. I don't want to have inherited that side of you.

I went over to Dillon's later and I felt *guilty* when I saw Lara. They were being kind of weird over there too, which didn't help.

'So how do we top that?' Dillon leaned back on the kitchen chair as he posed the question.

'You know they're after us now, right?' Jez propped his chin on his hand.

'They won't find us. Our boy here knows how to cover his tracks.'

They looked at me and I smiled and nodded.

'What do you think we should do next?' Katrin asked with that barbed tone she always uses with me. And only with me. For whatever reason, she doesn't seem to like me much.

Lara was by my side, her fingers linked with mine. She squeezed gently and I smiled for no reason at all other than she was there and I was with her.

'Spot hits next,' I replied. 'We proved how extensive we can be. Now let's focus on serious damage.'

'What do you mean?'

'Denial of Service is one thing and it gets attention, sure. But it doesn't disrupt for long enough. What I'd like to do is get into one area and make a serious mess in there. Something that gives them a real headache to unpick.'

Katrin shrugged. 'I don't really understand what you mean, but if it makes our point then fine.'

'I want to cause enough trouble that they have to throw money at it to fix it. Hit them in the pocket! That's all they recognise, right, Dillon?'

'Right.'

'But isn't that going to take more money from the pockets of the very people we want to help? Because the cash they throw at it to fix it doesn't come from nowhere,' Jez said.

'How is that any different to how much it costs them when you guys start a riot?' I replied.

Jez shrugged. 'Yeah, I guess. But some of this is starting to leave a bad taste in my mouth. Is it what we're really about? It's beginning to feel like glory seeking to me.' His eyes shifted slightly off me when he said that, but they didn't quite rest on anyone else. He got up and walked softly from the kitchen.

'Is he with us or not?' Dillon snapped at Katrin. 'I can't afford any liabilities now.'

'He'd like to see some result from our campaigning.'

'We got a result! Everyone knows about us now. What more does he want?'

'Fewer children dying. More access to clean water. Little things like that,' Katrin said with an acid edge.

'Oh, come on! He expects that overnight?'

'He's been with us a long time. I think he expects to see something positive. And also I don't think he approves of the means to your end either.'

I swear Dillon coloured up as Katrin got up and followed her boyfriend.

'What? He doesn't want us to use cyber-attack?' I asked.

'Dunno,' Tyler said. 'Jez is a quiet one. You never know what's going on in his head. So this thing you've got planned . . . tell me more now the non-techies have gone.'

Lara stood with me later in the backyard of the house and we looked up into the night sky together.

'You can't see many stars in a city,' she said. 'I could see more where I lived when I was a child.'

'You don't call it home.'

'It was never home.'

'Why not?'

She switched her gaze from the sky to me in surprise. 'Do you know you're the first person who's ever asked me that? Because I never fitted. I wasn't the daughter they wanted. My sisters were, but not me.'

'You have sisters?'

'Yes. I was the middle one.' Her mouth twisted. 'Supposed to be difficult in other words, so I guess I was predictable.'

'You *were* the middle one?'

'Yeah. They're not dead or anything. It's just so long since I felt part of all that.'

'But now you're part of this and that's enough?'

She pulled my head down to kiss me, her lips against mine as addictive as ever. And I was in that space again where there are only the two of us.

'This is kind of corny,' she said when we eventually parted. 'Kissing under the stars.'

'I can live with that,' I said, my lips chasing hers again and finding them.

'Will you come away with me to Africa?' she said as we walked back to the train station later.

I nearly said something very embarrassing like I'd go anywhere for her. She would have hated that so I settled on a simple, 'Yes,' and it pleased her. She told me I was special, more than any guy she'd ever met.

Dad, I wish you were here. I wish if I asked Mum for your address, she'd give it to me. But that isn't going to happen.

I miss you,

Silas

RAFI'S TRUTH WALL

Doubt creeps in with stealthy, silent tread.

CHAPTER 51

I called it fate when Andrea cancelled our next appointment because she'd come down with flu. Josie called it an opportunity to practise more. I still hadn't tried again since Failure Night a few days ago. Josie spent half an hour trying to convince me to have a go, but I wasn't ready yet. Maybe tomorrow.

In the meantime, I had other things to worry about. Silas was still not hanging out with his friends, despite Josie's tongue-lashing, and the last two days he'd skipped school too. He said he had work to catch up on, but I wasn't convinced. He was holed up in his bedroom all the time. He didn't even go out to see Lara – she came round to him and they hid upstairs together in his room.

That wasn't all of it though. I'd picked up my mother's newspaper yesterday and read an article on 'the extraordinary cyber-crime of the year'. 'Previously no more than a raggle-taggle group of anarchist protesters, not necessarily given to violence, but not entirely averse to it either' was how one paper described them, but now apparently they were in the Security Services' most-wanted sights. And not just in this country either. The FBI considered them a potential threat.

It wasn't going away. That's what all this added up to and I couldn't keep hoping it'd all just fizzle out.

What had Silas got into? And how could we get him out of it?

'You mean what has that girl got him into?' Josie said with a sour twist to her mouth when I'd finally managed to explain all this to her through a combination of text and scribbling on a pad. She read through the article again. 'They're saying this is an incredibly sophisticated attack. If he did do this, did he do it alone? I know Silas is good, but is he really *this* good?'

I didn't know, but if he was it didn't surprise me.

'What do you want to do? Ask him?'

There was a time when if I'd asked, he would have told me the truth. Now I wasn't sure he would.

<No, follow him.>

JOSIE'S PINTEREST BOARD

It is a wise father that knows his own child.

(William Shakespeare)

CHAPTER 52

Silas left the house at 3 p.m. rubbing his eyes. He'd slept at some point a few hours ago, but before that not for a long while. Day and night were all mixed up now, his body clock hopelessly awry. This was a good thing for us as he was too spaced out to notice us slipping through the streets after him.

'It'll be harder once he meets up with her,' Josie whispered. 'We'll have to be really careful then.'

Whatever. I wasn't letting him out of my sight.

As we expected, he met up with Lara near the bus station. Josie and I managed to stay out of sight fairly easily as he and Lara walked hand in hand through town. The streets were long and straight so we could follow from a distance and they were too busy gazing at each other to notice us.

'She seems a lot keener on him than she used to be,' Josie said.

Was that because he was into all this stupid anarchy stuff now?

When they turned into the train station, Josie grimaced. 'This could be awkward. Hold back – I think we can see from here.'

But we couldn't see where they were getting a ticket to so we had to watch until they went down to the platform. Josie had a flash of inspiration. She dragged me up to the ticket booth that Silas had just been at.

'Hi!' She gave the ticket man a big, beaming, utterly innocent grin. 'My friends texted me to say meet them now on platform 2. We're going somewhere for my birthday surprise, but they forgot I won't know what tickets to buy – doh!'

'London train, departing in six minutes?' the ticket seller replied.

'Yes, that'll be it! They knew I wanted to go and see *Les Miserbles*. I bet we're going there. Oh, thank you, you're a star!'

She bought us tickets and then we scurried down to lurk on the platform near the toilets where they wouldn't see us.

'We can hide in there if they come this way,' Josie said.

When the train arrived there were only three carriages and we waited until Lara and Silas got into the far one. Josie managed to get a window seat near the door. 'We'll have to jump off quickly when we see them get off.'

But they got off before we reached the terminus in the centre of London, so Josie and I had to scramble out quickly and hurry after them as Lara set off out of the station with a much more purposeful march than she'd used before.

It was raining here. It's easier to follow someone in the rain, I discovered. They keep their heads tucked down and don't look round. We tracked them to a mid-terraced house on a nondescript street and watched them go in.

'Is this where she lives?' Josie said. 'Because it's not where she said she did.'

I made a motion with my hand, mimicking Lara pressing the bell. She'd have a key if she lived there.

'Oh yes,' Josie said.

We stood helplessly for a while, not knowing what to do next. Then a man hurried past us, knocking into us with a mumbled sorry as he tried to avoid a deep puddle beside us on the pavement. I caught a flash of fairish hair and goatee beard beneath his soaked hoody, and then he too went into the house.

'Now he did have a key,' Josie said. She sneaked closer to the house. 'Number 33. Come on, let's get the street name. And then we'll do some digging. We can't stand here all night getting wet, but there are other ways of finding out what we need to know.'

We found our way back to the station with some difficulty because neither of us had had the sense to notice where we were going once we got off the train, other than that we were following Lara and Silas. Josie had to stop someone for directions a couple of times. We were sopping wet by the time we got on the train, clutching giant paper cups of coffee with shaking hands.

'Nothing we've seen tells us if Silas is involved in that stuff or not,' Josie said with a groan, her teeth chattering on the plastic sippy lid as she gulped some coffee. 'We need to find out who lives at that house. I'm going to have to get tricky with Dad. But I'll need your help.'

When we finally got home, the most sensible thing to do was

346

run hot baths and get changed. 'Meet me at mine in an hour,' Josie said as she left me at the gate. 'I'll cook something.'

We hadn't eaten dinner yet so I was in a hurry to get back to her place. I threw my clothes in the laundry basket and soaked myself in a hot bath until I could feel my toes and fingers again, then I got out and put some warm, comfy gear on and dried my hair. Going out in the rain again wasn't the nicest thing, but I jogged so I was there in a couple of minutes.

'Hi,' said Josie, flinging the door open and pulling me in out of the bad weather. 'Dad's here,' she continued under her breath, 'so keep up with me. I'm going to put the plan into action.'

Her dad had eaten earlier, but he was definitely up for a helping of the chicken fajitas wafting a delicious scent through the kitchen. He sat with us at the big table when Josie served up.

'Dad,' she said when he was happily tucking into a chicken wrap loaded with salsa, sour cream and guacamole, 'how do you find out who lives at an address?'

'How do the police find out?' he asked after swallowing his mouthful.

'No, the public. Like me. How would I find out who lived somewhere?'

A slow frown developed. 'Now why would you be wanting to know that?'

Josie hesitated, just enough to make it look like this wasn't planned. 'It's Rafi's brother. She's worried about him.'

I nearly shot off my chair. What was she going to say? He was a policeman – I didn't want Silas getting in trouble.

'He's got this girlfriend. And honestly, Dad, she's dodgy as anything. We think she's cheating on him so we . . . we, er . . . followed her today. Oh, don't look at me like that! Really, she is messing him around. She went to a house where another guy lives and she stayed there. Silas thinks she's round at a girlfriend's and she so isn't. We just wondered if we could find out. He's so into her that he won't believe us unless we present him with the facts. Please, Dad. Rafi's really worried about him, aren't you?'

I tried to look worried and pleading as I nodded in response to the question. This was one time I was thankful I couldn't speak because I wouldn't want to have to lie to him. I didn't know how Josie was managing it.

'And say you're right, what if you give Rafi's brother this boy's details and he goes round there and thumps him? He could get himself into trouble!'

Josie shook her head and I quickly copied. 'Silas isn't like that. We're only doing it so he believes us. He won't make trouble.'

Her dad stared hard at her for a moment. 'OK, Baby D, we'll do a trade-off. I tell you that, but only public-access stuff, mind – don't you be asking me for classified because you know you won't get it!'

'Of course, Dad,' Josie protested.

'So I tell you then, right after you tell me just why it is that your other friends don't come round here any more, why you never talk about them, and what that useless waste-of-space boyfriend you were trying to hide from me has got to do with it.'

I have never seen anyone looked as shocked as Josie did then.

'You know about Lloyd?'

Her dad took another bite of his fajita and chewed on it frustratingly slowly before he answered. 'Yes, I know you were seeing him for a while. And that you stopped, just as I knew you would.'

'And you weren't mad at me?'

'Mad? I was furious. But then I thought to myself, what kind of father am I if my daughter has to hide things from me like that? And maybe it was time to trust that my daughter is the girl I thought she was and let her see for herself what that boy is. It looks like I trust you more than you trust me, Baby D.'

Josie's eyes filled up. 'Daddy?'

'But know this, sweetheart. If he's hurt you, I'm going to . . .' He stopped and smiled at her. 'Well, you don't need to know that part. So what happened?'

I gulped. There were no words to describe how glad I was that I was not Josie right then.

'I split up with Lloyd,' Josie said miserably, 'because you're right – he is a waste of space. Then he got mean and spread rumours about me. And my so-called friends stopped talking to me.'

Her father's face suffused with anger.

'Rafi's brother made him stop. That's why me and Josie have to help Silas now. Because I owe him, Dad.'

'And these girls who were your friends – they're still not talking to you?'

'Oh, them, yeah – they tried to be friends again. Like they never did all that horrible stuff when Lloyd was spreading the rumours. But I don't want to know, Dad. They're pathetic. Real friends don't act like that. They did me a favour really. They taught me that it's not how many friends you have that counts, but how good they are.'

'Then they taught you a good lesson.' His face still held the remains of his anger though. 'I wish this hadn't happened, sweetheart. I know how much this must have hurt you for you not to tell me any of it. But you've come out stronger and better on the other side, I can see that.' He held out his arms and she went for a hug. 'Mum would be proud.'

I breathed a sigh of relief.

'In answer to your other question, there's something called reverse directories online. If the boy's family has a phone number, or is registered to vote, they're probably in it. Do a search and you'll find it straight away.'

His anger seemed to have died now. All the same I wouldn't want to be Lloyd if Josie's dad ever came across him.

Love makes fools of us all, big and little.

(William Makepeace Thackeray)

CHAPTER 53

We ambushed Silas in the hall as he was about to go out. 'We need to talk to you,' Josie said, looking for a moment remarkably like her dad – all unquestionable authority.

Silas looked at his watch. 'I'll be late.'

'It won't take long.'

He sighed and went into the kitchen after me. 'What is it?'

'Rafi's worried about you.'

He looked baffled. 'Why? I'm fine.'

'She thinks you're doing something stupid. Something Lara has got you into.'

As soon as she said it, his whole body language changed, on the defensive, and I knew we were right. 'I'm not doing anything stupid.'

'Whose is that house you went to yesterday? We traced the address and it said no one lives there now. Is it Lara's house?'

'What's it got to do with you?' His brows snapped together in a glower.

'Don't take that tone with me,' she bit back. 'I had to lie to my dad to check that address and I *hate* lying to my dad. If I didn't owe you, I wouldn't have done it, but Rafi and I would quite like to keep your stupid arse safe even though you look like you're doing everything you can to get it locked up in prison.'

He was really jittery now, shuffling from foot to foot.

'So it is Lara's house?'

'No, it's not! Not that it's anything to do with you.'

Josie shook her head in disgust. 'Have you even been to her house? Do you actually really and truly know anything about her?'

'She likes her space and her privacy!'

OK, so what Josie said had nettled him – she'd hit a sore spot for sure.

She nodded. 'Yeah, you keep telling yourself that. It's all bull, Silas. She's spinning you a line. She doesn't love you.'

He slammed out of the kitchen and the front door.

Josie sank into a chair. 'That was horrible. Did you see his face?'

Destroyed was a good word to describe it.

I texted her. <Because somewhere inside he knows it's true or he wouldn't have reacted like that.>

'What next?'

<We keep watching and hope he has the sense that I think he has.>

'I don't know, Rafi. He does seem to love her an awful lot.'

I shrugged with the complete lack of sympathy of someone who's never been in love. <He'll get over it.>

'I hope so,' she said drawing a pattern on the table with her

353

finger. 'I hated seeing him like that.'

It was then I decided that, whether she knew it or not, Josie was a little bit in love with my brother after all.

I saw pale kings and princes too,
Pale warriors, death-pale were they all;
They cried – 'La Belle Dame sans Merci
Hath thee in thrall!'

(John Keats – 'La Belle Dame Sans Merci')

CHAPTER 54

Dear Dad,

This is a really hard letter to write. Forgive me if I can't do it all at once. You'll see why.

Josie.

Something she said about Lara, how she was bullshitting me. I can't let it go.

I went over to Dillon's with Lara to launch the next stage of our mission. I didn't say much on the journey and Lara didn't prompt me to.

Josie's words were like a beetle burrowing into my brain. I played back every moment with Lara, every moment of certainty and every moment of doubt. I remembered that fear I used to have that she was using me to pull herself further into the inner circle of ActionX. It seemed a crazy suspicion, but not so strange when you knew how much that would matter to Lara.

I glanced at her profile as she looked out of the train window, watching the houses speed by. We were close to our destination. She looked like a perfect porcelain doll, but the fragility was completely deceptive. She was as strong as steel wire and, like the wire, would never snap under pressure.

We remained silent as we walked to Dillon's house. What I would have called companionable silence before I now doubted – was it really indifference?

At least Tyler was pleased to see me. Dillon said he needed to speak to Lara about something, but would be up in a minute.

I set the computer up and started work. This was the most dangerous thing I'd done so far. I was about to hack into the Ministry of Defence computer system and pull classified information for Dillon to leak. Not my original plan, but what Dillon wanted at this moment in time. It was a challenge – I wasn't sure I could pull it off. Tyler tossed me a can of energy drink and sat down next to me, fascinated. 'This is so amazing, man. You're like a god on here. You can do anything you want.'

I thought about what Jez said. How was this saving lives in Africa? Because unlike the rest of them, possibly Jez excepted, I didn't buy into Dillon's status like they did. I was here for Lara.

And if Lara didn't love me, why was I here?

I thought I could wait forever when I didn't have her. But once she was mine, to find out that perhaps she really wasn't . . . I discovered that was a very different thing. My stomach churned at the thought.

Still, here was Tyler encouraging me, and to block out the treacherous thoughts, I got on with the job.

* * *

While Josie's dad was out at the gym, she and I were doing the unthinkable. Josie had tears rolling down her face as she unlocked the door to his study. She'd retrieved the spare key from its hiding place in the kitchen and the only other copy was on her dad's key ring. I think it was having to put the gloves on that upset her the most, but of course it was essential we didn't leave fingerprints. She opened his desk drawer – also locked, but she knew where this key was too.

'He'd never believe I could do this,' Josie said with a sniff. She tried to rub her eyes dry before opening the document wallet she'd pulled out. 'If he's got any info on the people Silas is hanging out with, it'll be in here. This is all the stuff he's working on at the moment that he takes back and forth from work with him.'

This had been Josie's idea – another reason she was so upset because the betrayal was completely her own. It wouldn't have occurred to me that they might still be looking for people involved in the riot and that her dad might have information on that. But sure enough as she went through the pile of documents, she found a briefing sheet sent out to local forces about the operation to locate possible suspects. There were even some mugshots. I looked down the list in panic, breathing again only when I got to the bottom. But Josie was ahead of me. She pointed a trembling finger at a picture of a man with a goatee beard and a shock of shoulder-length hair. 'Do you recognise him?'

Yes, I recognised him.

Josie looked up at me with horrified eyes. 'I think that could be the guy who followed Lara and Silas into that house.'

'I don't know. It could be, but I didn't see his face.'

'I got a better look,' Josie said. 'He crashed right into me. It's him, I know it is.'

'Extract from Security Services file,' she read. 'Dillon Armstrong – leader of activist group ActionX. Wanted in connection with terrorist acts spanning six years. Appears to be largely non-violent, but is suspected of involvement in attack on PC Hensford in student riots against tuition fees. Prefers to orchestrate attacks from behind the scenes. Location currently unknown.' She pushed the paper away. 'Oh my God, Rafi, what is Silas doing? I never imagined it was this bad. We have to stop him before . . .'

She didn't have to say it. We had to stop him before it was his name and photo appearing on a sheet like this.

* * *

It was harder than I'd expected, Dad, and I wasn't entirely sure the trail was completely clean. There'd been a moment there where I'd seriously messed up. My heart raced and beads of sweat gathered on my forehead as I fought to claw back from disaster. But I still don't know if I managed it.

Tyler held his breath beside me, not fully understanding what was going on, but knowing we were in trouble. He learned fast, did Tyler. He'd be able to help soon.

'This is why you're so good,' Tyler said when the tension finally left my shoulders. 'Because you're so clinical about it. You don't get caught up in how great you are to be able to do this. You just *do*.'

'I screwed up there.'

'Did you get it back?'

'I don't know. Mostly. But mostly isn't always enough.'

'If they can find us, we move.' Dillon's voice came from behind us, making us jump. 'We've moved before.' He walked over and looked down at me. 'Do we need to move now?'

I stared at the screen. 'Possibly,' I said after a while. 'If you want to be sure.'

Dillon shrugged. 'But did you get what I wanted?'

'Oh yeah,' I said, still watching the screen, 'I got that.'

We heard Jez and Katrin come in downstairs and then shouting. We hurried down. Jez was angrier than I'd ever seen him.

'What's up?' Dillon asked in alarm.

In answer, Jez slapped an object down on to the sofa beside him. 'That!'

Dillon picked up a cellophane-wrapped plastic bag with writing on it. 'Charity collection bag, Third World aid,' he said. 'What's up with that?'

Jez kicked a wooden chair, sending it crashing across the room. Lara scuttled out of the way as it nearly hit her.

'Look again!' Jez snapped.

Dillon read the wrapper more carefully. 'Oh!' He looked up. 'Yeah, I see what you mean.'

Lara came over. 'What is it?'

'It looks like a charity bag, but when you read the small print it's not. It's a private company who put these out and then collect them exactly like the charities do, but then they sell the stuff on at a profit to people in underdeveloped countries.'

'They even put this on the front to con you – look!' Jez grabbed the bag and turned it over. And they read the message printed there: *God will reward you for your goodness.* 'Scum!'

Katrin came over from where she'd been hovering by the door. 'These are the kind of people we should be after, Dillon. This is what we used to be about.'

'I've got more on my mind than that at the moment,' Dillon

snapped. 'Unless we get out of here, we might not be about anything so let's cut the righteous anger and cover our backs, OK!'

* * *

Josie and I sat around miserably in my room, waiting for Silas to come back. 'I can't believe I had to steal from my own dad,' she said, her eyes still red and puffy. 'You wait till I see that brother of yours. I am uber mad at him right now.'

I was pretty mad at him myself. What was he thinking? And however could you love someone so much that you could let them turn you into someone else? Because this was not my brother, it was *not*.

I asked Josie.

'I don't know,' she replied. 'I'm the wrong person to ask because I'm still trying to understand how I let it happen to me.'

<That's why you're exactly the right person to ask.>

'Oh, Rafi, I do wish I knew. Or that there was someone I could ask. I can't ask Dad because I'd have to tell him about Lloyd properly then. Or lie even more and I am not doing that.' She sighed. 'What I'm starting to think is there's two kinds of love: good love and bad love. The good kind's like Mum and Dad had – not all difficult and confusing. And the bad kind . . .' She tailed off.

<Do you think that's love at all?>

'I honestly, honestly don't know. It feels like it at the time. Or it feels like something so big I don't know what else it could be. And sometimes you feel happy. But not like Dad describes with Mum.' She held her hands up. 'It's just so confusing. How are you meant to know?'

<Maybe if you have to ask that question it isn't real love.>

She looked back sadly at me. 'Maybe you're right.'

* * *

The way Dillon scrambled us out of ActionX's HQ, I knew he'd done this before, maybe many times. He knew exactly how to get packed up in the minimum time frame. He got Katrin and Jez to work on locating a new base. 'Surely we don't actually have to go *now*?' Lara asked.

'You want to wait until they're kicking the door down?' Dillon demanded. 'This is how I don't get caught. I don't take chances. Now the fewer people here, the faster me and Ty can move, so you two should go. I'll text when we have a new safe place.'

I suspected he already had one lined up. I suspected he always had one lined up.

On the way home, I decided it was time to clear something up with Lara. Josie's words were still eating at me, even after everything that had just happened. 'I don't want to go back to mine just yet. There's some family drama going on there at the moment with my sister. Can I come and hang out at yours for a couple of hours?'

I knew what the answer would be before she spoke. The shutters came down as soon as I asked the question.

'No. I've told you why before. It's my space. I don't like other people in it.'

'Not even someone you love?'

She went red from her neck to the roots of her hair. 'No, not even then.' She turned away from me and ignored me until she was nearly at her stop. 'You should get some sleep when you get home anyway,' she said as she stood up. 'Just go to bed and ignore whatever's going on.' She bent and kissed me on the lips and then she got off the train.

I sat stock still, the memory of her soft lips on mine, until at the last possible moment I made my decision. I got up and shot out of the train doors just before they closed. Lara was disappearing up the stairs from the platform. I followed her.

She walked out into the street and looked at her watch. Then she got out her phone and sent a text. She waited, watching the screen. After some moments a response came back. She frowned at it and slammed her phone back into her bag, then she rammed her hands in the pockets of her parka and trudged off down the street.

After a while of wandering up and down identical streets, I began to realise she wasn't going anywhere in particular. I wasn't even sure she knew this place well for when she spotted a coffee shop, she sighed with relief and picked up her pace.

She got a seat inside by the window and I took up position in a bus shelter opposite, making sure I was out of her eyeline. I could see her checking her phone at regular intervals, but not much else.

She was in there hours, buying one coffee after another, then a sandwich, then a cake, more coffee – anything not to have to walk the streets again. I was on the verge of storming in there and asking just what she was playing at when she got the text she'd obviously been waiting for. She got up and hurried back to the train station. I checked the train at the platform she went to – heading back into a different part of London – and followed her on to it.

When she got off, I stalked her until she reached a rundown block of flats. She knocked on the door of a ground-floor one and it opened. I caught a quick flash of Tyler's face before she went in.

I went cold all over.

I forgot how cold and hungry I was. And I waited and waited, hoping she would come out soon and it would all mean nothing.

But she didn't.

In the end, it was Tyler who came out, leaving the door on the latch as he popped to the shop a few yards down the road.

I took my opportunity. I dashed over and slipped inside.

The flat was in darkness save for a dim light coming from under a closed door.

I knew I shouldn't, but I pushed the door with a shaking hand. It opened.

It was a bedroom, a mattress tossed on the floor with a small bedside light beside it. And under the duvet, staring back at me, Lara and Dillon, naked together.

My heart broke, Dad.

I saw their starved lips in the gloam,

With horrid warning gapèd wide,

And I awoke and found me here,

On the cold hill's side.

(John Keats – 'La Belle Dame Sans Merci')

CHAPTER 55

It was Tyler who found me, Dad, sitting in a gutter, heaven knows where, beside a pile of my own vomit.

'You OK?' He sighed and sat down beside me, on the opposite side to the vomit.

'How long?' I asked in a dead voice.

Tyler dropped his head on to his knees. 'You know, I'm sick of getting landed with his dirty work. First Deef. I get stuck with the job of visiting my best mate in prison every week and having to tell him no, we're not going to lift a finger to help him get out of there because lawyers cost money, and besides: free publicity, Deef! And I have to watch him getting lower and lower because he can't stand being caged, and his hope's gone. And now this . . .'

'How long?'

'Look, they've always been together. Ever since you knew her.'

'Then why . . . ?'

'Dillon wanted to hack into the government networks. He saw what you did with that guy from *Codes of War* who made that website about his ex. Actually, man, that was my fault and I'm sorry – I play *Codes* and I saw what you were doing. I just mentioned it to him, just chatting, you know, said

I reckoned you were local-ish. What you did on there was pretty epic. It got a lot of attention. Dillon saw that and it set him thinking that we could use some of that, if only we could get someone with those skills. He set me to work to track you down. I'm not you, but I'm pretty good with computers. And then me and Lara got down to the area on the ground and tracked you by following the girl. Dillon set Lara on to infiltrating your group, once we thought it was you for sure. You work the rest out – you're smart enough.'

He stood up and hesitated for a moment before putting an arm on my shoulder. 'For what it's worth, man, I'm sorry. I really like you and . . . I wish it wasn't . . . it hadn't . . . whatever . . . I just wish!'

He ran off up the street, back to wherever that flat was.

I sat there, the stench of vomit making me want to throw up again, but my legs felt too weak to hold me if I stood. I wished it would rain to wash the sick away, wash *me* away if that was possible. Right now I wanted to dissolve in the rain and cease to be.

A lie. The whole thing was a lie. She was a lie, every last bit of her. The Lara I thought I knew would never have done this, never allow herself to be used in that way. Where had she gone? She had to be in there somewhere. No one could fake as well as that . . .

But she'd faked loving me well enough to convince me . . .

Not the other girls though. Rafi and Josie had suspected.

Suddenly I knew what I wanted. More than anything I wanted to be home. Away from all of this deception.

I got up, feeling stronger with the decision, and made my way down the street. I asked a man how to find the train station and walked back as fast as I could. My stomach was still churning. My clothes stank . . . not with the stench of vomit but of lies and lost hope.

I got home a little before midnight. Rafi heard me stumble up the stairs and went out on to the landing. I held my arms out and she ran to hug me. She didn't know what had happened yet, but my face told her enough of it.

She made me hot chocolate and sandwiches and I ate them sitting on her bed. Then I told her all of it. Every last sorry word of the story. When I finished telling her, she gave me her marker pen. I got up and went to her wall:

'Even though it hurts more than I thought it was possible to hurt, somewhere someone is fighting to live and this hurt is nothing compared to theirs.'

I shrugged at Rafi. 'She taught me that much, even if she is a fake. There's more pain out there for other people than I can imagine. I'm not going to break apart over her, even though it feels like I am right now.'

So there it is, Dad. And the girl I loved never really existed.

Love, Silas.

And this is why I sojourn here,

Alone and palely loitering,

Though the sedge is wither'd from the lake,

And no birds sing.

(John Keats – 'La Belle Dame Sans Merci')

CHAPTER 56

Josie was incensed. 'So all the time she was with this Dillon guy? And they planned the whole thing to get Silas to do their dirty work for them, hacking into this government stuff. Is that girl insane? What kind of freak does something like that?'

<Obsessed with this political thing.>

'Yeah, and obsessed with this Dillon from the sound of it. I mean, it's just EVIL! But I feel so guilty. They found Silas because of what he did for me . . .'

I shook my head. She was not responsible for what they did.

I'd texted Josie early and she'd dressed and come round while Silas was having a lie-in. I made breakfast for us both and filled Josie in on what had happened. I had to write most of it, leaving out Silas's feelings of course and sticking to the main events.

'What now, then? Is he in trouble over this last thing he did?'

<Don't know. I'm worried if he isn't with them that they'll frame him for it.>

'Would he grass them up first?'

<Doubt it. Not like him. Also don't know how much trouble he'd be in for what he did.>

'I could ask Dad but it'd be difficult without making him suspicious.'

At that point, my mother walked into the kitchen. She had reached fairly comfortable speaking terms with Josie by now. 'Good morning. What has you two looking so agitated?'

I was surprised she'd noticed. Josie checked with me and I nodded. I knew she wouldn't say too much.

'Silas. He's upset. His girlfriend has been cheating on him all the time he's been seeing her.'

We'd agreed it was best to tell her this much. I was doubtful, but as Josie pointed out, he was hardly going to be himself and if telling Mum meant she exercised some tact around him, all the better.

My mother swore fluently and comprehensively. She said things about Lara that would make a feminist wince. I'd never felt closer to her than I did then.

We dragged Silas out later for pizza and ice cream. Josie told him that's what you did after a break-up. You got together with your girls and you hit the junk-food consolation parlour. Silas didn't have the energy to protest with anyone so determined, but sitting in front of a computer screen killing things just reminded him of her now, and what else did he have to do? Besides, he'd been neglecting me and he knew it, or so he said.

Josie made us see a film first and she'd picked it to appeal to Silas – some Terminator rip-off, but it was OK. Silas liked it, which was the main thing. He was quieter than usual during the food, but that might have been because Josie filled the silence non-stop.

'I talk too much, I know,' she said at one point.

'I don't mind,' he said with an odd smile. 'You know, really I don't. It's OK.' It saved him having to think, he told me later. He said it was kind of irritating when most girls did it, but with Josie it was more funny. I got that – I felt it too.

On the way home, Josie was still chattering away as we got off the bus and we didn't notice the guy approaching until he was right in front of us. We all started back when we saw his face. It was Silas who relaxed quickest. 'Sorry, you made me jump. Are we in your way?' We were standing right in front of the bus timetable.

'Remind you of somebody, do I?'

'Yes . . .' Silas replied, 'actually you do.'

The guy was about twenty, six foot and skinny, with a drawn, sunken face. He had muddy blond hair and cat-shaped eyes and I knew exactly who he looked like though he didn't have a beard.

'He's my brother,' the guy replied in a quiet voice with a soft Cornish accent. He held out his hand to Silas. 'I'm Deef.'

Silas took it, but didn't shake it, holding it as if he was in suspended animation. 'But you're in prison! Tyler said.'

'Was. Tyler doesn't know,' Deef replied. 'Out on parole as of today.'

'And I didn't know you were Dillon's brother.'

'Yeah, I bet Dillon didn't tell you that. But then there's a lot of things he didn't tell you.'

'Yes,' Silas replied bitterly.

'Don't be too hard on her. She's just a dumb kid who believes every word he says. Always has done. And he's been stringing her along for years. Even when he was still with Katrin, he'd let her mope around in the background after him. He knew she had a crush on him, used to laugh behind her back about it. He's a user, my brother. I reckon he thinks he's still in love with Katrin, but he's not. Just can't stand seeing her with someone else. It's like a continual bit of grit in his eye. But Katrin's better with Jez. She's all hair-trigger action and he's so calm he tempers her fire in a way that Dillon could never do.'

Silas nodded at the truth of it. But Katrin was Dillon's ex? That was another thing he hadn't known.

Deef quirked his mouth in a quick smile. 'He'll get what's coming to him and it's long overdue. But you, kid, you need to look out for yourself. See, some people who've been looking very hard for my brother are about to find him and you need to stay clear. Tyler told me what he had you doing.'

'Tyler told you?'

'Yeah, he came to see me this morning before they let me out. I knew he was due so I asked them to hold off on the release – I don't want my cover blown. I don't need Dillon after me. Ty wants to bail. He told me you'd found out about Dillon and Lara, and I managed to con him into telling me where you lived. That's the trouble with Ty – he's just too trusting. That's how come he's put up with Dillon for so long, but he's sick of him now. Says that Dillon's so far from where he pretends to be that he's lost the plot. It's all about Dillon really, see. All about the power. He's become what he says he's fighting.'

Deef clapped Silas on the shoulder. 'You stay away from there, you hear? Don't go back for her. She'll never leave Dillon. Not until she grows up one hell of a lot anyway. And keep your head down. You don't want the people who're after Dillon now coming after you.'

'But they'll be after her too,' Silas mumbled, as though he knew none of us wanted to hear that from him, but he couldn't help it anyway.

'And her rich daddy will buy her a good lawyer and they'll get her off . . . good girl led astray and all that. Don't worry about her.'

'So that part was true, the part about her family?'

'Sort of, but she bailed on them when she met Dillon and she shacked up at his place. Been living with him for four years, all the time he was with Katrin. And when Katrin left him, she finally got what she wanted.'

'I see,' said Silas. 'These people looking for Dillon – how do they know where to find him?'

Deef held his hands up with a laugh. 'They were prepared to

pay a lot for information. Not with money, but with a parole. He left me to rot in that prison. My own brother. I was his best man on the ground. Without me, there would have been no action on the streets. I trained Katrin up and I trained her well. But he never once came to see me. Just sent poor Ty to do his dirty work, and that's Dillon all over. I needed to get out of there before it killed me. I'm not ashamed to say, kid, I couldn't hack it, couldn't stand being caged.'

'What about the others though? You've grassed them up too?'

'They're not interested in the others. It's Dillon they want. Without him, the others are just a bunch of amateur protesters. I didn't give them much on the rest of the group and they didn't ask. See – they don't care. They asked about you though. You really managed to get them rattled with what you did.'

'And what did you tell them?' Silas's face paled under the street lamps.

'Nothing, kid, I told them nothing. Said I didn't know who he'd got to do his hacking for him, but whoever it was wasn't with them when I got arrested, so it was probably some poor sucker he'd hooked in with his lies. There's no trail to you so keep your head down. If they do find you, play the innocent and you'll get through it. That's what I've come to tell you. Ty says you don't deserve this and I don't want to see my brother get away with screwing you over. But if they do find you, don't hesitate to land him in it because believe me, he'd do it to you.'

'OK, I hear you.'

'My brother will never stop unless someone makes him. Never thought it would be me, but . . .' Deef shrugged. 'At two in the morning, he's like me – wonders if he's made the right choices. It'd be easier to live like all the others, content with the consumer conveyor belt, the capitalist dream, life on the inside. Instead, we chose this fringe existence, this half-life in the shadows. It worked for a while, but when we're thirty, forty? What then? When Dillon went down this road, he thought they'd never get to *him*. He'd run in this direction until the day he died. Or he'd die trying. Me, I don't have his ability to shit on my mates. And I guess I just don't care as much as he does.' He looked around us. 'That's not a bad thing – you can care too much and Dillon does.'

'Yes,' Silas said quietly.

Deef gave my brother a swift nod as another bus drew up. 'Look after yourself,' and with that he boarded the bus. It pulled away into the night and he was gone.

Every form of addiction is bad, no matter whether the narcotic be alcohol or morphine or idealism.

(Carl Jung)

CHAPTER 57

This time Silas did tell me he was going out to see Lara. He got a text from her — meet her at the bus station, she wanted to explain. I got a pad and paper straight away and told him he was all kinds of fool, especially after what that guy Deef had said.

'Rafi, it's OK. It's not going to change anything. I just want to hear from her why she did it.'

But she's a liar.

'I know, but I still need to hear it from her, lying or not.'

Just please don't believe her.

'I won't.'

They met in the café at the bus station. What they didn't know was that I got there first and positioned myself in a booth at the back with high-sided seats. I wasn't going to leave him alone with that witch to get her claws back in him. I thought she looked a little less composed than usual, but otherwise there was no change. She'd taken my brother apart, but it obviously hadn't affected her too much.

I got lucky. They sat down a couple of booths away and there was no one else in there. I couldn't see much without getting caught, but I could hear everything — a result I couldn't have planned, but was very ready to take full advantage of.

'So, you wanted to talk.' Silas could sound calm even when his insides were a pit of writhing snakes. I always envied him that.

'Tyler said you know.'

'Yes.'

Strange now how her Ice Queen persona didn't quite work, not after what we'd been told about her.

'Dillon was looking for a hacker because Tyler didn't have the skills to do what they had planned, so he sent you out to hook me in and you played your part, is that about it?'

Her voice was impassive, a frozen desert. 'Yes.'

'So your boyfriend used you like that and you let him.'

'It was for the cause. That is more important than personal loyalties. Sacrifices have to be made.'

'Yeah, you keep telling yourself that.'

'I believe in what we are fighting for.'

'I know you do. But I want to know about the girl you pretended to be, that girl who wouldn't take any messing from anyone, that tough fighter. I don't buy that she'd let herself be used like that. She believed, yes, but she'd have found another way. She'd have seen what a user Dillon is and not bought into that. Was none of her real? Or is she what you want to be when you grow up?' He stood up to leave.

'I need to know where you stand with the group!'

So that's why she was really here. 'I stand nowhere, Lara. It's over. I don't ever want to see any of you again.'

'Dillon thinks you might betray us.'

'I really couldn't be bothered to.'

'You never believed in it, did you?'

'I believed in some of it. I just didn't believe in Dillon's way. But I believed in you.' Then he turned on his heel and left.

She got her phone out as soon as he had gone. I stayed hidden and strained my ears to hear.

'He says he can't be bothered to inform on us . . . yeah, that's pretty much all he said. I don't think he's a threat . . . Don't you believe me? Don't you think I can judge?'

There was a long pause.

'So why can't you tell me what you've got planned? Why am I always left out of the loop? . . . I bet Katrin knows, doesn't she?'

Another pause, shorter this time, then . . .

'Oh go to hell!'

When I risked a peek round the seat, Lara was slumped across the table, her head in her arms, the phone lying beside her. I scooted back. What was going on?

When I risked another peek, she'd left.

I am but mad north-north-west: when the wind is southerly I know a hawk from a handsaw.

(William Shakespeare)

CHAPTER 58

Josie was cooking tea for her dad when his work mobile rang. He left the papers he was reading on the sofa and hurried to the table to grab it.

'Yes?'

He paced up and down, listening intently.

'That's great news . . . which one? Dillon?'

Josie nearly dropped the saucepan in shock.

'Oh right . . . never mind, this Tyler will lead us to him if we take this carefully . . . yes, I'm coming in now!'

He rang off. 'Put mine in the fridge and I'll heat it up when I get home. I've got to go back into work. The boys have just arrested an important suspect and I need to liaise with the Security Services.'

He was out of the house and driving through the gates within five minutes.

It could be coincidence, Josie told herself. And then she noticed the papers he'd left scattered on the sofa. She went to tidy them and caught sight of the name ActionX.

Josie sank down on to the sofa, her hand over her mouth, and began to read.

Meanwhile, round at my house, Silas was pulling on his coat

with me grabbing at his sleeve to hold him back.

'Rafi, pack it in! I'll be fine. It's OK.'

But it wasn't OK. It wasn't OK at all. I'd seen the text come through on his phone. It was from Lara, saying she wanted him to come and meet her, naming a place, saying she'd left Dillon for good. I had to stop him going. I tried pulling him back, but he was too strong and he prised my fingers from his arm.

'Stop it! What is wrong with you? I need to see her. I need to know if she really has left him!'

All my fear for him, my hate for her, my frustration at not being able to tell him why this was so wrong all built as he wriggled free and ran to the door.

I screamed.

He spun round, mouth open.

I. Made. Noise.

It stopped him. He stared in shock.

<What if it's a trap? Police could be there.>

'It's not a trap.'

I stood in front of the door.

He sighed. 'OK, I'll cover my back. Will that make you happy?' He ran upstairs and came down with a piece of paper and a pen. He leaned on the wall and scribbled some instructions. 'If the police are there, I'll text you. And then you need to wipe my computer. The only way to destroy the evidence that I was doing any hacking is to run this program. It'll clear everything. It's in the middle of my desktop – it's called Goodbye, picture of a skull and crossbones. I've had it there since I knew they were after me, just in case.' He gave me the paper and grabbed my shoulders. 'Now let me go.' And he moved me away from the door. 'The password is on the paper. Burn the paper afterwards.'

And then he was gone and I was left shaking in the hallway. As soon as I could pull myself together, I texted Josie.

She took longer than I expected to respond, but then <Coming> and she was at my door in a couple of minutes.

'What's up?'

<Silas is doing something stupid. Help.>

'Something Lara-stupid?'

I nodded furiously.

'He's not gone to see her? Rafi, we've got to stop him. Dad's just been called into work. He left some briefing papers by accident because he was in a rush. They're using the info Deef gave them to bust ActionX at their new place today. He took a phone call and I overheard – they've got Tyler. They're going to use him to get Dillon. If Silas is there . . .'

I texted her quickly to explain where he'd gone.

'Rafi, that's miles away. We'll never catch up with him on a bus, and really we need to be there before him in case the police have already found them. We need to head him off!'

I pleaded with her silently to find a solution.

'Do you know anyone with a car? No, stupid question. Me

neither, not any more . . .' And then the thought struck her and she looked at me in panic. 'Oh God, oh God, oh God . . .'

What?

'My dad will kill me for this if he ever finds out . . .'

What???

'Come on!'

I followed her as she sprinted back to her house. By the time I'd caught up, she was emerging with a set of car keys. She opened the door of her dad's old VW Golf – the one that was going to be hers. I gasped.

'Get in.'

I climbed into the passenger seat. She could see the question on my face.

'Lloyd taught me,' she said. 'Like I said, I was stupid when I was with him. And if it wasn't for your brother, I would so not be doing this.' Her hands were shaking on the wheel, but she pulled off without stalling and by the time we got out on to the main road, I thought it was possible that I might not die. We drove through the night in silence, following the directions on the satnav, Josie concentrating as hard as she could on the road ahead.

She cursed as she missed the junction on the roundabout and had to go all the way round again. 'What time is it now? No, never mind . . . I can't go any faster or I'll lose control. I just hope we're in time.'

It seemed like forever before we arrived at a deserted industrial estate. 'So this is it,' Josie said, 'but where is he? He could be anywhere. Didn't she give any more instructions?'

I shook my head.

'Hmm, she probably sent him more while he was on the way,' Josie said, getting out of the car. 'Come on, let's look around.'

We huddled close to the wall of one of the units and crept round the side.

Nothing. No sign of life. So we tried slinking across the car park to the next building, but there was still no one in sight.

'Never mind,' Josie said grimly, 'we'll find him if we have to check every one of these buildings.'

I looked around – there were loads. This could take ages and we didn't have ages – the police could already be on their way. What if Tyler had spilled it all straight away? Deef said he was mad with Dillon.

Josie nudged me in the ribs and pointed. Over at the next unit, figures appeared, coming from across the car park: Dillon, Lara and two others – a man and a woman. We flattened ourselves against the building and edged around the corner out of sight.

'OK, so Silas isn't with them. Where is he? He must be here by now,' Josie whispered.

I peeked out. They were carrying stuff, bags, a crowbar . . .

And then they stopped in the car park near the door of the unit we were hiding behind. Josie and I crept around the back and along the other side until we were close enough to hear what they were saying.

'Is someone going to tell me now what the hell is going on?' Lara demanded. 'What were you guys doing in that warehouse? Why did I have to stand guard outside?'

'We've been busted once today,' Dillon snapped, putting a large canvas bag down on the ground. 'You want us to get busted again? Isn't it enough that the filth got Ty?'

'But what were you doing in there?'

Dillon chuckled. 'Getting back to basics, that's what. OK, Jez, fill her in. This is your mission.'

'Remember that charity sack scam?' Jez asked, passing the crowbar to Dillon while he packed up his bag again. 'This is their base, where they collect all the donations. And we've just set . . . well, a little bonfire.' He grinned hugely. 'In a few minutes, when Katrin presses the detonator switch, there's going to be a tiny spark that is going to turn into a flame – we put some accelerant down to make sure of that – and then . . . yeah, Guy Fawkes will have nothing on this. That whole place is going up. And I can't think of anyone who deserves it more!'

'Minimal collateral damage too,' said the woman, who I guessed must be Katrin. 'Most of this place is derelict. No security guards at night. No one to get hurt.'

'Where the hell is Silas?' Josie whispered to me. 'We need to get out of here and call the police or something.'

As we watched, a phone rang. Lara reached automatically into her pocket. She pulled her hand out, empty.

'That's my ringtone. Have you got my phone?' she asked Dillon. 'I can't find it.'

Dillon made no move to get it. 'Oh yeah, you dropped it earlier so I picked it up for you. Forgot to tell you.'

'Give it to me then!'

'No time for that now. We're busy. Later.'

Lara put her hands on her hips. 'Dillon, give me my phone!'

He picked up the bag and began to walk away.

'Dillon!'

She chased after him and made a grab for his pocket. There was a scuffle and she went flying to the ground, but when she scrambled up, dashing away from Dillon, the phone was in her hand. She ran in our direction as Dillon came after her. He grabbed her arm, but she swung round and kicked out at him and he dropped to the floor, winded.

She didn't even seem to notice as she talked into her phone. 'What do you mean, where am I? I never told you to meet me anywhere. Where are you? . . . Oh shit, no, no . . . Listen you have to get out of there!'

Dillon reared up and tore the phone from her hand, smashing it to the ground.

'What have you done, Dillon? What have you done?'

Jez and Katrin looked at each other blankly. Beside me, Josie grabbed my arm, squeezing painfully tight as she closed her eyes and swore under her breath.

Dillon's face was an uncaring, guilty mask. 'He knew too much. He's betrayed our location to the police. Who knows what else he's said?'

'Are you insane? This is not what we are!'

Dillon reached over to Katrin and took the detonator from her unsuspecting hands. He flicked the switch.

'NOOOOOOO!' Lara screamed. 'No, you can't do this.' He made a grab for her, but she evaded him. 'I won't let you do this!' and she ran across the car park towards a warehouse on the other side.

Jez and Katrin called out, but it was Dillon who pursued her. Lara might be small, but she was fast – he couldn't catch her. Josie and I hovered uncertainly by the building, still not fully comprehending what was happening, still stunned. The other two ran after them, yelling at Lara to come back.

Lara wrenched open the door of the warehouse – she was a speck in the distance beside the huge building but as she pulled the door back we saw flames lick out.

'Fire!' said Josie. 'It's on fire.'

'SILAS! SILAS!' Lara screamed and disappeared inside, still shouting. Dillon stopped dead, staring at the door. Jez sank to his knees, holding his head.

Josie looked at me, horror spreading across her face as we

finally worked out amid all the confusion that Silas . . . Silas!

We ran out into the car park towards the warehouse. And then there was a loud bang.

'Stop!' Josie cried, yanking my arm to halt me. She got her phone out and dialled 999 frantically. 'We can't go in there! It won't do any good! Hang on! I'm calling for help!'

I could hear her on the phone, her terrified voice begging them to come, but it was like an echo down a long tunnel, like she was a long way away. I fixed my eyes on the warehouse and prayed because there was nothing else I could do.

I died a thousand times from fear in the minutes before a figure came running out of the smoke and fell to its knees, coughing. It turned back to the door . . . And then there was an explosion so massive that it shook the ground we were standing on.

I heard the figure yell, 'NOOOO!'

It was my brother's blistered voice.

'Silas!'

Josie and I ran towards him. She was still yelling into her phone.

The girl sank down on to the tarmac next to the man, howling. Dillon let out an inhuman cry of rage. Silas plunged back towards the flames.

Dillon cried out again as he went after him. 'IT SHOULD HAVE BEEN YOU!'

And he brought the crowbar down on Silas's head.

Once.

Twice.

Three times.

RAFI'S TRUTH WALL

In real life, destiny does not arrive to the sound of trumpets. It creeps up to whisper silently in the ear.

RAFAELA AGAIN

I

As I finish writing Silas's story, I can smell once again the hideous stench of burning. I can smell the blood on my clothes when I reached him and scooped his limp form into my arms. I can hear Josie's sobbing voice on the phone calling for an ambulance. And Dillon's feet slapping on the tarmac as he ran away.

It was Jez who pulled the crowbar off Dillon. Who pulled Dillon away from my brother's battered body. He told the police everything. He felt responsible, he said. No one was ever, *ever* meant to die.

They tell me he was at Lara's funeral. He begged to attend and they let him go.

Dillon wasn't there. He took the car and he drove off into the night, no one knew where, a wanted man.

My brother didn't go to Lara's funeral either. As I finish his story, I sit beside him in the hospital, wires and tubes all over him. They managed to save his life . . . for now. But they can't get him to wake up. So we visit and watch and pray – even though none of us really believe there's anyone listening – Mum and Josie and I, so between us he's never left alone. We do it in shifts.

Mum says if he does wake she wants him to see a face he knows. I feel love for her when she says that.

I did what he asked me to with his computer. But before I wiped everything, I looked through his files. As he said, his password got me in. I found a set of draft emails to Dad. I copied them, but then I wiped the rest. The police might not want to pursue a boy in a coma, but I was taking no chances. His emails to Dad stayed hidden in my room on a memory pen I tucked inside my box of stories.

Day after day, we sit there by his bedside. Mum and Josie talk to him. I play him his favourite music. The nurses say we should keep trying to make contact – it's important not to give up. He may be able to hear us even if he can't respond.

How useless I feel when they say that.

So I began to write down his story. It might be the most important story I ever tell, and Josie reads it to him when she visits. I hope it will help him understand what happened. I hope he'll understand we need him back and he'll find a way home. His brain is healed now, they say. But he's still hiding inside and someone needs to bring him back. The problem is no one seems to know how.

I wonder if Lara was alive, and he could hear her voice, if that would bring him back to us.

Toby comes to see him one day and brings some of the girls they used to hang around with together. Rachel cries when she sees Silas. They're not allowed to stay long, but they are allowed in for a while because maybe one of them will be able to rouse him. Our brother and sisters come too. Mum calls them and they pay flying visits to see him. It took this to make us a family, Silas.

It works like this: Mum does the night shift, I skip school and do the day shift and Josie comes over in the evening. At night I stay at Josie's house so Mum can be at the hospital. As Josie predicted, her dad went loco over her taking the car, but when he calmed down he could see it was something she would never do again. We were *in extremis* and had no choice. Still he was as mad as anything at her for putting herself in danger – far madder than he was that she could have caused him serious trouble at work. Except that no one cared about what she'd done, compared to Dillon. I think he was proud of her too though. They say if she hadn't called the ambulance so quickly that Silas might not have made it this far.

And every waking moment I spend writing this book for Silas. I try to write him back to me.

It's finished now and I don't know what to do.

He lies there so still, unwaking, and I don't know how to help him now.

It's Monday afternoon and the hospital is quiet. For once no bells and buzzers echoing along the corridors. I sit beside my brother and watch him as he sleeps, a machine breathing for him through a tube. I watch the rise and fall of his chest. I see how his lashes are still ridiculously, enviably long. And he's still as beautiful as when he was a child, though now his jaw has angles to it and stubble etchings. His hair has grown and is kicking up in curls. It's grown while he is sleeping and they haven't cut it yet, though they shave off his fledgling beard every few days.

He looks like a sleeping prince in a fairy tale, but there is no princess left to kiss him awake.

And his chest rises and falls, rises and falls, and he sleeps on and on . . .

I watch the hands of the clock move round, from one to two to three . . .

And then as the hand creeps round to four, I know . . . I know with utter certainty, no revelation was ever clearer than this . . . I know what will wake him.

It is as if every moment of failure of my life coalesces into this to make it all worthwhile, to claw us back from the precipice. I don't have nerves. Me, who has been afraid of everything. The complete assurance that this is what my silence has been for saves me from that.

I *know*.

Andrea said the pressure of expectation stops me. There is no expectation here. No one to see me. No one to hear me except the one person who matters.

She would say, I think, that the pressure is too great. And

she'd be right – I have never felt more pressure to do this than I do now.

But she'd be wrong as well. Because I need to do this so badly, I cannot fail. I will not fail.

I take my brother's hand in mine. My voice is rusty with disuse and I don't even recognise it as my own, but it works. I say, 'Silas . . . Silas, it's me, Rafi.'

For a long, long moment there is nothing, and then he opens his eyes.

II

We are in the cemetery. I sit on a bench while Silas stands in front of the gravestone. Josie stands beside him and he has hold of her hand for comfort.

Lara's family gave her a beautiful headstone with a carved angel on it – I think it looks a little like her. I forgive her for what she did now, for she made sure my brother could come back to us and she lost herself to do that. I didn't know she had that in her. Silas is less surprised. It was the Lara she wanted to be, he said, and he told us what happened inside the factory:

Lara ran through the warehouse, yelling Silas's name until she heard him call back in return. He was heading towards her, coughing and choking from the smoke. Around him, piles of clothing were aflame.

'This way! This way!' She grabbed his arm. 'I didn't know, you have to believe me. It wasn't me. We have to get out!'

Silas nodded, pushing her forward. 'Go!'

She ran back towards the door, with him following. The fire was spreading fast. They had seconds and no more.

Then Lara caught her foot on something and sprawled headlong on the floor. Her chin cracked against the concrete. Silas hauled her up. She got her balance again, blinking as the smoke got thicker, and she lost sight of the exit. Silas lit up the way with the torch on his phone.

'Go, go, I'm following you,' she spluttered.

He held the light up so she could see and they stumbled on again.

They could see the door now, see the smoke pouring out of it into the fresh air. The flames were right behind them, all around them, ahead, licking so close. They leaped over them from space to space as they ran.

Silas hurdled one last heap of burning debris on the floor and he was out – he was safe. Lara had done it – she'd got him out.

He turned to see her make the jump herself. As she gathered herself, something with scorching flames fell from above . . . he saw her felled, pinned to the ground beneath burning debris. He lurched up from his knees to get her – he had to get to her – and then the place exploded.

I wonder if she did love him a little after all.

We spend a lot of time together, the three of us, now Silas is well again. I can even talk a bit sometimes. Josie has dragged me back to see Andrea and she's delighted with how I'm doing. So is someone else: I managed to say 'Mum' last week. I spoke to my mother for the first time in ten years, and she cried and hugged me and said it was the sweetest sound she had ever heard. We still don't understand each other, but Silas says sometimes you don't need to understand to love. Josie says he might be right about that.

They're talking as they stand looking at Lara's grave.

'When I look back at everything, some of the stuff she believed in, some of the stuff I came to believe in, it was right, you know,' Silas says. 'Just because they went about it wrong doesn't make the heart of it any less right.'

'So what do you want to do about that?'

He shrugs. 'Rethink my plans. Maybe do some volunteering abroad like she talked about doing. Get my degree and try to use it to help people. Give back, not *consume*.'

Josie nods. 'You should follow your heart. It'll lead you the right way in the end.'

He reaches forward and brushes the headstone with a finger. 'I feel like there's nothing left of me to love anyone again the way I loved her. It's in there, buried with her.'

'Love isn't a well that dries up,' Josie answers. 'You can never run out of it. But you can feel too bruised and lost to try again for a long time. I think that's where you are now.'

Silas studies the ground at the foot of the grave. 'I could lose someone important in the time it takes me to heal, couldn't I?'

'No. If someone is that important, they'll wait.'

And I see him shift and stand a step closer to her, and see the barely perceptible squeeze of his fingers on hers.

Above us, an oak tree sheds some yellowing leaves to carpet the path and herald autumn. There's a briskness to the breeze and a faint chill in the air that tells me the season of renewal is coming, where the land makes itself over again from fallen leaves and fruits and buried things, to lie fallow through the winter and be strong again for spring.

RAFI'S TRUTH WALL

I believe in happy endings. If it's not happy, it's not the end yet.
(Rafaela Ramsey)

ACKNOWLEDGMENTS

As ever, thanks to my agent, Ariella Feiner, for looking after me, especially this year in what has been a transformational twelve months. Thanks to my editor, Stella Paskins, for shaping the raw material into a real book, and for all at Egmont involved in getting the books out there, especially Jenny Hayes.

The book would not have been possible without technical advice, so for Silas's wizardry with a computer, my grateful thanks go to AndyB of the Enemy Boat Spotted (EBS) community. Additional thanks to Garry Griffiths for advice on a police matter, and to Paul for helping with my eleventh hour plot holes again.

Finally, thanks to my family. To my mum for reading the first half and telling me it wasn't dreadful at all, because I can tell if she's lying and she wasn't. To Paul, for keeping everything together in a few months of very tight timeline to get the book finished. To Joshua, for understanding when I was busy. And to Orlaith, for sleeping like an angel so I could get the book written at all. It has been a very special year for us and I am so lucky to have all of you.